Order of S

Getting Away with Murder

Book Five of the
Brian Sadler Archaeological Thrillers

Bill Thompson

Published by
Ascendente Books
Dallas, Texas

Order of Succession
All Rights Reserved
Copyright © 2016
V.1.0

Published by Ascendente Books

ISBN 978-0996467100

Printed in the United States of America

DEDICATION

This book is dedicated to my wife Marjorie, who patiently puts up with me when I'm writing. We've traveled to places I'm sure you never expected to go. We've climbed Mayan temples in Belize, experienced the wonders of Petra and the pyramids of Egypt, navigated ancient tunnels in Israel and seen the sun sink like a ball of fire into Banderas Bay at dusk. And we've just begun. We have many more things to see! I love you and appreciate you more every single day.

ACKNOWLEDGEMENTS

As always, I thank my beta readers Bob, Peggy, Jeff, Ryan and Margie. Each of your efforts contributes to the critical review process and I appreciate your time and willingness to help.

CHAPTER ONE

The First Day
Tuesday, March 31, 9:30 p.m. Eastern time

We interrupt this program to bring you breaking news.

When one of ABC's senior newscasters, a man with decades of experience, appeared flustered and uncertain, it could only mean one thing – something catastrophic had happened. The familiar anchor behind the news desk had obviously been pressed into service quickly. His shirt collar was open and he wasn't wearing a jacket. His microphone had been so quickly affixed to his collar that it hung to one side.

We go now to the White House for a special briefing.

The press secretary walked to his usual place behind the podium, glanced at his notes and began to read.

Air Force Two, with the Vice President and the Secretary of State on board, disappeared from radar less than half an hour ago over the Pacific Ocean southwest of Hawaii. The plane was en route from Honolulu to Hong Kong, where Vice President Taylor and Secretary Clancy were meeting tomorrow with Xi Jinxing, President of the People's Republic of China, to discuss economic issues.

The last radar transmission showed the plane near the Mariana Trench, the deepest part of the ocean. There were no apparent weather issues. A squadron of military aircraft is en route to the area.

At the moment, President Harrison and his family are aboard Air Force One en route to the United States from the Caribbean nation of Barbados, where he attended a conference. The President has been briefed on the situation and he urges citizens to remain calm. For now we simply don't know what has happened.

The Secretary of Defense announced that as a precautionary measure, the nation's security level has been raised to DEFCON 3. The President ordered the level increased from DEFCON 5, the lowest level, where it has been for many years. The last time the nation was at DEFCON 3 was after the attacks of September 11, 2001.

The press secretary ended the news conference without taking questions for which there simply were no answers. How could a Boeing 747 simply disappear? Had there been mechanical trouble? Did the plane explode? Americans prayed this wouldn't end up as a terrible tragedy.

President William Henry Harrison IV was in his office aboard Air Force One when the head of the National Security Agency and the Secretary of Defense called to report Vice President Taylor's aircraft missing. Secretary Clark recommended the President's plane immediately divert from its flight plan, aborting the trip to Dallas and instead flying directly to the nearest air base, the Naval Air Station at Key West. The President concurred, and within minutes the radar station at Marathon, Florida, noted the aircraft's new course.

The night's second horrific announcement came just twenty minutes after the first. This story sent the world into a tailspin of dread. This day would be remembered forever, just like that beautiful Tuesday morning, September 11, 2001, when one horrific plane crash became two, then three, and everyone realized this was all part of a plan, the largest terror attack ever waged against the United States of America.

Shortly after the world learned that the Vice President's plane was missing, the media watched the White House press secretary as he returned to the podium for his second news conference in thirty minutes. This time he brushed away tears before he spoke.

———

Please bear with me as we get through this together as a nation drawn into confusion. Now tears were streaming down his face. *A few moments ago Air Force One disappeared from radar, exactly as Air Force Two did earlier. The President, his wife and children, the Chief of Staff and the plane's crew were over the Caribbean Sea en route to the Naval Air Station at Key West. After the Vice President's plane disappeared, President Harrison's plane was immediately diverted to the closest military installation.*

Massive search-and-rescue operations will soon be under way at both locations. It's daytime in the Pacific where Air Force Two was last on radar, but there are several hours of darkness left in the Caribbean Sea where Air Force One disappeared. Regardless, massive efforts are already beginning.

The press secretary paused to compose himself. President Harry Harrison was loved and revered by his staff and most American citizens. He was a man whose vibrant personality and quick wit made him seem more like an average guy than the wealthy former senator he was. The press secretary had become particularly close to Harrison, and he choked back a sob as he read the next words.

Speaker of the House Chambliss Parkes is next in the order of succession to the presidency. Although no final word about the President is known at this time, the Speaker and his family have been moved to a secret location until more information develops. Several agencies, including the Department of Homeland Security, the National Security Agency, the FBI and CIA are working jointly with the Department of Defense in the ongoing investigation.

The press secretary paused as an aide walked to the stage and handed him a piece of paper. He looked at it. The people seated in front of him couldn't miss the involuntary shudder as he read what was on the note.

The Defense Secretary contacted Speaker Parkes moments ago. The Speaker ordered security raised to its highest readiness level, DEFCON 1. The United States has never before been at DEFCON 1.

As the news conference continued, the correspondents began furiously typing on their cellphones, searching to see what impact the highest threat level carried.

I will now read a brief statement from Speaker Parkes. I quote, "Although we have no tangible reason to believe the country could be threatened at this time, both the President and Vice President are missing. The Secretary of Defense recommended we go to DEFCON 1 as a prudent measure and I agreed. I urge the American people to remain calm. There is no reason to panic." End quote.

The press secretary paused, wishing to God there would be no questions, yet knowing that wasn't going to happen. The handful of reporters who had been hanging around the White House this evening were suddenly the world's news sources. Hands flew into the air and reporters shot rapid-fire questions with the urgency that accompanied fear and lack of understanding.

He called on a reporter who glanced at his phone and said, "I'm reading verbatim from the Defense Department's website. 'DEFCON 1 means the nation will be at maximum readiness for what could be an imminent nuclear attack.' Does implementing DEFCON 1 mean Speaker Parkes and Defense Secretary Vernon believe there's an imminent possibility of nuclear war?"

I'm giving you what information has been made public at this point. The Speaker asked us to remain calm and not panic. I think that's important now as we try to learn what's happened tonight.

"Is Speaker Parkes going to be sworn in as President? If so, when will that happen?"

All of us in this room know that two years ago we went seven days without a President. Tonight there simply isn't enough information yet to say what's happened to President Harrison and Vice President Taylor. We can't jump to conclusions. We have to wait for now.

"This is obviously no coincidence. Two planes are missing. Has any group claimed responsibility?"

I'm not aware of anyone claiming responsibility at this time. We're not even sure if there's anything to claim responsibility for. We just don't know right now what happened.

4

ORDER OF SUCCESSION

The beleaguered press secretary did his best in a situation he never envisioned having to face. He told them there simply was no more information available. With his shoulders slumped, he walked out of the room.

———

The nation had heard the first report – news of the disappearance of Air Force Two – at 9:30 p.m. Eastern time on a Tuesday. After that sobering press conference, Wall Street experts predicted the stock markets would open significantly lower the next morning. No one had an inkling how shortsighted that prediction would be. As bad as things were, just thirty minutes later they were multiplied a thousandfold when a second news flash took the events from horrific to unfathomable. Governments around the world braced for a panic of global proportions, and it took very little time to happen.

On October 19, 1987, the day of the stock market's greatest crash, the Dow Jones Industrial Average dropped twenty-two percent. This time investors would have been thrilled with that number. Although US markets wouldn't open until tomorrow morning, the Asian exchanges were in the middle of their trading day when the news was announced. Stocks plummeted twenty percent before the closing bell rang. The same thing happened in Europe. When their markets opened, fail-safes designed to avoid a crash like 2008 shut the exchanges down within minutes.

The Fed convened an emergency meeting at 3:30 a.m., considering moves to prop up the market if necessary. Their efforts would be for naught; no one could stem the tidal wave that would hit in a few hours. When the market opened the next morning, the experts knew exactly what was going to happen. Sell orders from around the world would flood the Internet as investors large and small rushed to beat the hysteria that always seemed to accompany a catastrophe.

Many people didn't hear the story until they woke the next morning to a horrific reality. The top leaders of the United States were missing. The Dow Jones had closed yesterday above seventeen thousand. This morning it opened down an astounding six thousand four hundred points. Nothing before had ever remotely approached the magnitude of panic that was unfolding worldwide. There was no stopgap – no fail-safe – to deal with massive selling and zero buy orders to offset it. Investors around the world were literally hysterical and in panic mode.

Just before the New York Stock Exchange opened, the Hong Kong exchange announced it would not open for the rest of the week, a total of four trading days. That monumental announcement was the last straw for the markets. The massive computer system serving the New York Stock Exchange crashed thirty seconds after the opening bell. In a fruitless attempt to create order from chaos, the exchange stayed open seventeen turbulent minutes before the governing board pulled the plug. An orderly market required both buyers and sellers, but today only one side of the market existed. When the Stock Exchange closed at 9:47 a.m., the Dow was down seven thousand six hundred points, a mind-boggling, paralyzing forty-three percent loss from yesterday's close.

CHAPTER TWO

Brian Sadler and Nicole Farber had begun that Tuesday morning eager to see Harry and Jennifer Harrison and their girls Lizzie and Kate. The President called Brian around noon to confirm they would leave Barbados after he spoke at a dinner. They looked forward to seeing everyone tonight around ten at Love Field in Dallas.

Since their days as college roommates, Brian and Harry had maintained a close friendship while one became a renowned antiquities dealer and the other rose quickly in politics. Harry had first been a congressman from Oklahoma, and then he was elected to his father's Senate seat when Henry Harrison retired. Republican presidential nominee John Chapman picked Harry as his running mate, and the two were swept into the White House by a comfortable margin three years ago.

That afternoon Brian spoke with the head of the Secret Service detail that would be handling security for the President. The agent had briefed him earlier on this evening's plans; this call was to nail down the specifics.

A government sedan would pick up Brian and Nicole at nine p.m. They'd go to the nearby airport and wait in a VIP lounge for Air Force One's expected arrival around ten. They would greet the President and his family and ride in their limousine to the Crescent Hotel, where the first family was scheduled to spend the night. After a quick nightcap, Brian and Nicole would go home to their condo in the Ritz-Carlton, a couple of blocks from the President's hotel.

Love Field had both commercial and private aircraft traffic, and there were a dozen operations along the airport's east side that catered to corporate jets. For the rest of his life, Brian would never forget what happened just as he and Nicole were being escorted into the VIP lounge. He'd glanced at his watch and saw it was 9:16. Suddenly both Secret Service agents with them stopped, pressing their earpieces, alert to the communication they were hearing.

"Code Orange!" They all heard the yell from the next room as the agents grabbed Brian and Nicole by their arms and roughly pushed them forward. Six more agents were rushing from the tarmac into the lounge through large glass doors. Everyone's weapons were drawn.

"What the hell?" Brian yelled as they were told to sit.

An agent said, "There's an emergency situation, sir! Sit down! Now!"

The Secret Service men waited for orders as their chief, the one who'd spoken to Brian, was on his cellphone. The evening news on CNN was on a muted TV opposite them. Suddenly Brian saw a breaking news flash and pointed to the screen.

"Turn that up!" the lead agent shouted.

As they heard about the disappearance of Air Force Two, Brian and Nicole realized that Code Orange was a signal that the Vice President was in trouble. They knew this could change Harry and Jennifer's trip completely. Now wasn't the time to ask – the agents were huddled in a corner opposite them, getting orders from their leader.

Moments later six of the agents left the building, returning to a stretch limousine sitting near the aircraft parking area outside. It was undoubtedly the vehicle intended to carry the President and his family. The senior agent came over to them and said, "I apologize for the inconvenience, but we're going to take you both home. For the President's safety, Air Force One's being diverted to a base in Key West. They won't be coming to Dallas."

"Not at all?" Nicole asked.

"That's my understanding, ma'am. It's too early to know anything and things can change, but I'd say President Harrison's going to be in a secure facility until people figure out what's happened."

They talked quietly as they rode back to their building. The two agents who'd brought them over were in the front seat. Brian and Nicole could hear static and chatter from a radio mounted in the dash. They were five minutes or so from the Ritz-Carlton when the words CODE RED, repeat CODE RED were broadcast loudly through its speaker.

"Oh God!" the driver said, activating red lights and turning on his siren. "We've got to get you home!" He accelerated sharply as his partner's phone rang.

"What's going on?" Nicole screamed. "What's happening? What does Code Red mean?"

The agents said nothing. One concentrated on driving and the other spoke quietly on his phone. When they pulled under the porte cochere at the Ritz, the driver screeched to a halt, jumped out and walked around the car. The building's doorman, startled at the red lights and the siren still screaming in his driveway, opened the back door, and they hopped out.

The driver was obviously frazzled and in a hurry. "Apologies, folks. Sorry, there's no time to explain." He ran back to the front and the car sped away.

Brian asked the doorman if there was any more news about the Vice President's plane. Something had just happened, but they had no idea what it was.

"Nothing since the news conference. The news is on in the lobby." He pointed to the screen just as the same words – Breaking News – appeared again.

Half a dozen residents who were coming or going joined Brian, Nicole and the doorman in the lobby to watch the report. Nicole began to sob as they heard the President's press secretary solemnly announce that Air Force One, carrying the President, his wife and two children, the Chief of Staff and a crew of seven persons, was missing too. It had disappeared less than thirty minutes after the first plane vanished.

BILL THOMPSON

CHAPTER THREE

The Second Day
Wednesday, April 1

The stock market was only one manifestation of the hysteria that swept the nation. The people who had been asleep when the events unfolded learned the news the next morning. It was April Fool's Day, and some listeners wondered for a moment if this was someone's idea of a tasteless, insensitive joke. But it couldn't have been. The news was literally everywhere, and it was devastating. This was no joke.

The frustrating part was how little anyone knew. The plane on which the President was flying – the one dubbed Air Force One – was a Gulfstream G650 jet put into service less than nine months ago, and Air Force Two was a Boeing 747 less than two years old. They vanished from radar within thirty minutes of each other on opposite sides of the globe. A coincidence? Impossible. An act of terrorism? Possibly – probably even, but no one knew.

The 747 carrying Vice President Taylor and Secretary of State Clancy was last reported near the Pacific's Mariana Trench, while the Gulfstream had vanished over the Caribbean Sea. The areas where the planes disappeared were two of the deepest places on the planet and hundreds of miles from land. Unprecedented search and rescue efforts were under way, but nothing had been spotted.

The nation's borders were locked down the moment DEFCON 1 was implemented. No one entered and no one left. Every airport, public and private, was closed. For the first time in history, the entire country was under a no-fly order. The mass transit systems in New York, Boston, Washington and Philadelphia were closed and Amtrak cancelled every train in the nation. National Guardsmen carrying loaded automatic rifles were deployed in America's larger cities.

Some Americans reacted with violence. During the night, there were riots in Detroit, Los Angeles and Miami. A mosque was torched in Knoxville. In Chicago people roamed the streets, smoking marijuana, drinking whisky they'd stolen from liquor stores, and using bottles, trash cans and rocks to shatter storefronts along posh Michigan Avenue.

Many feared that the next step would be an attack inside the United States. Many steps were taken, including an order by the governor of Nevada that all casinos be closed. The mayor of Las Vegas also directed that the millions of lights that made the Strip and downtown visible from space be extinguished.

By daybreak the mechanics of DEFCON 1 were creating chaos in the lives of ordinary citizens. Workers couldn't get to work, commuters couldn't use Amtrak, and flyers were stranded in airports all across the country.

The Department of Homeland Security ordered schools and all nonessential governmental offices closed on Wednesday. DHS also urged private businesses to close for at least today, until the threat could be properly assessed. No group had claimed responsibility for what was tentatively being termed an act of aggression, but citizens of several Middle Eastern countries were clearly thrilled. They were on TV, gathering by the thousands in public places and praising Allah for the gift from God. The media filmed thousands of people shooting guns into the air and screaming defiantly as they burned United States flags in Iran, Syria and Pakistan.

When Air Force Two disappeared at 9:30 p.m., Speaker of the House Chambliss T. Parkes, a Democrat from Austin, Texas, was still in his office in the Capitol. He was puffing on the last of three fine Cuban cigars he allowed himself every day. Staff and visitors alike complained about the Speaker's nasty habit and how much his office stank, but it made no difference to Parkes. The Speaker was a crude, quick-tempered man accustomed to having his way and oblivious to the needs, concerns and opinions of others.

It wasn't unusual for Parkes to be in his office at this hour. He often returned to the Capitol after a dinner engagement with friends, constituents or colleagues, and he'd have a nightcap and a cigar before heading home to bed. Ten minutes ago the Secretary of Homeland Security had called, alerting the Speaker that Air Force Two was missing with the Vice President and Secretary of State on board.

"Keep me advised," the DHS Secretary would later tell people was the Speaker's only comment.

On this monumental night when the fearsome events were headlined on every channel, the TV in Cham Parkes's office was muted. He wasn't watching the news; he was looking at his computer, scrolling through comments about last night's Democratic presidential debate. He thought he'd done very well, but the hosts of tonight's shows had vehemently disagreed. He never gave a damn about what Fox said, but when the liberal networks criticized him, it pissed him off.

An online CNN panel reflected on Cham's three decades in the House, contrasting his years of service against his much younger opponent's first term as governor of Delaware, one of the nation's smallest states. They pointed out the Speaker's vastly greater experience, but noted that his braggadocio demeanor and condescending attitude toward his rival had caused many former supporters to switch to the younger candidate with fresh, new ideas. There were just four months until the Democratic National Convention; polls showed Parkes and his opponent in a dead heat. What a defeat it would be for the Speaker, CNN reported, if a young, likable newcomer beat an irascible, ill-mannered career politician.

Screw them. Screw the damned media. They'll pay for this when I'm President.

Cham took another deep drag off his Churchill and thought again about last night's debate. His opponent was a weakling who had smiled every time the Speaker interrupted or berated him. When Parkes had called his opponent a baby who needed diapers, the wimp just stood there and took it. *Calling him a baby was clever,* the Speaker reflected. *I thought that was my best remark.*

Obviously not everyone had agreed. By all rights, Cham Parkes should have been ahead in the polls by thirty points, maybe forty. But he wasn't. He was dead even.

These idiots – the stupid voters – actually feel sorry for the wimp I'm running against.

Before last night his advisors had recommended toning down the rhetoric, but the Speaker only had one speed – full blast. It didn't matter anyway. There would be no problem because he had an ace in the hole. Before the convention in four months, he'd be so far ahead of his rival that the vote would be a foregone conclusion. Cham T. Parkes would be both the Democratic nominee and the next President of the United States.

Suddenly his office doors slammed open. This was unheard of; no one entered without the Speaker's permission, but there was clearly something different happening tonight. Three Secret Service agents rushed to his desk and said, "Code Red, Mr. Speaker! Code Red! Put the cigar out! We have to go! Now!"

Parkes calmly rose from his chair, stubbed out his cigar and quietly muttered only seven words, a sentence that one of the Secret Service agents would recall much later.

"This has been a long time coming."

For now those words were lost in the frantic hubbub. The agents surrounded the man who was third in line to the presidency and ushered him out of his office. Their guns were drawn and their faces showed grim determination. In the broad hallway outside, ten Capitol policemen with semiautomatic rifles surrounded them as the Speaker was shoved into an elevator in front of a dozen stunned staffers who were pulling all-nighters for their bosses.

Parkes never asked a question about what was happening and never raised an eyebrow about the sudden extrication from his office. He knew what Code Red meant. This wasn't about the Vice President's missing plane. Code Red meant the President was in trouble.

Those in the security detail surrounding him would remember how uncharacteristically impassive and calm the Speaker appeared. Typically he'd be barking orders laced with profanity. During the elevator ride to the Capitol basement, the man said nothing. Perhaps it was the gravity of the situation. Maybe he was lost in the knowledge that he might soon become leader of the free world. Whatever it was, this was not the behavior of the Chambliss T. Parkes the world knew.

A few minutes ago Pennsylvania Avenue had been closed to traffic. Now it was deserted as the motorcade pulled away from the Capitol. Soldiers in riot gear stood on every corner as the SUVs raced the two miles to the White House. The director of Homeland Security was on the line with Parkes the entire time, telling him what they knew about the missing planes, which was extremely little.

When they pulled through the White House gates, Parkes noticed sharpshooters on the roof. The last time he'd seen that was on 9/11. The SUV raced across the grassy lawn toward a helicopter sitting with its rotors idling, ready for takeoff the moment he boarded. A second chopper hovered overhead. It was crammed with heavily armed Marines and would provide increased security.

As the vehicle pulled up next to the helicopter, one of the agents got a call. "It's the Secretary of Defense for you, sir," he said as he handed it over. Parkes listened for a moment, and then he ordered implementation of DEFCON 1. When the Secret Service agents heard the words, they knew that history was being made tonight. America was in a dangerous, perilous situation, facing an unknown threat. And Chambliss T. Parkes was the senior person in the United States government.

More than one of them fervently prayed that this situation wouldn't last long.

When the call ended, Speaker Parkes pulled a piece of paper from his jacket pocket, handed it to the agent and said, "Give this to the press secretary." The paper was his handwritten statement approving threat level DEFCON 1 and asking the people to remain calm.

This is exhilarating, Parkes thought. From now on, the media would leap upon every comment he made. He was the *man,* the leader of the free world, beginning now. And he was looking forward to every minute of it.

"Stay in the vehicle a moment until we get in place, sir," the agent said. "Your wife's already on board, but we have to go to full readiness before we move you to the chopper."

Of course you do. I'm numero uno. How satisfying!

Karen, Speaker Parkes's wife, had gone to bed early so she hadn't heard the news. Suddenly her bedroom door had slammed open and the four agents who guarded the house burst in, screaming, "Code Red! Code Red! We have to go, Mrs. Parkes. Now!"

Karen Parkes was supposed to know what Code Red meant, but she'd forgotten. She asked for time to dress, but they told her to grab a robe and come with them.

"Is it Cham?" she asked, hoping Code Red didn't mean something had happened to her husband.

"It's Harrison and Taylor," the agent replied urgently. "Go! Let's go!"

The President and Vice President? "Dear God! What happened to them?"

"They're missing. There's no time, Mrs. Parkes! We have to go now!"

Two black SUVs idled in the driveway, their red lights flashing in the darkness. Six Secret Service agents sat in the front car; Karen Parkes and the four agents got into the second one. They all had their weapons drawn, and that scared her. She hoped Cham was all right, wherever he was. The SUVs pulled into the street and were met by four Virginia state troopers with sirens screaming.

16

"Can you tell me where we're going?"

"We're going to the White House, ma'am. Agents are bringing the Speaker there."

The White House? She had no idea what was going on, but she'd just wait to find out. Cham would explain everything like he always did.

She watched the two SUVs coming across the lawn and hoped one was carrying her husband. They both stopped, but nobody got out for a few minutes. Suddenly a dozen agents jumped from the vehicles and ran toward the helicopter, lining a pathway through which the Speaker was herded like a football player entering a stadium before the big game.

When Cham climbed into the helicopter, he saw her robe and slippers and grunted disapprovingly. She didn't notice; she reached to touch him and wiped away her tears.

"I'm so glad you're here. What's going on? Why's there so much security? I'm so scared! They wouldn't even let me dress!" She tried to hug the man she'd been married to for decades, but he pulled away as usual.

"Didn't you hear the news?" he replied curtly. "Calm down, Karen. It isn't the end of the world. This could be the best thing . . ."

"One of the men said Harry Harrison and the Vice President are missing. Is this a terrorist attack? Where are they taking us? How can you be so calm?"

He shook her roughly. "Stop it! That's not what this is. Just calm down!"

"How do you know it's not a terrorist attack? What have they told you?"

The pilot turned to them. "Sorry to interrupt, Mrs. Parkes. Mr. Speaker, please put on your headphones. We're going to Rapidan. Your sons are being moved to that facility as well."

Mrs. Parkes screamed when she heard that her adult sons were involved. She began to cry.

"The *boys?* Why them? What's happening, Cham?"

As the pilot lifted off, he could hear the Speaker's response through his headphones.

Parkes spoke to his wife as if she were a child. "Listen to me and try to understand, darling," he snarled sarcastically. "Do you know what Code Red means? It means there's something bad that involves the President. Right now he and the Vice President are both missing. We're being relocated to Rapidan out in rural Virginia. It's the most secure bunker in America, and they're taking the boys there too until they can find out what's going on."

"*You* certainly seem to be taking the news calmly," she noted, still gasping between sobs.

"Shut up, you stupid cow! I'm about to become the President of the United States! Can't you understand *anything*? Sit back and enjoy the ride!"

The pilot had only flown Cham Parkes once, but the man's vulgar, brash demeanor was legendary inside the Beltway. He could hear everything the Speaker said, and he wondered how the man could be so unconcerned about the fate of two American leaders, even if they were from the other side of the aisle.

He doesn't seem the least bit upset that the President and Vice President may have died. In fact, he's about as upbeat as I've ever seen him even though he's treating his wife worse than I treat my dog. He actually seems to be enjoying all this. But it's none of my business. I'm paid to fly the arrogant son of a bitch, not to figure out what's in his head.

With the implementation of DEFCON 1, every plane in the United States had been ordered to land immediately at the nearest airport. Now there was no other traffic as the two choppers, flanked now by four fighter jets, flew west toward the Shenandoah Mountains. Those fighters were armed and ordered to destroy anything that appeared to be a threat.

They arrived at the Rapidan Wildlife Management Area forty minutes later, setting down on a helipad near a beautiful rustic hunting lodge built in 1929 as a retreat for President Herbert Hoover. The remote site consisted of several hundred acres of dense forest and a few outbuildings surrounding a lodge. Few people knew that in the 1970s a twenty-room underground bunker had been added to serve as a combination bomb shelter and secure hideout for the government's top officials. The facility was constantly maintained and kept stocked with food and water in the event of a national emergency.

Tonight would be the first time the bunker would serve its intended purpose. Vice President Cheney had almost been taken there when 9/11 broke and President Bush was aboard Air Force One, but instead he'd gone to a different secure facility in Virginia called Mount Weather.

A cadre of Secret Service and FBI agents had flown to Rapidan the minute news broke about the Vice President's plane. If this turned out to be the first step in an attack against the United States, this facility would house the President and his family. Now that Air Force One was missing too, the Speaker's family would become its residents.

There was no sleep for anyone for the rest of that night. Parkes spent over an hour on the phone with the Secretary of the Treasury. The Secretary's immediate concern was the likely collapse of the stock market, but he advised opening anyway in an attempt to maintain normalcy. That would turn out to be a mistake that resulted in the brief seventeen-minute market session and the huge drop in the Dow.

All the other cabinet members reported in, and everyone was cautious and tentative. This was a sticky situation – President Harrison and Vice President Taylor, two Republicans, were unaccounted for but technically still in office. Parkes, a Democrat, had no power to order anything, but he was next in the order of succession, as much as Harrison's appointees hated to face that reality. Parkes would soon be President if, God forbid, Harry and Marty Taylor were gone. They detested him, but they had no choice but to seek his guidance and opinions.

By late Wednesday afternoon, around twenty hours after it all began, the nation still reeled from a day like none other. Doomsday predictions abounded; in parks and squares people brandished signs that said "Repent Now!"

while rioters, drunk on whisky from liquor stores they'd looted, mocked them. At least five Wall Street brokers committed suicide, apparently unable to cope with massive personal financial losses. As frantic citizens packed the National Cathedral in Washington, dropping to their knees and praying, an angry mob outside chanted, "Why pray to God? There is no God!"

It turned out to be a busy day at Rapidan. At five p.m. Parkes took a break from the constant calls and updates. He joined his wife and their two unmarried adult sons in a comfortable living room thirty feet underground. Everyone had a cocktail, and the Speaker, typically oblivious to everyone else, puffed on today's cigar number two, a fat one that filled the upper half of the room with dense smoke. The seventy-inch TV nearby was muted. They'd heard the repetitive reports all afternoon, and there was nothing but bad news. The Speaker didn't need the TV for news anymore. The second any information became available he'd be the first person in the world to know it.

Around noon, the last time Cham had seen his wife before now, she was still wearing her robe. Now she had a dress on; obviously someone had brought out her clothes. That was a positive, he thought for a second. It didn't look good for the first-lady-to-be walking around in a bathrobe.

"Dad, are you worried about the market crash and our family investments?" one of his sons asked. It was a legitimate question – for years they'd known that their parents were heavily invested in stocks.

"The market always comes back, son. How many times have I told you that? This is a momentary aberration in the big scheme of things."

There was a little secret no one knew. He didn't own one single share of stock anymore. Over the last three weeks he'd liquidated his entire portfolio – several million dollars in common stocks – and the proceeds were safely tucked into CDs at a dozen of the nation's largest, safest banks. There was also the other thing – the secret account Cham called his retirement fund. No one knew about that either. *Wouldn't be prudent*, as George Bush the first would have said.

President of the United States, he repeated to himself for the hundredth time, relishing the words. *I'm going to be President of the United States. Not bad. Not bad at all.* He took a long pull from his Bourbon and water and settled back in his chair. So far things were going very well indeed.

BILL THOMPSON

CHAPTER FOUR

Edlib, Syria
Six months ago

In a heavily fortified basement, two men were meeting in the war room of the militant organization al-Nusra Front, also known as al-Qaeda, in Syria. Above them on the street, the bombed-out building gave no indication that a sophisticated operations center had been built twenty feet below.

Much of this section of Edlib had been destroyed in the country's brutal, never-ending civil war. Rubble and debris were simply bulldozed aside to create a narrow lane for traffic, but this part of Edlib was so infiltrated by rebels – so dangerous – that ordinary citizens didn't venture into this part of town anymore. The damage to buildings was so extensive it was unlikely anything would be rebuilt for decades. It was a perfect place for Nusra, the leaders of which had chosen this unsafe, menacing part of the city as its headquarters.

Three youths armed with Russian Kalashnikov rifles sat on overturned pails in front of the ruined building. They blended in perfectly – they looked just like hundreds of other unemployed militants who were loyal to the Nusra Front and who roamed the streets of Edlib looking for excitement or trouble, or both. These three smoked cigarettes and laughed among themselves, but they missed nothing going on around them. They were guards, and their leader, a ruthless killer named Abu Mohammad al-Joulani, was conducting an important meeting in the basement room. As carefree as they seemed to be, chatting and smiling, each of these boys not yet twenty years old would willingly give his life before allowing an assailant past him.

Since 2013, when the violently Sunni Islamist group split from ISIS, Islamic State fighters had exterminated nearly a thousand al-Nusra soldiers. The carnage only served to bolster the splinter group's popularity among the youth of Syria. These young men were tired of poverty, sick of lies from the government, and angry at the establishment. It was a perfect breeding ground for jihadist militants, and training camps were established in the areas of northwestern Syria that the Nusra Front controlled. Weapons training was carried out using photos of President Assad and President Bush as targets. Within weeks al-Nusra Front was designated as a foreign terrorist organization by the USA and the United Nations. Those designations only helped Nusra's recruiting efforts. Militants flocked to join, and soon the group was the most powerful and dangerous jihadist organization in the Middle East.

Today's meeting in the war room was the culmination of months of planning. The most stunning attack against the Great Satan in history was moving from the planning stage to action.

Mohammad al-Joulani was afraid of no man. That said, he was always cautious when dealing with the thirty-year-old who sat across the table from him. He'd created this monster – Joulani had personally taught the man known as Tariq the Hawk to be ruthless, beholden to no one and loyal only to Joulani himself. He'd been systematically cleansed of feelings, memories, emotions and concern for others. Tariq was a carefully engineered killing machine.

For two years Tariq had been the leader of a shadow group within Nusra called the Falcons of Islam. The Falcons consisted of just twenty young fanatics, each handpicked by Joulani and trained in secret to become suicide jihadists for Allah. The al-Nusra Front was formidable, but the Falcons of Islam was a terrorist group on steroids. Joulani had created it for one purpose – one complex, multifaceted plan that would shake the very foundations of the West.

As they talked, Joulani thought his young protégé looked for all the world like a nondescript, scraggly-bearded Arab university student. Tariq would have fit in perfectly on the campus at Harvard or Cambridge or the Sorbonne. And that was exactly the idea. In a Western world gripped by Islamophobia, Tariq would be the least likely person one should fear. But in reality he was the one they should fear the most.

Not only was Tariq cunning and fearless, he was a poster child for terrorism. Joulani had trained him how to garner funding from sympathizers around the globe. At his mentor's suggestion, Tariq had turned the Falcons of Islam into contract mercenaries, tackling projects that were totally outside Nusra's primary mission, the Syrian war effort. Many of these jobs were virtually effortless – an assassination here, a suicide bombing there – but others were highly complex. For the latter, Tariq's ragtag band of soldiers-for-hire earned good money, which they used to fund further regional terrorism.

Mohammad had taught Tariq well, sadly perhaps too well, he was beginning to see. The man was getting cocky, full of himself, forgetting that his newfound stature and position in the terrorist world was solely because al-Joulani had allowed it to happen.

Listen to him, Joulani thought as the youth talked. I've *done this.* I've *done that. Look at the money* I've *made for the Falcons. How about thanking* me – your mentor – *without whom you'd either be still living in poverty or more likely dead.*

The Falcons had successfully completed several missions-for-hire and sat on a war chest of nearly five million US dollars. Joulani's feelings for his protégé were mixed – while he was proud of the boy, he was becoming increasingly wary. Joulani had handed him the mission they were discussing today – the most difficult job Tariq would ever encounter. If the Falcons of Islam was successful with this next project, its bank account would contain ten times what it did today. That was both a blessing and a curse, Joulani thought. This job was incredibly complex, multifaceted, rife with possible problems, and its successful conclusion would have worldwide repercussions. Mohammad would oversee everything, despite Tariq's

25

insistence he could handle it. When it was over, Tariq would share the money with the Nusra Front. If he refused – if the impetuous young man's brash arrogances continued – Mohammad would deal with Tariq. He had created this bright young terrorist. He could create another.

He forced himself to stop thinking about the negatives. Logistically, everything was coming together well, Joulani thought as the meeting wrapped up and they sipped coffees. Making solid connections inside the United States had taken over a year, but alliances that appeared tenuous just a few weeks ago now seemed firmly in place.

Only one thing was left, and this last part wasn't under their control. They had to wait for a particular set of events that would allow the mission to happen. This exact combination of things came about only rarely, but they had plenty of patience. When the time was right, they would be ready to execute.

CHAPTER FIVE

Washington, DC
Present day

It was a singularly sobering time in American history. Vice President William Henry Harrison IV had assumed the top office just two years ago when his own predecessor, John Chapman, disappeared in southern Mexico under strange circumstances. At that time, America had gone for seven days with no President. Now a stunned nation was trying to grasp the incredible truth that it had happened again. This time Harrison himself was the one missing and the nation faced the same dilemma.

How long should the country go without a commander-in-chief? The network panels had debated the question last time this happened. This time it was different – this time the Supreme Court acted quickly. Despite the insistence of Senate Republicans that the President could still be alive, a prompt decision was handed down. Without going so far as to declare him deceased, the highest court ruled that Harrison and Taylor were presently unable to carry out the duties of their offices and instructed that successors be expeditiously appointed.

With that simple, unprecedented and historic ruling, the Democratic Speaker of the House was going to become the President of the United States.

The day after the planes went missing, the Parkes family returned to Washington. Although the White House would be their home now, the personal effects of President Harrison and his family were still exactly where they had been when the four of them left. Cham and Karen lived in Georgetown, but the Secret Service insisted they move into the White House immediately. With the country at DEFCON 1, protecting the President was top priority. For the time being they would sleep in the Lincoln Bedroom on the second floor of the White House, just down the hall from the private residence that would be theirs as soon as

President Harrison's personal belongings were removed. That was just fine with Cham Parkes; he coveted nothing more than to be living in the White House.

Without the fanfare he would have relished, at three o'clock on Wednesday the chief justice of the Supreme Court gave Chambliss T. Parkes the oath of office. Only his family and Chief of Staff A. J. Minter were in attendance. The new commander-in-chief was a Democrat from Texas, a man whose cronyism, favoritism, self-dealings and lust for power were legendary, and he was now exactly where he had always yearned to be. The only thing that would have made it sweeter was if the Republicans hadn't controlled the Senate, but that would only be a minor inconvenience.

Cham knew how to work the system. He had only seven months of Harry Harrison's unexpired term to serve, but President Parkes was planning far beyond the upcoming election. Now that he was the incumbent, he was sure he'd win the nomination this summer. Four months later, this coming November, he'd win the whole thing. He'd be elected President, earning his own four-year term. After that, nothing could stop him. He just had to be careful and make no mistakes until he snagged the victory.

Fifteen minutes after the ceremony ended, his cellphone rang. He glanced at the number and asked his caller to hold. He shooed everyone out of the Oval Office. Once the doors were closed and he was alone, he said curtly, "Don't you ever call me again on this phone."

"And hello to you too, Cham. Yes, it is also good to hear your voice." The caller spoke in cultured but heavily accented English.

He spat, "What do you want?" There was one person on earth who might keep him from being elected President next January, and he was talking to that man now. Cham intended to put him in his place. He was the President, after all.

"That's not the tone of voice I expected from you, *Mr. President*." The title was tinged with sarcasm. "I'm simply an old friend, a loyal supporter, calling to congratulate you. I prepared a little present for you – a little inaugural gift – and I've sent it off. It should already have been delivered by now."

This is going to stop right now, Parkes thought smugly. He didn't need help from this "old friend" any longer. Cham had agreed to make something happen if he became President, and he'd honor that commitment. After all, his old friend had made it well worth his while. But they didn't need to start being phone buddies, and he would have nothing to do with this man once he'd delivered what he promised.

"Fine. Done deal, then."

"Until next time." The caller hung up before Cham could comment. A deal was a deal, and this one was, in fact, done. There wouldn't be a next time.

At six o'clock President Chambliss T. Parkes gave his first address to the nation. He was eager to assert his new authority, and his advisors thought the nation needed to hear from him. In his distinctive Texas drawl, Parkes promised that every resource available to the government was being employed to learn what had really happened less than forty-eight hours before.

"If this is an act of terrorism, we will leave no stone unturned in our quest to find and kill these people," he asserted. "If it is something else, we must learn what happened so we all can put this tragedy behind us. It is my fervent hope that we come together not as Democrats or Republicans, but as Americans, unified in our desire to keep our homeland safe, great and impregnable."

BILL THOMPSON

CHAPTER SIX

The Third Day
Thursday, April 2

Two days after the incidents, debris was spotted two hundred miles west of Puerto Rico within a few hundred miles of what had been Air Force One's flight path. A naval vessel plucked a Gulfstream aircraft seat from the water. Two hours later the DHS chief announced that a seat from the plane had been found. It was positively identified. Within minutes the world saw the familiar seal of the President of the United States on the chair's back cushion.

Shortly thereafter, President Parkes held his second news conference. Without a hint of compassion Parkes declared that the President, his family, Chief of Staff Bob Parker and seven others had perished in what was assumed to be an act of terrorism. The President had no authority to declare a person deceased, but this one did so anyway.

Once the President had read the remarks his speechwriters prepared for him, the briefing should have been over. But Parkes wasn't finished. He very deliberately folded his notes, put them in his pocket and continued speaking extemporaneously. What came next was strictly Cham Parkes doing whatever he wanted since he was now the leader of the free world.

All of this was undoubtedly a massive plot, the President said matter-of-factly. Although no wreckage had been found from the second plane, Air Force Two was unquestionably part of it, and he declared it had been destroyed as well. Although he halfheartedly promised the search efforts would continue, the President opined that given the remote area where Air Force Two disappeared, he didn't expect that debris would ever be found.

The reporters in front of him were wide-eyed with astonishment. Some looked as though they were in shock, others whispered into their recorders. Never before had a President stepped out like this. Parkes was offering his own personal opinions about the most serious crisis in American history!

As if things couldn't become more bizarre, Cham Parkes still wasn't finished. Next came a startling announcement that infuriated his advisors, his cabinet members and many Americans. He lowered the nation's threat level to DEFCON 3 and announced it was back to business as usual in America. Aircraft, planes, borders and schools would all reopen by dawn tomorrow, Parkes ordered, pointing out that nothing had happened since the planes disappeared and there was no longer a continuing threat to America.

Without taking questions, the man who'd been President less than twenty-four hours walked away from the podium. Fox News later called his news conference "astounding to the point of insanity and given without a hint of emotion. After only one day in office we can say this is a President unlike any other the nation has ever seen. America can only hope he will listen to the advice of the many qualified individuals whose job it is to run our government." The inference was unmistakable – President Parkes was going to do things his way. It wouldn't be long, a Fox panel said later that day, until every Harrison appointee was replaced with cronies of Chambliss Parkes.

─────

Two hours before the President's press conference began, Lydia Beckham, a seventy-three-year-old grandmother from Merrickville, Ontario, was accomplishing something that had been on her bucket list for years. For three months she'd been taking flying lessons at a local airport, and today she was going on what was called a "cross-country." Flying solo, she'd go to a nearby small airport, land and get her logbook signed, take off again, do the same thing at another airport and then return to home base. It was a rite of passage for student pilots, and she was both apprehensive and ready to get it done.

Today she was alone in a four-seater Cessna 172 trainer, flying from Merrickville to Kingston, Ontario, seventy miles away. Although the weather had been beautiful when she left, spring could bring rapid changes. Storm clouds began building ahead and Lydia became nervous. She wanted to talk to her instructor on the radio, but she panicked. Forgetting everything she'd been taught, she was turning the dial frantically when a sudden downdraft buffeted the plane for a few seconds. She screamed and banged on the radio, but it wasn't working at all now. She knew she'd turned the wrong dials. Lydia had never been this scared in her entire life. She prayed to God to let her live. Trying to calm herself, she steered away from the cloudbank between her and Kingston. She turned her little airplane south toward clear skies.

When the Cessna reached a broad expanse of water, she knew she had come to Lake Ontario. Still addled, she thought she should turn around, but now there was lightning behind her. Suddenly it began to rain fat drops that splattered hard on the windshield. She turned right again, desperately trying to get to the clear skies she could see in that direction.

She was so confused that she couldn't remember how to interpret the instruments that told her where she was going. Where she was now didn't matter anyway to Lydia. What mattered was finding an airport – *any* airport. If she could just land, she promised God she'd never get in an airplane again. Finally she saw dry land coming up ahead of her. *Thank God!* She put the plane into a steeper descent than her instructor would have liked, but she desperately had to land as soon as possible. Suddenly she let out a shriek. An enormous black airplane of some kind, flying very, very fast, shot by on her right side, less than a hundred feet away. Seconds later there was another one directly in front, coming straight toward her until at the last minute it veered sharply to her left. She pushed the yoke harder to increase her descent. She wanted to be down, now.

Unfortunately the little grandmother from Canada had made a mistake. She had entered United States airspace over the state of New York. President Parkes ordered the threat level lowered to DEFCON 3 just half an hour later, but at the moment Lydia's plane entered New York the country was still at its highest level, DEFCON 1. The control tower at Kingston, Ontario, frantically tried to contact her, but she couldn't hear them.

A tiny airplane that might be packed with explosives, its pilot perhaps on a suicide mission, had just flown into the United States and was maintaining radio silence. Two F-16 fighters had been scrambled to intercept her when she entered US airspace. As they flew very close, they could see an elderly female pilot, but she ignored their orders to turn back. Instead, the pilot had put the plane into a very steep descent, something that seemed to the military pilots to be a kamikaze dive.

At 3:22 in the afternoon a frazzled, confused and upset Lydia Beckham saw the last thing she'd ever see. A Hellfire missile streaked across the sky directly toward her windshield. She didn't even have time to scream as the Cessna exploded into a million pieces.

———

"Remember what took old Tricky Dick down?" President Parkes sat with his feet propped on the presidential desk in the Oval Office. His Chief of Staff A. J. Minter sat on the other side. Minter had been Parkes's faithful lapdog for twenty years. Those around him didn't understand why anyone would be willing to work for a boorish ingrate like Cham Parkes, but once they saw the Chief of Staff in action, it made sense. Minter's lack of self-esteem made him a perfect fit for his boss's constant nagging and criticism. The job was so far over his head that it was embarrassing, but he'd do whatever Parkes demanded, and that suited the two of them just fine.

A President's Chief of Staff was typically the backbone of operations in the White House, a leader to whom the staff looked for guidance and the gatekeeper to the President. It wasn't going to be that way during this term. The only man with backbone in the Oval Office today was the one whose shoes were scuffing the top of the most famous desk in America.

It was the afternoon of the first full day of the new President's term. He was wasting no time making changes. He barked at his subordinate, "Did you hear me? What took Nixon down?"

Minter hung his head and replied, "Uh, Watergate, I suppose." Whatever he said was going to be wrong. It always was.

"Shit, son! Do you need a history lesson? The *tapes* took him down. He recorded everything. Why the hell he did that, I'll never know. But we're not making the same mistake again. I want this office swept twice a day for bugs. I want to know how to circumvent the White House operators when I use the phone, and I want to find out how they archive emails so we can figure how to deal with it. They may have jumped Hillary's ass for having a private email account, but I'll guaran-damn-tee you I'll use mine whenever I want. And one more thing – that son of a bitch Homeland Security Secretary – what's his name, I never can remember – said I shouldn't use my personal cellphone anymore. Screw him! Write this down – replace that guy. Hell, I'll replace 'em all. Who's going to stop me from doing whatever I want? I'm the President of the goddamned United States!"

The Chief of Staff quietly took notes as his boss spewed venom. It would have been so much easier, he reflected to himself, if there had been the usual few months of transition between the election and the inauguration. Teams on both sides usually worked together to ensure a smooth transfer of power, especially when the new chief executive was from a different party. It was in the nation's interest to make things as easy as possible, not that Cham Parkes would have been cooperative anyway.

Regardless, this time things weren't smooth at all. One minute Harry Harrison had been President and the next minute Cham Parkes was. It was unprecedented and it threw everything off. Every appointed official and every single person working in the executive wing had been chosen by the Republican, a man whom Cham openly detested. In normal transitions the new President's Chief of Staff would have solicited recommendations for cabinet posts, offered his boss ideas for staff positions in the White House and supervised the transfer of duties. A.J. not only had no idea how to do something like that, he was powerless if he *had* known how. Cham Parkes didn't give a damn what Minter thought and Minter knew it. This President would make his own decisions.

Parkes's assistant buzzed him, asking if the press secretary could come in for a moment with some important news. The obviously frazzled young man told President Parkes about the grandmother whose plane had been shot down over western New York moments ago.

"It appears it was simply a mistake on her part," he continued. "Do you want to issue a statement?"

"My God, that woman was stupid," Parkes said without a tinge of feeling. "Here's my statement. Wrong damn place, wrong damn time. Write something yourself and make it be from me. Now get out. We have work to do."

Oh boy, the press secretary said to himself as he prepared a statement of regret for the woman's error that resulted in her death. *People in the White House thought President Clinton's shenanigans around here were bad. At least he cared about people, unlike this jerk I work for.*

CHAPTER SEVEN

Two days after the planes disappeared, Master Sergeant Jeremy Lail, a twenty-year veteran of the United States Air Force, failed to show up for work. Taking a sick day would be nothing unusual, but Lail hadn't called in at all. A high-ranking NCO, he'd never been a no-call, no-show in the fifteen years that he'd worked at Andrews Field.

Lail was the base's senior line operator. It was his job to sign off on preflight checks for government-owned aircraft. Last week the master sergeant had scribbled his signature on the checklists for both Air Force One and Air Force Two. His signature was the final part of the process before the President's plane had departed for Barbados and the Vice President's left for Honolulu, then on to Hong Kong.

Command Chief Master Sergeant Jim Perkins, the highest-ranking NCO at Andrews, not only was Jeremy's boss, he was his close friend as well. When one of Jeremy's co-workers called to say the man hadn't come to work this morning, Perkins was worried. Ordinarily he wouldn't have gotten involved chasing down absent employees, but this was different. This was his friend and this was a guy who never failed to report.

He hoped nothing was wrong, but he grew more concerned when his call to Jeremy's cellphone went to voicemail. He sent a couple of men over to Lail's house in nearby Prince George's County, Maryland. Jeremy lived out in the country near a little town called Morningside. Perkins knew the house well. He'd played poker there every other Saturday night for the past two years.

Most people who knew them wouldn't have paired the men as friends. They had only two things in common. Both were from New York City and both were high-ranking NCOs who tended to fraternize more with others of their rank than with subordinates. But there the similarities ended.

Jim Perkins had come out of a broken home in Harlem, attending New York University on a scholarship and graduating first in his class. He never knew his father, and although his mother loved Jim and his sister more than life itself, things had always been tough for them. He'd fought hard for everything he ever accomplished, he'd been married and divorced twice, and now Perkins was the top non-commissioned officer at what once had been called Andrews Air Force Base. He was in charge of nearly six thousand men and was a capable, efficient soldier who was on top of his game.

Jeremy Lail had grown up in vastly different circumstances. He was the son of a wealthy Wall Street investment banker. From his birth Jeremy's father told everyone his only child was someday going to be a high-powered lawyer. Jeremy went to the best preparatory schools and enrolled at Princeton, his father's alma mater, where he skipped class so often that he flunked out after one semester. Now his enraged father told friends Jeremy had been a loser his entire life, and he threatened to disown him. Jeremy's mother intervened and he enrolled at Nassau Community College. When that didn't work either, Jeremy's dad declared him an embarrassment to the family and said he never wanted to see him again. While his wife cried, the man tossed Jeremy's belongings out a second-story window onto the lawn, leaving a broken, tearful young man to gather his things in front of shocked neighbors, who watched it all.

Jeremy kept in touch with his mother, who secretly sent him money to get by. He moved to Virginia and enrolled at a vocational-technical school, finally finding something that excited him: aircraft maintenance technology.

He got a degree, joined the Air Force and worked at one base after another, rising in rank until he became a master sergeant and a senior line operator at Andrews four years ago. Although his mother told him how proud she was of his accomplishments, all his father would say was that he should have been an officer instead of an NCO. *But that would have taken initiative*, his dad said loudly and spitefully in the background more than once as Jeremy and his mother talked by phone. Jeremy got the message loud and clear.

He and his up-the-line boss Jim Perkins had met over drinks one night at the NCO Club and soon became friends. When the Saturday card game started, Jim became one of the regulars at Jeremy's house for beer, pizza and low-stakes poker. There were a few others who were faithful attendees, some of whom also worked at the base.

The men Jim Perkins had sent to Jeremy's house this morning reported in. No one answered the door and the carport was empty. The back door was unlocked, so Perkins told them to go inside. Within minutes he learned his friend wasn't there.

This is crazy. It can't be the way it looks. Given the situation, he knew what he had to do. Two aircraft from this facility had gone missing the day before yesterday, carrying the leaders of the free world. The National Transportation Safety Board had been camped out at the base ever since. For the hundredth time, he looked at the two sheets lying on his desk. The preflight checklists for Air Force One and Two bore the same scribble at the bottom – the signature of Master Sergeant Jeremy Lail, a man who was now unaccounted for. As bad as it looked, Jim was beginning to have tinges of fear. This could be monumental. He called his boss, the commandant of Andrews Field, who in turn called the Secretary of Defense. An hour later President Parkes had been briefed and federal agents were combing Lail's house.

The FBI issued an all-points bulletin, calling him a person of interest in the disappearance of the planes. His picture and description headlined the nightly news worldwide. As soon as the media learned what Master Sergeant Lail's job had been at Andrews, there was intense speculation about his potential involvement in the crisis. This man could be a key part of whatever had happened, and the networks began digging into his past to find out who Jeremy Lail really was.

BILL THOMPSON

CHAPTER EIGHT

The Fourth Day
Friday, April 3

"How about a brandy, Lou?"

Senator Louis Breaux, Democrat of Louisiana, sat across the desk from the President. Breaux glanced at his watch out of habit. It was 10:30 a.m. Cham saw him and raised his eyebrows.

"Too early for you, son?"

Lou laughed heartily. "It's never too early, Mr. President. It's five o'clock somewhere, as some intelligent man once said!"

Although the hidden bar was barely twenty feet from Parkes's desk, there was no way he'd fetch the drinks himself. There were people for that now. This new position of power brought with it a heady sense of entitlement, and no one was going to enjoy it more than he was. Cham pressed a button. A door across the room opened and a steward emerged from the pantry adjoining the Oval Office.

"How may I help you, sir?"

"Get Senator Breaux and me a couple of brandies," Parkes ordered.

"Right away, Mr. President." *Isn't it a little early?* the steward thought to himself as he retrieved two Baccarat snifters and carried them and a bottle to the desk.

As the man finished pouring in both snifters, Cham said, "We're going to get to know each other really well, boy, and here's your first lesson. You need to learn something about me. I'm a two-fisted drinker. You didn't pour enough brandy in those glasses for a girl to drink. Fill the damn things up halfway and be quick about it. I'm getting thirsty waiting for you!"

Senator Breaux laughed heartily as the President pulled out a seven-inch Churchill, clipped the end and lit it, exhaling satisfying puffs that drifted in gray clouds to the ceiling of the most famous office in the world.

"They let you smoke in here?" Beaux quipped.

"By God, who's going to stop me? With a four-trillion-dollar budget, I guess we can afford to clean the drapes now and then."

The steward pulled the pantry door shut behind him. In his thirty years here, he'd served several Presidents. Each one had been different. Some were outgoing and friendly, others occasionally condescending, and still others moody and dark. But none of them had been a total asshole. Not until now.

What the hell is this country in for? He shuddered at the thought.

The two old friends clicked glasses across the President's desk and sipped slowly. After a moment Parkes asked, "How'd you like to be Vice President?"

Senator Breaux popped his head up in surprise. He and Cham Parkes had been friends for thirty years as they rose in seniority in Congress. They'd brokered a lot of deals together. Some had been widely publicized and politically popular back home in their neighboring states of Texas and Louisiana. Others were done secretly, benefitting not only important donors but the men themselves. They shared big secrets, and neither could afford to hurt the other.

Louisiana was a place where politics played out in back rooms with a handshake or a nod and a wink. Many politicians from the Pelican State had gone to prison for their dirty deeds. Others should have been jailed – most of those got away with nothing more than a misdemeanor ethics violation. Louis Breaux had cleverly managed to keep his dirty laundry hidden. He was one of Cham's best friends, a man whom the Speaker always enjoyed drinking and dining with. Now the senator from Louisiana was being offered the second-highest job in the land.

"I'd consider that an honor, sir," the senator replied in his slow, syrupy Southern drawl. "My, my, Cham. Look where you are today. Sitting over there behind the desk of the President of the United States. How can I turn you down? Just think of the things we can do together!"

President Parkes walked around his desk, stuck out his hand, raised his glass and said, "To prosperity, to good friends and to a more perfect union, one with you and me in charge!"

They clinked glasses, shook hands and Breaux responded, "Damn right. Let's figure out . . ." He paused. "Do you sweep your office for bugs?"

"Who are you talking to here, Louis? Do you sweep *your* office for bugs? Hell yes, you do. And that's the first thing I ordered A.J. to do here. I might have been born at night, but it wasn't last night!"

The senator bellowed with laughter. "All right then. What I was going to say was, you know that four-trillion-dollar budget that's going to help clean your drapes? Let's figure out how to get some of that working for us personally."

"My thoughts exactly, Lou. My thoughts exactly."

BILL THOMPSON

CHAPTER NINE

The person who knew Jeremy Lail best was Joe Kaya, the owner of a chain of auto salvage yards in the suburbs around DC. After Jeremy's boss notified his commandant that Lail was missing, Jim called Joe next.

Perkins and Joe Kaya knew each other well because they both played in the poker games at Jeremy's house. They often sat next to each other and engaged in typical male banter about football, women and life in general. Jim had learned a lot about Joe's background from those conversations. Joe was a first-generation American, born in Baltimore to Iraqi immigrants, and he spoke both English and Arabic. His father had started a salvage business and became well-off thanks to his customer base of emigrants from Europe and Asia. These new Americans stuck together, trusting and preferring to deal with others like themselves.

Joe was an intelligent boy and had been salutatorian of his high school class. The first in his family to attend college, Joe was admitted to Georgetown University on a full scholarship. The institution was an unusual but perfect fit. Although being a Catholic wasn't a requirement for matriculation, Joe converted and attended Mass far more regularly than many of his friends who'd been raised in the faith.

Georgetown's Walsh School of Foreign Service trained students to become diplomats and work in embassies and international business settings. Joe majored in international relations and graduated with honors. His degree, coupled with his fluency in Arabic, caught the attention of State Department recruiters. Joe accepted a position at the embassy in Baghdad and spent two years in his parents' home city.

When Joe's father died suddenly of a heart attack, he returned home for the funeral and decided to stay. Leaving behind a promising career in international affairs, Joe took over the family salvage yard. Fifteen years later there were half a dozen offshoots spread across the suburbs, and Joe, a confirmed bachelor, was comfortably wealthy.

He and Jeremy Lail had met because of the latter's interest in restoring old cars. Jeremy had shown up at Joe's yard one Saturday looking for a particular part for a 1955 Chevy. The clerk pointed out the same model, this one beautifully restored, on a rack in the bay. "It's the boss's car," Jeremy was told, and when Joe heard him gushing with admiration over the condition of the automobile, he stepped out of his office to meet him. That conversation led to a few beers occasionally and then an invitation to the poker game. Over time they became best friends.

When Jim called Joe's cellphone, the first words he heard from Joe were lighthearted and jovial. "Ready to get your ass whipped at poker Saturday night?"

There was no friendly response. In a somber voice Jim said that Jeremy was missing. He hadn't reported for work today and he wasn't at home. Neither was his car.

"This is so unlike him," he told Joe. "Did he mention anything to you about going somewhere?"

"Damn, this sounds bad. He didn't say a word to me. What in hell could have happened? Do you think he's in trouble? Could he have been kidnapped? It feels weird to say this, but something's wrong, don't you think? This isn't like Jeremy."

"I'm going to tell you something that has to stay between us until it becomes public. Two days ago Jeremy signed off on the preflight checklists for Air Force One and Air Force Two. His signature gave them official authorization to fly. That's the part that has me worried."

"Holy shit! What are you saying? Are you thinking Jeremy was involved with the disappearances? Could somebody have planted bombs and forced him to sign off on it?"

Perkins wiped sweat from his brow. "Frankly, I have no idea what to think. But I'll tell you this. It doesn't look good."

Joe signed off with a promise to see what he could find out. His stomach began to churn. He'd always been a macho guy, but with things unfolding the way they were it was scary – terrifying, if you really let yourself think about it. He ran to the restroom and threw up his breakfast.

BILL THOMPSON

CHAPTER TEN

One week later

This afternoon in a church near downtown Oklahoma City, Brian and Nicole would attend a unique service – a combined funeral for a family of four, one of whom was the President of the United States. There would be no caskets because there were no bodies. It was an eerie, surreal time for the nation, and certainly for those invited to attend the service.

Brian had hired a sedan and a driver for the three-hour trip to Oklahoma. Security and logistics would be a nightmare since news agencies from around the globe were on hand to cover the funeral. More importantly, Brian had lost his closest friend. Driving for three hours was the last thing he needed to do.

As they traveled north from Dallas on Interstate 35, they reminisced about Harry and Jennifer Harrison and their two girls. Brian had been Harry's freshman roommate at the University of Oklahoma. Nicole had met the couple when she and Brian began dating several years ago. Once Harry became President, the four of them remained close, even though it became more difficult to see each other often. Brian and Nicole spent the night in the White House every few months after private dinners in the family quarters, and when Harry had to be in Dallas or London, he made sure Jennifer came along so the four of them could get together, even if only briefly.

Sometimes they'd grab an hour at Love Field in the living area aboard Air Force One before Harry and Jennifer flew back to DC. Other times they'd have a quiet meal at Nicole's condo in the Ritz-Carlton. Less often they dined out. The logistics required for the President of the United States to have dinner in a restaurant made that the most difficult choice, but occasionally they did it anyway. The memory of their being rushed by Secret Service agents through the kitchen and into a private room at the Mansion on Turtle Creek six months ago brought smiles to their faces.

There had been so many good times. Brian recalled memories of the hilarious predicaments the college boys had gotten themselves into. Nicole had heard all the stories before, but today she laughed all over again. Brian needed to talk and she wanted to listen.

Emotions ran high. There were smiles one minute and tears the next. "It's just so crazy that we're going to Harry's funeral," Brian commented, wiping his eyes. "And not just Harry but his entire family. My God, how will his father and mother ever cope with this? How could someone lose a son, daughter-in-law and grandchildren and be able to go on living?"

Henry Harrison, the President's father, was a retired US senator whose son had succeeded him. He and his wife Julia loved Jennifer as if she were their own daughter and they adored the girls, their only grandchildren. Nicole sobbed as she thought of losing an entire family in a flash, then having to move ahead without even knowing what had happened.

Earlier in the week the President's personal secretary had called about funeral arrangements. Harry's mother and father had requested Brian and Nicole sit with the family. She explained that admittance to the sanctuary was by invitation only, but a nearby auditorium that seated two thousand people would broadcast the service on closed-circuit TV for the huge crowd that was expected.

The scene in front of the church was more chaotic than they expected. Security was high today even though President Parkes had again made a unilateral decision to reduce the threat level back to its lowest point, DEFCON 5. At a barricade two blocks from the church, Oklahoma City police officers checked their names off a guest list and waved the sedan through. They saw two dozen news trucks, their satellite dishes aimed skywards, lined up on a side street. Announcers giving live reports stood nearby, the church providing the background. Out of deference to the President's family, this was as close as the news media would be allowed. They were near enough to see the guests arriving and offer commentary, but too far away to speak to anyone in person.

At the bottom of a staircase leading to the entrance of the church, a cadre of armed Secret Service agents double-checked their names. At the top of the stairs stood twenty Marines wearing flak jackets and cradling automatic rifles. President Parkes's decision to stay in Washington had been criticized by many, but Vice President Breaux was there. He shook hands and patted shoulders of many of his acquaintances as he shuffled down the aisle between his two Secret Service men and took a seat behind the family.

Brian nodded to several people he recognized as they were ushered to the front. He saw members of Congress and the Supreme Court, several cabinet officials and the governor of Oklahoma. When they reached the pew, the usher whispered that they should move to the middle. The two aisle seats next to Brian were reserved for Henry and Julia Harrison.

As soon as the President's parents were seated, the service began. Reverend Franklin Graham gave the opening prayer, the pastors of both this church and a one in Washington that the Harrisons attended gave eulogies, and there were solos by an acclaimed opera star.

The Vice President was impassive, but virtually every other person in the room was moved by emotion. Tears flowed and muffled sobs could be heard frequently during the forty-five-minute service. Julia Harrison took Brian's hand more than once during the most difficult parts. When the ending prayer was given, commending the lives of these four people into the hands of God, she cried out, literally in pain. It was heart wrenching to Brian and Nicole to watch the grief of this mother and grandmother whom they loved so much.

BILL THOMPSON

CHAPTER ELEVEN

After every event, no matter how tragic and overwhelming it is, the population eventually moves ahead. People desperately want things to be as they were before. They want structure, order and normalcy. They want the calmness of everyday life. It's simply human nature, even in the most turbulent of times.

In the weeks following the tragic loss of twenty-five Americans – its two senior leaders, the President's family, a cabinet secretary, the Chief of Staff and the crew of two aircraft – Parkes's decision to quickly lower the threat level seemed to have been a good, stabilizing move. Americans weren't typically a fearful people. They were optimistic, encouraging and positive. The President had urged the nation to get back to normal, and people were enthusiastically embracing his suggestion.

To many Washington insiders, it appeared the new President was following his own advice a little too much. He seemed unconcerned about what had happened to the planes, unwilling to commit significant resources to the recovery effort, and convinced nothing was ever going to turn up to solve the mystery of two aircraft that had simply disappeared.

When the line chief at Andrews went missing, the FBI initiated a search of transportation databases, looking for a hit on his passport and credit cards. They discovered that on the very day Parkes lowered the level to DEFCON 3 and travel restrictions were lifted, he had bought a train ticket from Washington to New York. Descending on Union Station downtown, agents quickly found Lail's SUV parked in the lot, but they learned nothing new.

In New York he'd paid by credit card to take a cab to Kennedy airport, where he used his credit card and passport to buy a coach seat on Delta's overnight flight to Athens. Up to this point, Lail didn't seem concerned about hiding his whereabouts, but that ended sharply.

He arrived in Greece at 8:15 a.m. the next morning. He was seen on video walking out of customs with a suitcase, exiting the building and getting into a private car that had been idling at curbside for several minutes. There was no shot of the black Volvo's tag, and the local police initiated what was ultimately an unsuccessful search for the car.

After that, Jeremy Lail hadn't used his passport or credit cards again. For the authorities looking for him, the trail ended, but for Master Sergeant Lail, the adventure was just beginning.

CHAPTER TWELVE

Six men sat in the White House Situation Room, listening to an update from Rodney Stang, head of the CIA's Arab desk. Born in Beirut to parents in the diplomatic corps and fluent in Arabic, Stang was the nation's top intelligence official for the Middle East. This quickly arranged meeting was the most urgent since Chambliss Parkes had become President. There was important news: at last someone was claiming responsibility for the incidents.

In addition to the President and Stang, there were four others around the table. They were Ken Upton, the head of the National Security Agency; Upton's boss, Secretary of Defense Clark Vernon; CIA Director Donovan Case; and A. J. Minter, the President's Chief of Staff.

Except for Minter, everyone was a holdover – a person who had been appointed by Harry Harrison – and all the holdovers in the administration knew exactly where they stood. Cham Parkes demanded loyalty, and he was already actively, systematically replacing Harrison's people, indifferent to their competence or value in dealing with the current crisis. Parkes didn't want to hear about how things used to be done or what President Harrison once thought about a particular issue. Everyone in the room knew his turn would come, but for today they were still part of the intelligence team. The President simply hadn't dealt with them yet. They all knew why – with only weeks until the Democratic National Convention, Parkes had been out of town on the campaign trail. Fortunately when the news broke this morning, he happened to have slept in his own bed last night.

Since the planes disappeared a few weeks ago, intelligence teams in Western countries had intercepted literally tens of thousands of texts, emails and phone calls from the Middle East. Regardless of potential importance, every single transmission emanating from the area was logged and shared among the agencies. There was lots of chatter, but today's news was a surprise.

Thirty minutes ago the Arab news network Al Jazeera had broadcast a live interview. From a remote outdoor location said to be in Syria, a reporter interviewed the leader of a group claiming responsibility for the destruction of Air Force One and Two. Things had been completely quiet since the disappearances, but now at last the United States government had new information.

Today's meeting began with a viewing of the newscast on the Situation Room's ninety-inch television. Although this was at least the second time each attendee had seen it, the video gave everyone goose bumps just like repeated viewings of the tragedy of 9/11 had done.

A young man sat in a chair under a tree with a tent in the background. He was dressed in blue jeans and a white shirt and a black hood covered his head and shoulders. Only his steely, dark eyes were visible. He called himself Tariq the Hawk, the leader of the jihadist organization Falcons of Islam. The man's Arabic words were in the background as a translator spoke tonelessly in English. The man said Falcons of Islam was responsible for planning the destruction of both aircraft, planting bombs on them and murdering the top leaders of the loathsome American government.

The man brandished an AK-47 toward the camera as his final words, the words that chilled the Western world, were spat out with unmistakable hatred and contempt.

"What has happened is only the beginning. Listen to my words, people of America. Your women and your children are going to die. For as long as even one of us still lives, our purpose is to exterminate every one of you. Today, yes, today, we are already in your cities, your towns and your villages. But you do not know us, and you cannot recognize us. You no longer need to fear people who look like Muslims – people who look like I do. Our brothers in your country look like you and act like you, because they *are* you. The Falcons of Islam is not just Arabs. It is also

American citizens – men, women and children who will gladly die for jihad against the Great Satan. The next strike, like the last one, will be when you do not expect it. Your foolish President has lowered your country's threat level to DEFCON 5. Thanks be to Allah for his stupidity. Now it is even easier for us to wipe your bloated, capitalistic nation off the map. And it shall happen soon, Allah willing. Sleep well tonight, America, for we will be awake, watching. Allahu Akbar."

Stang had listened to the interview first in English, then in Arabic. He confirmed the translation was accurate, adding that Tariq's words were cold, calculating and without any hint of emotion. He said that the Falcons of Islam was an offshoot of the notorious al-Nusra Front or al-Qaeda in Syria, and Western intelligence agencies knew almost nothing about the group or Tariq the Hawk.

He passed out a briefing packet on the Nusra Front and its leader Abu Mohammad Al-Joulani. The newscast might indeed have come from Syria, Stang explained, because the headquarters of the Nusra Front was in Edlib in the northwestern sector of the country. Recon satellites were being redirected to the twenty-five-hundred-square-mile area of Edlib Governorate in hopes something helpful might turn up.

As the briefing continued, those in the room reflected over the past few weeks. Cham Parkes hadn't been President when the planes disappeared. He'd had almost no input about the situation since then, because there had been nothing new. The only two actions he took were decisions every person present today thought were wrong. Two days after the tragedies, long before anyone could speculate on exactly what had happened, Parkes lowered the readiness level to DEFCON 3. It was far too early for such a decision, and it should have never been made without consulting his advisors. But the pros on his team kept their opinions to themselves. It was better to keep your job and work to hold things together than to infuriate the President.

But then the crazy bastard had done it again. Only days later he'd announced it was time to give Americans back their comfort zone. Again without consulting a single advisor, he had lowered the level to DEFCON 5, the bottom of the scale. That time one man had had enough. The Chairman of the Joint Chiefs of Staff, a dedicated career officer who had served four Presidents — two from each party – told Parkes he was wrong.

That was two weeks ago. Today there was a new Chairman of the Joint Chiefs of Staff.

They were thirty minutes into today's briefing, and it appeared to Director Case that Parkes was no longer interested in it. His eyes flitted around the room, his brief note taking at the beginning had long since stopped, and he glanced at his watch every few minutes. It reminded Case of the White Rabbit who was late for a very important date. Only at the end of the newscast, when the terrorist called him foolish and stupid, had the President perked up.

It surprised no one when Parkes muttered, "Jackass. We'll slaughter every one of you A-rab bastards." He pronounced the word Arab with two syllables and a long A. He wasn't the first leader to mispronounce words, of course. President Bush couldn't say the word *nuclear*. But Bush could laugh at himself. This was different. When Parkes did it, no one dared laugh even though the word sounded like it came from a redneck holding a beer in one hand and a rifle in the other.

If the shoe fits . . . Case thought, his mind turning back to the men around the table as Defense Secretary Vernon said, "Mr. President, I suggest we raise the threat level back up to DEFCON 3. As long as there's a possibility they really have sleeper agents . . ."

"Are you kidding?" Parkes interrupted, shouting at the career Army veteran who had held his position under both Harrison and his predecessor John Chapman. "Are you out of your mind? We're not going to let these assholes push us around. It's business as usual around here, gentlemen. I made the decision to go to DEFCON 5. We're safe as hell. We're in America, for God's sake. Who in this room's afraid of a bunch of A-rabs making idle threats?"

Hoping Parkes meant the question rhetorically, Secretary Vernon asked, "So sir, what are you suggesting we do?"

"Nothing! That's exactly what we're going to do. Are you scared of this guy sitting in the desert a million miles from nowhere? I can't believe I'm the only one in this room out of all you *professionals*" – he spat that word sarcastically – "who knows that little shit is lying. They couldn't have pulled off an operation like this. A bunch of ragged people in some third-world country figured out how to bomb Air Force One and Two? Somebody did, but it damned sure wasn't these amateurs. Seriously? You seriously believe this guy? I can't believe it." As an aside he muttered loudly enough for everyone to hear, "And these are supposed to be the advisors I depend on?"

He leaned forward with his elbows on the table and said, "I should replace every single one of you *men*" – he said the word with disdain – "in this room right now. It'll come soon, I promise, but for now you're going to listen to me, and you're going to do what I tell you, because I'm the goddamned commander-in-chief. You may not like it and I'm happy if you resign now and get the hell out of this room. We're going to do nothing. *Nothing.* We're going to sit tight and act like grown-ups. We're not going to let these ragheads push around the greatest country in the world."

He stood up, shoved his chair back so hard it slammed into the wall, and stormed out of the room. Minter meekly gathered his things and followed like a cowering dog.

Stunned, the others sat without speaking. The same thought was going through the minds of every one of them. They should resign. They *should* get out now. But no one would, because each loved his country and was dedicated to preserving liberty. Despite the fact that this President seemed hell-bent on destroying what the founding fathers had created, they would do everything in their power to hold it together for as long as they could. It might not be long, they feared; either they'd be replaced soon or there wouldn't be a country left to run.

Everyone sat lost in thought until Case cleared his throat and said, "Well, I suppose this meeting is over." They walked out in silence, each considering the inherent danger of the President's opinions.

Back in his office, Defense Secretary Vernon recalled the disturbing aspects of the meeting. The President was not only dismissing the Falcons of Islam as amateurs, he had given the order that nothing would be done. The country would remain at its lowest threat level, and the terrorists' claim to have sleeper agents inside the United States would not be investigated. It was almost as though the President were indifferent to the potential menace.

Vernon had been having the same thoughts about Parkes's stance for a while, and today merely solidified his hands-off position on terrorism.

What if his opinion wasn't indifference at all? What if it was something far more insidious?

Back at Langley, Don Case was having the same trepidation. He had to report what had happened. Parkes was far too dangerous. He made a call.

CHAPTER THIRTEEN

I am a blessed man, Tariq the Hawk said to himself. His mentor Mohammad al-Joulani had taken a boy and formed him into what he was today. Tariq had grown to manhood under the tutelage of his mentor, but like the hawk, there always came a time to spread one's wings and fly on your own. Tariq was ready to fly.

Allah had blessed him six months ago when Mohammad introduced him to the plan that would jolt the world. His mentor had trusted him with this monumental project, and Tariq had performed stunningly well.

The few who knew the plan had told Tariq it was impossible, crazy beyond belief. No one could guarantee the schedules of the President and Vice President. No one could get aboard the government's airplanes at the most heavily guarded base in America. No one could successfully plant not just one bomb, but two.

But Tariq had accomplished the impossible.

He brought people, materiel and plans together, infusing his enthusiasm and skill into every aspect of the plan and creating a loyal team who believed it would actually happen. He masterfully guided a dozen separate parts until they were joined to create the final piece of the puzzle – the installation of small boxes in the cockpits of each plane. These could be detonated via the Internet using the aircraft's Wi-Fi.

Things could go wrong, of course. The biggest problem would be a last-minute change in scheduling. Since the devices would be detonated remotely, no one would be around to know exactly when they should be fired. Instead of disappearing over the ocean, the plane might explode while parked on a tarmac somewhere with no one on board. That was a chance the Falcons had to take. If by Allah's grace they didn't kill the Great Satan's leaders, destroying their two planes would still send a message about America's vulnerability from within.

But the plan had worked perfectly, and now Tariq was a legend among his countrymen. Since the bombings, he had moved to an oasis in the Syrian desert near the Iraqi border. The Falcons of Islam had been fanatics before the attack on America. Now they were absolutely rabid in the fervent adoration of their leader. These men protected Tariq. They would gladly die for him because Allah had blessed him with success against the enemy.

Tariq's cellphone rang; he glanced at the number and answered a call from a man he considered the most important person in the world to the cause.

They hadn't spoken since the planes went down. Today Tariq listened with pride to words of praise – respectful words he hadn't heard before from this powerful individual. The caller told the young man that he was a true leader and a soldier of Allah.

"I promised to help you if you could make this happen, and I will. Shall I send my contribution to the account we discussed earlier?"

Tariq took out a slip of paper he kept in his pocket. It contained nothing but numbers, banking information he now confirmed. Before the attacks, his benefactor had set up a Swiss bank account for Tariq. He knew nothing about such things; the only bank account the Falcons had was the one Mohammad set up in Morocco, the one that had almost five million dollars in it. This new account was in Tariq's name, not the Falcons of Islam. It was a dangerous move, but it was time for the hawk to fly.

The next morning Tariq awoke early, as eager as a child to know if the caller had told the truth. He opened the bank's app on his phone, entered his ID and password, and saw a number that literally gave him goose bumps.

The bank account – *his* account and his alone – now held fifty million dollars.

Tariq knew one thing for certain. Having the fifty million dollars in his personal bank account would result in an excruciatingly painful death once Mohammad al-Joulani found out. By the time he did, Tariq would be ready. One person would surely die, but it would not be the Hawk.

His mentor had prepared him well. He needed no one now.

BILL THOMPSON

CHAPTER FOURTEEN

Senator Henry Harrison III and his wife were participating in their nightly ritual, the five o'clock cocktail hour, on the porch of their country house. They had owned the thousand-acre ranch for years. It was only an hour's drive from their beautiful home in the exclusive Nichols Hills area of Oklahoma City, and for the Harrisons it had become their refuge since the funerals two weeks ago. Well-meaning friends kept them busy when they were in the City, but the solitude of this place, its silence broken only by their quiet conversation or the honking of geese heading north, was what they craved now. In the weeks since the disappearance, they had stayed at the ranch most of the time. Every evening they sat out here on the porch; tonight they watched a blazing red sun slowly sink into the horizon as cattle lowed nearby. Both of them found comfort in the rolling hills and green pastures that seemed to go on forever. Right now they didn't want anything else from life but the ranch and their memories.

"Harry and Jennifer and the girls loved this place," Julia remarked wistfully. Lost in reverie, her seventy-five-year-old husband nodded and sipped his Bourbon and branch water. He'd been remembering the fun times they had out here, teaching little Lizzie and Kate how to ride a horse and packing tents in their old pickup to do overnight campouts on the back forty acres. He thought about the Christmases spent in the great room in front of a tree they had cut themselves, singing carols and roasting marshmallows in the fire they always kept going in the winter.

The couple had no other children, and they were private people with no really close friends. Since Henry's retirement, the grandchildren had become the main thing that gave them fulfillment. They had kept their townhouse in DC so they could be involved in the girls' lives. They were always picking up Lizzie and Kate, taking them places and attending recitals, performances and football games with them.

Things had gotten more complicated when Harry became President. The requirement for security upended the simple life they'd enjoyed since Henry's retirement, and this place – the ranch – became their retreat. Even here there had to be changes, of course. A level section of pasture half a mile from the house was paved, and a runway long enough to accommodate a private jet was built. Air Force One would land sixty miles away in Oklahoma City, and the smaller jet or a helicopter would ferry them out to the country.

While Harry, Jennifer or the girls were at the ranch, Secret Service agents occupied the guest bunkhouse. The agents were very good at what they did – they were masters at remaining watchful without being intrusive. Everything was perfect until that awful morning. What had been normal would never be normal again. Jets no longer landed and the Secret Service agents were gone. Now there was no President here to protect. All that was left was the two of them. The family retreat was now a place of silence for two aging people who had lost everything.

The house phone rang. They looked at each other in surprise – it happened so seldom that they wondered what it could be. They knew who the caller was. Now that the kids were gone, it could only be the answering service. No one else had the number.

Calls to any of the Harrisons' residences were picked up by a service who emailed a message to Henry. He looked at them now and then; it was rare that anything required even same-day attention. The ringing phone this evening meant something different. The only time the service called was when there was an emergency.

Henry pushed himself unsteadily up from the porch rocker and walked into the house. Julia didn't hear anything for several minutes.

"Are you all right, Henry?" she called to him.

She turned as he rapped on the screen door. He was holding the cordless phone to his ear and he gave her a thumbs-up. She settled back into her chair, rocking slowly and wondering what in the world had happened this time. However serious it might be, it didn't matter anymore. Nothing could ever be as horrible as that call – that life-ending call – had been.

In a moment Henry came outside carrying refreshed drinks. The squeaky sound of the porch door opening and slamming was comforting, she thought briefly. It made her feel at home.

They talked quietly for over an hour. Henry explained about the call, what he'd agreed to do, and what would happen next. The conversation was occasionally interrupted by Julia's outbursts of uncontrollable sobbing. At last he squeezed her hand and said, "Let's go inside and fix dinner, sweetheart. We have a big day tomorrow." She smiled and kissed his cheek.

The next evening as Brian and Nicole watched the news, they saw a ten-second clip about former President Harrison's parents. They were heading to the Mediterranean for a month aboard a private yacht.

They must have been invited by one of the many very wealthy people who he'd gotten to know during his time in the Senate, Brian figured. But he also knew how much the couple valued their privacy, so he was a little surprised they'd chosen to be with others so soon.

Good for them. I can't comprehend their loss and the grief they must still feel every second. Brian hoped the change of scenery and time with friends would speed the healing process.

BILL THOMPSON

CHAPTER FIFTEEN

Brian Sadler was better known than many Hollywood actors. Since he had assumed ownership of Bijan Rarities a few years ago, Brian had become a regular on cable networks such as History and Discovery. A worldwide cadre of loyal viewers eagerly heard his opinions about the provenance, authenticity and value of unique archaeological pieces. When he and Nicole were in restaurants in Dallas, New York or London, people often stopped by their table to meet him.

Bijan had become the gallery of choice for well-heeled collectors who wanted to acquire or divest priceless pieces. Sotheby's or Christie's handled art, wine and collectibles, but Bijan Rarities surpassed both in the sale and auction of ancient relics and artifacts.

Brian had become enamored with Bijan from that day he first visited the Fifth Avenue gallery and met its owner Darius Nazir, an Egyptian respected worldwide among his fellow dealers. When Brian arrived, Nazir was finalizing preparations for a television broadcast. Soon millions of armchair travelers eagerly watched archaeologists enter a newly discovered tomb in Egypt's Valley of the Kings and marveled as the sarcophagus of a long-forgotten pharaoh was auctioned. By the time the show aired, Brian was one of those eager fans. Fortuitously, through a strange turn of events, he became sole owner of the prestigious gallery.

Brian continued the tradition of his predecessor, holding auctions every six months. The other major houses couldn't compete with Bijan's popularity – each wildly popular auction was aired on a prime time cable network. There was always a theme – his next one was called *The Wrath of Vesuvius* – and the networks eagerly bid against each other for exclusive rights. This morning Brian read the latest contracts sent over by his attorney that would solidify the Vesuvius auction four months from now. That one would be broadcast live from Bijan's Old Bond Street gallery in London.

As he stood in the showroom, directing his second-in-command Cory Spencer and two staffers about the display of a new piece, his cellphone rang. He looked at the word "blocked" on the screen and refused the call. He had neither the time nor the patience for some auto-dialed sales pitch. Suddenly he got the ding of a voicemail. He listened a moment; then he walked out of the showroom, closed the door to his office and sat down at his desk to wait.

The voicemail had been brief. "Brian, this is Henry Harrison. I need to speak with you urgently. I'll try this number again in exactly five minutes. If I don't reach you, I'll call every day at nine a.m. and three p.m. your time until I reach you."

Senator Harrison and his wife should be somewhere in the Mediterranean, cruising on a private yacht by now. A ship-to-shore call might show up as blocked. Whatever it was, it sounded urgent. While his employees waited for him in the showroom, he waited for the call.

Three minutes later his phone rang. Brian answered immediately.

"Good morning, Senator. I hope you and Julia are holding up all right, given the situation."

"It's as good as it can be," the President's father said more tersely than Brian had ever heard him. "I don't have much time, so I'll get to the point. The government needs your help. You can't imagine the resources being deployed around the world to solve the mystery of Air Force One and Two. You can help, Brian, and I'm personally asking for your assistance."

"Anything, Senator. You know I'd do anything. I'm sure every agency on earth is trying to find out what happened, and I can't imagine how I can help. But if you think there's something I can do, I'm ready."

"You have an auction coming up soon involving pieces from Pompeii. Is that right?"

"Yes, but I don't understand . . ."

The President's father interrupted. "And you won't understand for a while. You're going to get a call Saturday morning at 8:30. What they ask you to do may sound strange, but I can't emphasize enough how urgent this is. If you want to help with the mystery of Harry and the family, I'm convinced what these men ask will be a critically important contribution. Someday I can tell you more. For now I have to go. Thanks for your help and, Brian, don't say anything to Nicole about this call."

Brian sat for a moment looking at his phone. He was baffled.

BILL THOMPSON

CHAPTER SIXTEEN

As the former President's father had promised, Brian's phone rang at exactly 8:30 on Saturday morning. Even though he'd been waiting at his desk for fifteen minutes, the sound still startled him.

Three hours later he walked to the United States Embassy in Grosvenor Square, just a couple of miles from his gallery on Old Bond Street. He was brought to a small office, where a man in jeans and a sport jacket sat. He rose and offered his hand.

"Please sit down, Mr. Sadler. I'm Donovan Case, director of the CIA. Thanks for agreeing to help us."

Their meeting lasted just over an hour. Brian signed a confidentiality agreement at the outset, although afterwards he wondered why, since he had been given very little information. The CIA wanted his help to accomplish something he was uniquely qualified to do. He had agreed – what the director asked would be simple to accomplish, presuming the circumstances were right. Certain things had to come together to make everything work, and those things might never happen. If they did, Brian would be helping in the quest to determine what happened to Harry Harrison and the rest of the people on those airplanes. Of course he'd help. He had an obligation to do whatever he could.

Once the meeting ended, Case reminded him to keep their discussion confidential even from his fiancée. Brian agreed, knowing the less she knew about this, the better.

As he walked back to work, he asked himself how they knew he had a fiancée. It really made no difference, but it did surprise him. But then they were the CIA, after all. These spooks supposedly knew everything.

BILL THOMPSON

CHAPTER SEVENTEEN

Joe Kaya had made the decision to betray the country of his birth sometime during his sophomore year at Georgetown University. It happened soon after 9/11, but he'd forgotten the details after all these years.

His college roommate Adam was from Syria and was the son of the deputy ambassador to the United States. As college kids do, Joe and others studying in the Foreign Service School spent many evenings drinking beer, discussing religion and contrasting the politics of the United States against that of the Middle Eastern countries where many of these kids were from. Adam was one of those who vocalized the American aggression many of them felt but rarely discussed. Most students were afraid to speak out. They wanted futures – jobs as diplomats and embassy workers – and an education in the United States. They consciously distanced themselves from the brutal jihadists back home. Even Joe Kaya did something to make himself more "American." He converted to Catholicism.

One evening in the second semester of their freshman year, Adam asked Joe to meet some friends. They drove half an hour to a suburban mosque where a group of men in their late twenties welcomed the boys. They used Joe's birth name Yusuf – no one but his father had ever called him by that name. They drank tea, smoked strong Turkish cigarettes and talked until after midnight. Joe enjoyed the discussions so much that he and Adam went back several times before the summer break. Two people in particular – Ali and Mo – took an interest in Joe from that first night, but he didn't pick up on it.

Joe would later recall that those early meetings were full of mostly tame criticism about American tendencies like how rednecks in the south seemed to hate Muslims just because of where they had been born. Despite the fact that Joe was at an impressionable age, a lot of what the men said made sense because it was true. Many Americans really did treat Muslims differently.

After the summer, the boys roomed together again for their sophomore year. They moved back to campus in early September, bought books and did a hundred other things. Classes resumed on Monday, September 10, 2001.

The next day at 8:46 a.m., everything changed completely. American Airlines Flight 11, flown by an Egyptian hijacker named Mohamed Atta, hit the North Tower of the World Trade Center, and Islamophobia suddenly became a familiar term. In an instant, citizens who were as American as anybody else – people who had been born and educated here, men and women who belonged to churches, PTA groups, Rotary Clubs and Masonic lodges – became the subjects of fear and hatred. Because of how they looked or where they came from or how they spoke, some Americans ostracized others who in truth were as American as they were. It didn't matter if they were Little League coaches or deacons in the Presbyterian Church or Cub Scout den mothers. None of that mattered to some people. Those people – those different ones – were Muslims, just like the ones who had perpetrated the most egregious attack ever on American soil.

Georgetown University's Foreign Service School was a very cosmopolitan, ethnically and socially diverse place. There were kids from a hundred countries and a hundred backgrounds. Even so, the two Arab boys felt a little self-conscious walking around campus after 9/11 even though no one ever said anything negative to them.

Two days later Adam revealed that the mosque they'd visited had been shuttered. People had marched in front of it and threatened some of the worshippers.

"Come with me tonight. I know where Ali and Mo are hiding out."

This was exciting stuff for a college sophomore. In a garage apartment somewhere in Virginia, they talked until dawn. This time it was different. The men explained 9/11 as a retaliatory strike against a nation that had supported the Jews every time an issue arose. The USA got involved in Middle Eastern civil wars, coups and bombing missions, always taking sides and protecting its own interests. The downtrodden were always left behind.

Once again all this made sense. Was he an American first, Ali asked Joe that night, or was he a Muslim? He could not ignore the issues much longer, they insisted. The time was coming when strong men would make a choice, standing and revealing who they really were inside. Soon men would fight for what they believed, right here in America.

At some point soon after that, Joe made the choice. His friends Ali and Mo were a huge help, as was his roommate Adam. Joe chose his heritage over his nationality.

He said he would renounce Catholicism immediately, but they told him not to do it. It would help, they said, if he fought the battle in secret. Just blend in and be like everyone else. Graduate, get a job, do everything every other loyal, red-blooded American citizen does. Some day – maybe a day far in the future – he would have the chance to stand for his beliefs.

That was the day Joe agreed to be an undercover fighter for the cause. The men who recruited him – Ali and Mo – shifted roles. They were no longer casual friends – they were his handlers. It was a subtle but important change. He belonged to them now.

When he graduated and went to work at the US Embassy in Baghdad, translating documents and transmissions the CIA intercepted every day, Ali and Mo put him in contact with some of the very people whose texts and emails he was translating. He gave them information about what was going on inside the embassy. He never knew if it was important or not; they wanted whatever he could give them.

He juggled the two parts of his life very carefully. It was exciting and he felt as though he was making a contribution to his people, but if he made a misstep, he would pay dearly. He knew the Iraqis would kill him if the Americans discovered what he was doing. That was simply how it was, and it didn't make Joe any less fervent in his desire to aid the cause.

Two years later his father died and he returned to America for the funeral. He planned to return to Baghdad immediately afterwards, but his handlers thought he was ready to move on. He had become exactly what they wanted – an extremely valuable commodity. He had been born and raised in the United States, and Joe was a citizen whose loyalty was unquestioned.

Joe had been told to wait until the time was right. For all these years he had done just that, and at last he was asked to do something that turned out to be very simple. He was asked to enlist his best friend Jeremy Lail for a special project.

CHAPTER EIGHTEEN

Franklin and Sarabeth Ives were having a quiet dinner on the veranda of their suite. They were both in their seventies, and the transatlantic crossing on the opulent ocean liner had been tops on their bucket list for twenty years. This was the third evening of an eight-day trip from New York to Southampton and they were enjoying every minute of it.

George W. Bush had appointed Justice Ives to the Supreme Court in 2003. Over the past decade he and his friend Antonin Scalia had been the most conservative voices on the bench. After Scalia died, the next appointee moved the conservative justices – Ives and three others – into the distinct minority. That had disappointed him, but this new President's possible appointees were downright frightening. Parkes was a loose cannon. Thank God the Republicans controlled the Senate, he'd said to Sarabeth more than once lately. That might keep Parkes in check.

This was the first time the couple had been really alone with each other in years. At home in Washington they were always accompanied by Supreme Court police officers. When Ives traveled to one city or another to make a speech, the US Marshals were his bodyguards. The only time justices had an option about security was when they were on vacation, and the Ives hadn't taken a vacation in a long, long time. Instead of traveling to places they might have enjoyed, they saved their money for the cruise of a lifetime. They had packed tuxedos and long dresses, but they left their security detail – their shepherds, as Franklin called them – at home.

The couple had dined formally the past two evenings, meeting new friends around their own ages in the beautiful dining room. Ives wasn't as well known as some justices, and this sophisticated crowd of mostly Brits wasn't into celebrity-gawking anyway. Sarabeth was pleased that no one gave them a second glance. It was refreshing.

Tonight they'd decided to order room service and eat on the patio outside their suite. The weather was pleasantly cool and the dinner had been really special. They clinked wineglasses, held hands for a prayer before the meal and dined as the full moon illuminated smooth seas stretching endlessly in every direction.

Around nine Sarabeth yawned, stretched and said, "I think I'll take a shower and read until I fall asleep. Are you going to go upstairs for a brandy?"

Last night after dinner they had taken a stroll and discovered a tiny British pub tucked away on the tenth level. It was quiet and cozy and they had enjoyed a nightcap. Franklin told his wife that was exactly what he wanted to do. He put on a sport jacket, kissed her goodbye and told her he'd be back shortly.

When Sarabeth was too sleepy to read any longer, she glanced at the clock. It was after ten and Franklin had been gone over an hour. Where was he?

Fully awake now, she looked up the number of the pub in the ship's directory. A man with a distinct British accent answered with a cheery greeting. She asked if her husband was in the bar and described him and the jacket he was wearing.

"He was here, madam, but he's been gone, oh, I'd say half an hour. I wouldn't worry much. There's a lot to do on the ship. He's probably found a place to listen to music somewhere!"

This wasn't like Franklin at all, she thought as she dressed. She wasn't sure where to start – the ship was massive. She left him a note that she was looking for him and would be back here at eleven sharp. If he returned, he'd wait for her. That was her Franklin and she knew what he'd do.

She wandered around for fifteen minutes, sticking her head inside public areas here and there with no luck. She went back to the room and saw the note where she'd left it.

She changed the time on the note to 11:30 and opened her door to leave again. At that moment the steward who was in charge of this block of suites happened by.

"Good evening, Mrs. Ives. Is there something I can get for you?"

"I'm actually looking for my husband," she said, her worried voice filled with anxiety. "He's been gone a lot longer than he said, and this just isn't like him."

The steward offered to get a security person to accompany her, and she quickly agreed. She felt more at ease – two sets of eyes and all that. They searched all the public areas: the bars, nightclubs, theater and even the men's grill, where some passengers congregated for an after-dinner cigar. Franklin didn't like smoky rooms, but maybe he'd gone there anyway. They didn't see him anywhere.

Around midnight the security officer notified the bridge that a passenger was missing and a squadron of men began searching the ship floor by floor. Franklin Ives was nowhere to be found. At 2:30 a.m. the captain called the company's New York offices and told the night operator to contact the US Marshals Service. A passenger was missing – not just any passenger but a Supreme Court justice.

Passengers who were up and about at daybreak felt the ship come to a full stop. Those on the starboard side saw a helicopter touch down on the top deck's landing pad. Six agents interviewed Sarabeth Ives and began an intensive search.

At 8:30 every morning the captain's voice came across the intercom system to deliver his daily briefing to the guests on board. Today he announced that a passenger in his seventies was missing and asked if anyone might have seen or heard anything.

Only one person came forward to speak with the Marshals. Around 9:45 last night, he said, he was on his veranda, smoking a cigarette, when he thought he saw something dark fall into the sea from somewhere above him. He wasn't sure if he really saw anything and even now couldn't say for sure that it happened.

The man's stateroom was situated four decks below the British pub where Ives was last seen. Outside the pub was a ten-foot sidewalk with a rail for strollers to pause and look at the ocean. No one saw anything unusual up there last night, no one volunteered any further information, and Justice Franklin Ives was never seen again.

The cause of death listed on his death certificate was "presumed drowning." Ives had apparently fallen overboard accidentally and the matter was considered closed.

CHAPTER NINETEEN

Parnell Varney loved to fish the old-fashioned way his dad had taught him back in Pennsylvania. This morning he sat in a folding chair on the bank of the pond that lay behind his mountain cabin. He'd owned these forty acres in Vermont since the sixties, and he treasured the limited time he got to spend here with his line in the water and a red-and-white bobber floating lazily on the still water.

Justice Varney liked this time of day best. At six in the morning here in the hills, things were just about perfect. A seventy-nine-year-old confirmed bachelor, Parnell loved the solitude, listening to birds call to each other, hearing bullfrogs sing in throaty hums, and watching the occasional bass jump out of the water just out of range of the worm on his hook. He loved the Supreme Court, but compared to the hubbub of Washington and the reserved dignity of the court itself, this was paradise. He could wear his old jeans, a faded hat and boots that had seen better days. Up here he wasn't Supreme Court Justice Parnell Varney. To his friends in the little town a couple of miles away he was simply Parnell.

Less than two weeks ago his good friend and fellow conservative Justice Franklin Ives apparently fell from the deck of a cruise ship. After that mysterious incident, the US Marshals dramatically ramped up security for all the justices. They wouldn't let him drive alone anymore, not even up here in the boondocks, and this very minute an agent sat in the old rocker on the porch a hundred yards behind him.

The guy means well, and if he had his way, he'd be standing here next to me. He's just doing his job, and up on the porch is fine. At least I can have a little peace and quiet.

Suddenly the bobber sank as a fish took the bait.

"Gotcha!" the agent heard Varney yell as he watched him pull back hard on the pole to set his hook. Then he heard a sharp crack from off in the distance. It echoed across the water. The agent jumped to his feet and saw the justice fall. He ran to him, knelt down and saw blood flowing from a hole in Varney's chest. Parnell Varney was dead.

Agents combed the dense woods that ringed Varney's pond, but they found absolutely no clues. US Marshals and the state police concluded that, for reasons unknown, a shooter had stood in the trees across the pond and fired once, murdering the justice.

President Chambliss T. Parkes hadn't yet nominated a replacement for Franklin Ives, and now he had two vacancies to fill. Two conservative voices on the court were silenced now. There was no hurry to find replacements. For now the Supreme Court would consist of four liberal justices and three conservatives.

And that fit Cham's plans just fine.

Public reaction to the loss of two Supreme Court Justices in as many weeks was swift. The financial markets that had just begun to recover swooned again as fear and uncertainty gripped the American people once more.

Parkes issued statements every day, assuring his fellow Americans that the deaths were nothing more than a strange coincidence. Ives's death had been ruled accidental, and although Varney was murdered, there was no reason to read more into the situation than it warranted.

Prior to all this, the economy in the United States had been robust. All the numbers were trending in the right direction and the stock market had been near its all-time high. Stay focused on the positives, the new president urged the nation, and don't let fear and panic overpower your basic American instincts.

Over time, the people agreed. It was slower this time around but over the next couple of weeks there was no additional bad news. Things got back on the right track – the road to normalcy.

CHAPTER TWENTY

Master Sergeant Jeremy Lail stepped into a black sedan idling curbside at Athens International Airport, dragging his rolling suitcase in next to him. With a wide grin and a firm handshake, the driver greeted him effusively in broken English.

"I am so glad to meet you! You are a true hero, sir! I will be taking you to the house where you will stay until tomorrow. If you have a cellphone, please give it to me now. The GPS function will give you away. And do not use your credit cards again. They told me to give you these euros." He handed Jeremy an envelope stuffed with currency.

Lail was too tired to do anything but nod his head and hand over his phone. He didn't even care who "they" were – the people who'd given him the euros. His body felt like there had been a brawl inside it. The flight had taken just over ten hours, and he'd been stuck in a window seat with two boys in their early teens next to him. He hadn't gotten even one minute of sleep. The kids put their tray tables up and down, up and down all night long, their music was so loud he could hear it through the earphones, and their Greek parents across the aisle ignored them completely. The parents were sleeping well, he noticed as he glanced over more than once. They slept and he was trapped. Even going to the bathroom was a struggle maneuvering over backpacks on the floor beneath their feet and gathering up bottles and snacks in order to raise their tray tables. After all that was done, he could snake his way out to the aisle. When he returned after the most recent trip to the head, one kid had spilled Coke in Jeremy's seat and was half-heartedly attempting to wipe it up while his fat brother giggled uncontrollably.

The biggest part of his inability to sleep was the overpowering remorse about what he had done. As soon as he heard the news about the disappearances, Jeremy knew what had happened. He had helped murder the President and Vice President of the United States and two dozen other innocent people. Without his signature on the preflight checklists, Air Force One and Air Force Two wouldn't have disappeared. He knew something very unusual had happened, but he signed off anyway. He'd made a serious mistake with monumental consequences.

As the driver negotiated through the dense traffic in Athens, Jeremy put his head back and rubbed his tired eyes. *How in hell did I end up here, running away from the country I've served for years and being betrayed by my best friend?*

All this had started with Joe, he reflected with deep sadness. They had identical '55 Chevy Bel Airs. Jeremy's was red and white, just as it had come from the factory, but Joe's had been painted black. They were both bachelors, and from that first day when they met for a beer after Joe's salvage yard closed, they began to spend time with each other.

Although Joe was five years younger, he became both a good friend and a counselor as Jeremy struggled with depression and his overwhelming lack of self-esteem. They had long talks about Jeremy's father and how he had demeaned every positive thing the boy ever did.

"I worked my ass off and became a damned master sergeant, for God's sake, and all he could say was why didn't I have the initiative to be an officer?"

Joe had grown up differently. His had been a home filled with love and respect, but he listened and tried to offer helpful advice. It seemed to be good for Jeremy; he became more upbeat, gregarious and social. Jeremy even started a Saturday night poker game at his house, inviting his boss and others from the base. Joe sometimes included his own friends too. One night he introduced everyone to his friend Ali. Ali – who was actually Joe's handler – fit in well and everyone seemed to enjoy his company.

A few days after that poker game, Ali had arranged a meeting. Joe hadn't seen much of Ali or Mo in years, but he remained as committed to helping his Muslim brothers now as he'd been just after 9/11. Islamophobia in America wasn't getting any better in the twenty-first century. As his countrymen in the Middle East fought civil wars and rebel insurgencies, they also attacked the West in places like Paris and Brussels. That did nothing to endear them with America, although Joe truly believed the jihadists were fighting a righteous holy war for Islam.

No one would have imagined how he really felt. Joe vehemently denounced radical terrorists when the subject came up, just as every other red-blooded American did. He engaged in spirited discussions with his employees at the salvage yard, always taking the side of the USA. No one would have believed that this Catholic American was a totally different person in his mind and in his heart.

Joe was instructed to go to a park not far from his salvage yard. He walked along a shady trail that led to a secluded area with benches facing a small lake. Ali and Mo were waiting. They shook hands and he sat down. They began to explain the first task they'd ever required of him.

When he had left the poker game that Saturday night, Ali felt like he'd won the lottery. Once he reported to his superiors about the evening at Jeremy Lail's house, they were ecstatic. It turned out Lail was a master sergeant in the Air Force and he was in charge of final preflight checks for the most well-protected aircraft in the world, the planes that carried the leaders of the United States. And Lail's best friend was Joe Kaya! Allah had truly blessed their cause by handing them a perfect opportunity.

Ali and Mo explained what they wanted Joe to do. He listened, asked questions and offered suggestions. It would take time – perhaps a long time – but this was exactly what Mo and Ali's bosses had been hoping might happen someday. The men told Joe to take his time – eventually things would be right and it would happen.

Jeremy had known none of the background, of course. All he knew was that his best friend Joe became more and more of a mentor. Joe was a rock-solid man on whom Jeremy could rely for sound advice. Most of all, Joe guided his friend along the journey to rebuilding his confidence, self-esteem and sense of worth. Joe believed in him, and Jeremy believed he was a better man because Joe was in his life.

At that point Jeremy would have done anything for his best friend.

Then one day it happened. Joe asked him for a favor. It was unusual, illegal and bizarre, but Joe presented it more as a daring stunt. And it was something Jeremy could easily cause to happen as a favor to his friend.

Joe had a distant relative by marriage who also worked at Andrews, he told Jeremy. He hadn't mentioned him before because Joe rarely saw him. Thousands of people – civilian and military – were employed at the base, and it didn't seem odd to Jeremy that one of them would be a third cousin Joe had never mentioned.

According to Joe, his cousin was chained to a desk job while his lifelong ambition was to sit at the controls of the two most famous aircraft in the world. From his desk, the cousin often watched the planes soar into the sky, carrying the leaders of our country, and he wanted to experience – just for a moment – what it would be like to sit in the left seat of the cockpit like the pilots did.

The planes that carried the President and Vice President weren't designated Air Force One and Two until shortly before they flew. There were always several aircraft available and ready to go. No one knew exactly which would be used until two days before a scheduled departure. If the President was leaving day after tomorrow, today the plane he was using would be designated as Air Force One. It was also the first time that anyone would know for certain on which plane the President would be flying.

Jeremy hadn't been aware that soon President Harrison and the Vice President would be away on trips at the same time. This part of his job – the last preflight check – was so routine that he never paid attention to the passenger manifests. These planes weren't "Air Force anything" to him – they were just 747s, or Gulfstreams, or whatever.

Apparently it was important to Joe's cousin to be on the actual Air Force One and Two after they were designated, not just one of the planes that occasionally was used to haul the top brass. It surprised Jeremy when Joe told him his cousin had learned that both leaders would be away at the same time. Apparently his cousin had heard it on the news. The President would leave for Barbados, and a couple of days later the Vice President and Secretary of State would head out for Hong Kong. It was a perfect opportunity for a selfie photo op on both planes, all in the same week!

"Sure," Jeremy said. *What could it hurt? The guy would only be on board each plane for a minute, just enough time to climb into the left seat, snap a picture and get out again.* He was doing a favor for his good friend Joe, and helping Joe's cousin achieve an odd – but not that crazy – dream.

The man had shown up on two different days, gone into the cockpits of Air Force One and Two, and left again, his lifelong goal apparently satisfied.

I let him put bombs on those planes.

The worst part was afterwards, when he'd called Joe. He knew his old friend would be astounded at what his cousin had done. He wanted the two of them to go to Jim Perkins and explain what happened so Jeremy wouldn't appear to be complicit in all this.

That was when he finally understood Joe was a part of all this. Joe told Jeremy he'd be branded a traitor.

"What cousin? I didn't say anything to you about a cousin. It's all on you, Jeremy. You can't prove anyone else was involved."

Joe had known all along what was going to happen. That guy wasn't Joe's cousin – he was a terrorist. That meant Joe was too. Jeremy could see it all now, but it was far too late.

"I can help you," Joe had said. "I have friends in Greece who can help you disappear."

Jeremy had nowhere to turn. He was so far out of his element that he made another serious error. Instead of going to the authorities, he listened to Joe and bought a plane ticket to Athens.

Any way you looked at it, Jeremy was a traitor and an accessory to twenty-five murders. Maybe more than an accessory. If there was no cousin, then only Jeremy could have planted the bombs. Any jury in the world would convict him of treason without a minute's thought.

He fought back the feelings – the loss of someone else he felt close to, the betrayal by his best friend, the knowledge that he'd been a part of a conspiracy all along – and tried to concentrate on what was ahead. As remorseful as he felt now, there was no turning back. What's done was done, and he knew he would never see his country again.

CHAPTER TWENTY-ONE

The driver pulled up in front of a four-story building in an area of Athens called the Plaka. There were hundreds of apartment buildings, taverns and cafés in these streets situated just below the Acropolis. Right now all Jeremy wanted was a bed.

The affable Greek lugged Jeremy's suitcase up two flights of stairs and unlocked the door to a pleasant studio apartment. He opened a pair of doors revealing a sunny balcony. Light breezes wafted through the room.

Jeremy pulled out a wad of one-dollar bills and offered them to the man, but he declined.

"It has been a pleasure to serve you," he said enthusiastically. "I will pick you up here tomorrow morning at seven for the next part of your journey."

"Where am I going?"

"Until tomorrow, then," the man replied as he walked out the door.

Jeremy stayed in the shower for ten minutes, letting hot water stream all over him as though the scalding liquid would erase his sins. He pulled down the bedcover, slipped beneath the sheets and slept straight through until late afternoon.

The sun was setting and it was much cooler outside when he awoke, so he closed the balcony doors. He felt rested, but he was also famished. He was ready to walk around the area and find a restaurant. He turned on the TV, flipped until he found CNN in English, and began to rummage through his suitcase for clean clothes.

Suddenly he heard his name. He whirled around in horror and saw his picture emblazoned on the screen. He stared in shock and learned that there was a worldwide search under way for Master Sergeant Jeremy Lail, the man whose signature had allowed the planes to depart Andrews Field. He had arrived in Athens, Greece, this morning, and the airports and train stations were under tight surveillance.

Local and federal police had joined Interpol to scour the city for the international fugitive.

Holy shit! He should have expected this, but he hadn't allowed himself to consider the consequences of suddenly leaving the United States. In his entire life, Jeremy Lail had never had so much as a parking ticket. Now he was a man on the run, wanted for questioning in connection with a horrible crime against the United States of America.

How proud must his father feel now?

Why the hell am I thinking about him? And how can I even go out to get something to eat? Everybody in this city is looking for me!

Overwhelmed and scared, he sat on the bed shaking uncontrollably, completely lost in the enormity of what he was facing.

There was a quiet knock on the door.

Jeremy was petrified. He sat silently, afraid to even move.

"Mister Lail," a voice said, "I'm the man who brought you here. Let me in!"

He wasn't sure if it was his driver's voice. Maybe it was, but he wasn't positive.

What the hell? If it was the police, then all this would be over. He opened the door. His driver rushed in and closed it quickly.

"We must leave now! Everyone is looking for you! We have to go at once. Leave everything and come with me. There is very little time."

"How are you going to get me out? They're watching the airport and the train station."

"By ship. So far they haven't made it to the docks. It's impossible to watch every boat in the harbor. But we must go quickly!"

Jeremy grabbed his passport, the envelope full of euros, his wallet and a jacket. As he walked out, he thought briefly that he was leaving behind not only his belongings but his entire life as it had been. Nothing would ever be the same.

The driver had him wait in the vestibule while he went out and looked up and down the sidewalk. He opened the car door and motioned for Jeremy to get in. He ran around to the front, started the car and handed Jeremy a cheap cellphone and a white baseball cap.

"You'll get a call tomorrow from the people who are meeting you. Wear the cap. It's the way our people will find you."

"Where am I going?"

"Cyprus. You should be there by this time tomorrow."

Cyprus. From geography classes he knew roughly that it was situated in the eastern Mediterranean Sea not far from Turkey. *What a perfect starting place for a traitor who's going to spend the rest of his life on the run,* he thought with another wave of remorse.

They drove along the busy docks of Piraeus, past a number of small boats and several decent-sized yachts. Finally they came to the commercial zone. Ships of every size were lined up along the dock one by one for a mile or more. When they stopped, the driver accompanied him to a gangplank. His ship was an aging cargo vessel with a few containers on its deck. A couple of crewmen were untying ropes in preparation for an immediate departure. No one gave Jeremy a glance.

The driver pointed to a swarthy, dark man with a scraggly beard. "This is your captain. He will take things from here." The man's T-shirt and jeans were filthy, and he simply nodded his head toward his passenger.

As soon as the driver walked off the ship, the crewmen pulled up the gangplank. With a groan and a creak, the old vessel began backing out of its berth. Soon it was heading into the Mediterranean Sea for the five-hundred-mile trip to Cyprus.

Jeremy stood at the railing for thirty minutes, lost in thought. A crewman came up and addressed him in Greek. Finally realizing Jeremy didn't understand, the man guided him down a flight of stairs to a tiny cabin. He saw a bed with stained sheets and a dirty blanket, a table, one chair and a half-empty bottle of water. The crewman left and Jeremy was alone.

There was no way he was staying down here. First of all, it smelled dank and musty. Secondly, being alone with your thoughts when you'd done something that made you hate yourself wasn't a good thing. He went back on deck to a refreshing, bracing sea breeze. That was the only thing about this trip that was refreshing, he reflected.

He was absolutely starving and hoped he'd eventually be offered food. He stood around for a while and watched three mates doing various chores as they chain-smoked cigarettes. At last a man came up from below deck, carrying a rickety folding chair and a sack. Jeremy sat down and looked inside.

There was a white bread sandwich with some kind of meat and a slice of cheese. There were grapes, a sack of American potato chips and a can of orange soda. He attacked it like it was a filet mignon and a fine cabernet, eating everything there was. When he finished, one of the men offered him a cigarette. He hadn't smoked in ten years, but tonight seemed like a perfect time to start again. He zipped his jacket as the breeze turned cool, sat in solitude and smoked.

By nine they were well out to sea and there were no lights from shore. It was a pitch-black, moonless night, and the star-filled sky created an amazing spectacle. He would have been awed if he hadn't felt so singularly lost. As he gazed upwards, he thought for a moment about heaven, but he forced that thought out. There would be no heaven for him. If God ever chose to cast judgment on a human being, he thought, that man would be me.

Just as he had betrayed his country, he'd been betrayed by those he considered closest to him. His father had never understood or cared about him. They never had a father-son relationship. Instead, he'd cut his own kid loose because he didn't measure up. The same thing happened with the man who'd become his closest friend. Joe had seduced him. He'd become Jeremy's advisor and mentor; then he'd carefully planned how his friend would betray his nation. He'd been a willing participant, of course. Even though it was wrong, he'd agreed to let a man on the planes – a man who had obviously planted two bombs.

Joe wasn't running for his life now. Only Jeremy was. He had given up everything. Everything. And for what? A life looking over your shoulder every minute? A life in the squalor of a war-torn Middle Eastern country? Would they – whoever *they* were – even *let* him live?

Again, like so many times before, he was completely alone.

At last he went to his cabin. As much as the nasty bunk repulsed him, he needed to get some sleep. Jeremy itched and scratched all night long as tiny bugs invaded his T-shirt and shorts, leaving red bites all over his torso. *Thank God I rested all day yesterday,* he thought as he spent a fitful night tossing and turning.

At some point he fell asleep. When he awoke, he glanced at his watch. It was 6:45 a.m. and there was an aroma that smelled heavenly. Coffee was brewing somewhere nearby. He pulled on his clothes and went upstairs.

With the sun not yet up, it was frigid topside. The captain tossed him a heavy coat that he gratefully donned as he and the crew drank coffee. As cold as it was, he didn't want to go back to the dank cabin. Breakfast consisted of an assortment of meats and cheeses with hunks of brown bread. Still hungry from yesterday, he ate everything they gave him.

Jeremy spent the day sitting on deck. He had absolutely nothing to do – no smart phone, no tablet and nothing to read. There was a TV on the bridge on which the crew watched one American game show after another, the English-speaking contestants now speaking dubbed-in Greek. He had a lot of time to think – far more time than he'd have wished.

At noon the news came on. He could see the TV from the deck, and he watched his picture appear along with the word INTERPOL. He pulled the ball cap lower on his head, but it was too late. As the crewmen watched the news, two whispered, turning and pointing in his direction.

For the rest of the trip he was uneasy and watchful. The crew looked like ex-convicts in the first place. Now that they knew their passenger was an international fugitive wanted by Interpol, who knew what they might do? Was there a reward for his capture? He couldn't read Greek, so he didn't know what the words on TV had said. He sensed danger all around him although admittedly in his entire life this was the only real danger he'd ever faced.

He had decided to get rid of the things that could hurt him. Regretting losing the security they represented, he tossed his credit cards into the sea one by one. They were a liability now; if he dared use one, he'd be found immediately. He held his passport in his hand for a long, long time, knowing it was an even greater liability than the cards. If anyone demanded to see his identification at this point, he was better off having nothing than to hand over the passport of a wanted man. It went overboard too.

In the late afternoon he jumped as his new phone rang. He'd never heard it before and he'd almost forgotten that it was in his jacket pocket.

The caller spoke passable English. He said that a man would meet Jeremy at the dock in Limassol and take him by car to Nicosia, fifty miles away.

"Wear your cap so he will know you," the man said.

He also could look for the only American international fugitive getting off a tramp steamer at a seaport in southern Cyprus, Jeremy thought.

An hour later the ship pulled into the harbor at Limassol. He'd never heard of the place and was amazed at the volume of marine traffic. Huge container ships moved slowly toward the docks alongside giant ocean liners with passengers lounging on their verandas. The port was teeming with activity, and their tiny cargo ship maneuvered its way to its assigned area. The crew secured it and lowered the gangplank as Jeremy stood on the deck.

His phone rang again and a man said, "I am just below you on the dock. I am wearing a red shirt."

"What do I do about customs and immigration?"

"You're still in the EU, my friend. There's no border inspection here. Now get off the boat."

Fifteen minutes later he was in the backseat of an old Citroen that was chugging along the busy highway toward Nicosia. Within the hour they pulled up in front of a small hotel just off the town square. His driver, the man in the red shirt, had said absolutely nothing. He handed Jeremy a room key and a manila envelope, got back in the car and drove away.

The sun was setting as Jeremy walked upstairs to a refreshingly comfortable room and looked inside the envelope. It held a thousand more euros, even though he still had all the money he'd been given in Athens. With the money was a handwritten note telling him he would be picked up from the lobby tomorrow at seven. He recalled that had also been the plan twenty-four hours ago in Greece. He hoped things would work out better tomorrow morning; he needed some rest.

The first thing he did was to find CNN. He had to know what was going on with Interpol. The sports news was on, so he stripped and showered, trying to wash off the grime and dirt from his night on the ship and trying to ease the knots in his muscles caused by anxiety. The bug bites around his groin and legs itched like hell, but he didn't scratch them. He wanted a drink and a good dinner, toiletries and ointment from a pharmacy, in that order.

He put on the clothes he'd worn for two days – the only ones he had – as the story about missing fugitive Jeremy Lail came on the news. Authorities believed he was still in Greece. He had not used his credit cards or passport since his arrival yesterday morning, and every means of departure from the country had been secured. The man would be found soon, the director of Interpol promised.

Thank God I got out when I did, he thought as he watched a clip showing policemen combing the very dock from which his ship had left. With so much traffic it would take a long time to check out every vessel that had departed from the port, and he knew his wasn't one that carried passengers anyway. Maybe the authorities in Cyprus wouldn't be on the lookout for a man who was supposed to be five hundred miles away.

It was time to move. He pulled his ball cap down low and walked out into the street. He had two days' growth of beard, and that helped change his appearance a little. The nearby square was full of people, many speaking English. Tourists. He was grateful for the anonymity afforded by blending in with others like him.

It was a pleasant evening and he wanted to sit outdoors. He entered a sidewalk café, took a table away from the crowd and ordered a beer, then another. At last he began to relax and he asked for a menu.

An hour later he strolled the quaint old town and found a pharmacy and a men's clothing store. He bought everything he needed and went back to his hotel for a long soak in a real bathtub. He didn't shave; the beard was now part of his disguise.

He got the first night of rest he'd had in two days.

The next morning he was met by the same driver, taken to the airport and put aboard an old twin-engine Cessna 402. He and the pilot were the only ones on the plane. They took off, flew across the water for about an hour and descended for landing.

"Where are we?" he shouted over the noisy engines as they prepared to land in a large coastal city.

"No English."

He pointed down and shrugged as though he didn't understand.

The pilot nodded. "Latakia."

"Turkey?"

The pilot shook his head.

"No Turkey. Syria."

CHAPTER TWENTY-TWO

The Cessna taxied to a stop next to two men standing in front of a dilapidated building. Jeremy ducked out and turned to get his duffel.

Suddenly one of the men grabbed his arms and the other threw a cloth bag over his head. His hands were cuffed behind him and he was pushed roughly into the backseat of a car.

"What the hell's going on?"

"Shut up," one of the men said calmly in English. "You belong to us now."

Six hours later Jeremy had posed for dozens of still photos and videos. He had stated his name, rank and serial number, he had confessed to his crime, and he had denounced Americans as evil, lying, hate-filled murderers of Muslims.

At first he refused to speak against the United States, but a few well-placed blows to his kidneys changed his mind. He wanted to be brave, but all this was so far beyond belief, he capitulated quickly. He was forced to stand up straight and tall for the pictures, even though he had been doubled over in pain from the beatings. His captors looked to him like stereotypical terrorists. Seeing them on the video, Americans would be reminded of Jihadi John, the shoe bomber or the 9/11 hijackers. The men wore ski masks and carried automatic weapons. They laughed and mocked and spat on him.

One of them spoke excellent English. Jeremy was forced to kneel, and the man stood next to him, facing the camera and explaining that the Air Force master sergeant had done an excellent job for the Falcons of Islam. He had been a loyal servant and Allah would bless and receive him.

A fleeting thought flew through Jeremy's mind. *I guess I'll find out about those seventy-two virgins.*

Jeremy wasn't afraid anymore. He was past afraid. He knew exactly what was coming.

He had seen one man standing behind the others and holding a saber. Even that didn't scare Jeremy. It was all over, and he was resigned to what was coming.

They took pictures right all the way to the very end. As Jeremy heard the long sword begin its swish through the air, the cameras were rolling and the terrorists laughed and pointed at him.

Afterwards they sent the footage to the Western news media. On the seventh day after the planes disappeared, the missing senior line operator from Andrews was executed. The world saw the grisly scene and grew afraid once again.

It took investigators almost no time to connect Joe Kaya to the missing line chief. Jeremy's boss had told FBI agents about the Saturday night card games at Jeremy's house, and everything fell into place. By now Ali and Mo, the men from the mosque who'd recruited Joe, were long gone. Agents would never learn their real names or where they went, but finding Joe was as simple as going to the salvage yard and arresting him.

CHAPTER TWENTY-THREE

During the six months prior to the disappearances of the planes, the crew on Air Force One and Two had experienced a subtle but critical change. The pilots and chief engineer were the same seasoned veterans, but the support staff positions – the people on each aircraft who served as cooks, stewards, secretaries and the like – had turned over one hundred percent. Every single one had been replaced by someone new.

Although there was no discernible difference between the new staff and the ones before, there was, in fact, one thing the new crew had in common. Each of them was a trained military professional skilled in a particular craft, and none had close family. They were loners who were recruited for Operation Condor and required to sign ironclad confidentiality agreements. Divulging even a single word about their mission would land them in a federal prison for the rest of their lives. There would be no trial, no judge or jury to hear evidence and learn what they knew. They had waived every right traditionally guaranteed to persons charged with a crime in the United States, and violators would be prisoners within their own nation.

Only six people knew what Operation Condor was about. Three of them – the President, Vice President and Secretary of State – had agreed to it in the most top-secret meeting ever held. The others who knew were the director of the CIA, the Senate Majority Leader and the chief justice of the Supreme Court.

For six months the CIA chief and President Harrison had met weekly to develop an unprecedented plan. It was so fraught with danger and uncertainty that others who would ordinarily be included in such an operation – the FBI director, the head of the National Security Agency and the Chairman of the Joint Chiefs of Staff – were excluded. Meetings were held in the White House Situation Room, a five-thousand-square-foot bunker in the basement of the West Wing that was typically used by the President and his advisers to deal with worldwide crises. It was the most secure room in the world.

No records were kept of the meetings, and no emails, texts or phone calls would ever reference what was being planned. On the rare occasion when they had to discuss something outside the Situation Room, they used the code word Condor.

When the CIA director learned that the operation might be implemented soon, it was time to share the secret with four more people. Vice President Martin Taylor was an old friend of Harry's, selected by him to fill the VP role when Harrison assumed office two years ago. He'd been head of the Senate Intelligence Committee, and the President respected and trusted Marty implicitly. Taylor had been divorced twice and had no close family. There had been no children and his parents were long-since deceased. He had given his full support to Operation Condor the moment he was briefed. He thought it was brilliant.

Secretary of State Aaron Clancy was a native of California and another appointee of Harry's. They had been fellow senators and good friends for ten years. The implementation of Condor would be most difficult for Clancy to accept, given his personal situation. Unlike the Vice President, the sixty-year-old widower had a married daughter who was forty. Although there were no grandchildren, this mission would put a burden on him for a time. Even as the President explained how Clancy's involvement in Condor was essential, he empathized with Clancy's situation. He had the same issue, he explained, since neither of his elderly parents would be aware that the mission existed.

Travel schedules for the President and Vice President were typically made public several weeks in advance. Even though military intelligence was picking up more and more alarming chatter from Syria, that public disclosure continued. Although incredibly risky, it was required for Operation Condor's success.

Over the next few weeks, intel out of the Middle East skyrocketed. Intercepted transmissions from the al-Nusra Front revealed that something really big was about to happen and it was aimed at the United States. At last they got just enough of the jihadist group's plan to understand. The sworn enemies of the Great Satan had created a brilliant maneuver that would result in worldwide chaos.

Finally came the day when all the chatter went silent. The team went over everything one last time. They were ready to implement Operation Condor.

President Harrison, Vice President Taylor and Director Case sat in the Situation Room as the Secretary of State, the Senate Majority Leader and the chief justice were admitted by the sentry outside. Once the airlock on the door was sealed, the President explained that only the six of them – plus a group of people who would be a part of the mission itself – would know about Condor. You all are my team, he said as he explained what was going to happen. As bizarre as it was, as remarkable and terrifying as Condor would be, it was the only solution. And everyone agreed it was perfect – if it worked.

BILL THOMPSON

CHAPTER TWENTY-FOUR

The day of the disappearances

"Air Force Two, you are cleared to taxiway 34 right."

"Roger 34 right."

At ten a.m. Vice President Taylor and Secretary of State Aaron Clancy settled back in their plush seats as the engines on the huge Boeing 747 powered up. The plane moved slowly at first, then at a steadier clip. There were thirteen people on board. In addition to the VIPs, there were two pilots, a flight engineer, two Secret Service agents and six cabin crew – a chef and five attendants.

The plane made a turn at the end of the taxiway and idled at the head of the 11,300-foot western runway at Andrews Field. The copilot performed his final check, the pilot revved the engines, and the enormous plane strained against its brakes until it was freed. It quickly increased speed as it roared down the runway, lifting off gracefully into the skies and heading west towards Honolulu.

The almost-new 747 was usually in service as Air Force One, transporting the President. Since Harry and the Vice President would be on separate trips at the same time, the decision was made to swap planes because the 747 could fly greater distances without refueling. The President and his family had left two days ago on a Gulfstream G650 to attend a conference in Bridgetown, Barbados. Today Taylor and Clancy were heading nonstop to Honolulu, where they would refuel and continue to Hong Kong. It made better sense to use the bigger plane for the long-haul itinerary, and the Gulfstream was perfect for the President's short trip to Barbados.

The attendants aboard Air Force Two served coffee shortly after takeoff. Two hours later there was lunch and a California Merlot for the Vice President and the Secretary of State. Afterwards the cabin lights were dimmed and the men dozed. Although both knew exactly what to expect, they grabbed a nap before the unprecedented twenty-four hours ahead of them.

Five thousand miles away, Air Force One sat on the tarmac at Grantley Adams International Airport in Bridgetown, Barbados. Night had fallen, and the words *United States of America* running down the Gulfstream's gleaming fuselage were bathed in floodlights.

First Lady Jennifer Harrison and her daughters, twelve-year-old Lizzie and nine-year-old Kate, were on board, awaiting the President's arrival. Chief of Staff Bob Parker sat at the back in the President's tiny office, on the phone to his assistant in DC. The pilots ran through preflight checks in preparation for departure within the hour. A Secret Service agent sat with the President's family as two stewards served coffee and soft drinks. A contingency of agents had guarded Harry Harrison during the Barbados conference; all but one would fly back to the States on commercial planes tomorrow.

As soon as the President arrived, they would begin the four-hour flight to Dallas. His itinerary called for landing at Love Field around ten. They would spend the night at the Crescent Hotel, where Brian and Nicole would join them in their room tomorrow morning for a private breakfast. At noon the family would attend a fund-raiser and luncheon benefitting Republican candidates, then head back to Washington.

The trip to Barbados had been a combination of pleasure and business. Jennifer and the girls had enjoyed three days in the sun at a private villa where the presidential party had stayed at the invitation of his friend the Prime Minister. While they had a relaxing time swimming and surfing, the President had attended a conference of the Organization of Central American and Caribbean States, or OCACS.

Usually the President would have sent someone else to this type of meeting – the Secretary of State or perhaps the Vice President. But this had been different. Eight heads of state and a half dozen senior officials of territories and protectorates were gathering to discuss the increasing problems of human trafficking, drug smuggling and the impact of lifting the trade embargo against Cuba. President Harrison's senior advisors believed he should attend in person to emphasize how high a priority the United States government placed on these topics. Tonight Harrison was at the closing dinner, where he would deliver the keynote address.

As they watched out the window, the girls saw flashing red lights and a motorcade approaching the Gulfstream. They yelled, "Daddy's coming!" The agent on the plane moved to block the doorway, his hand casually resting on his pistol, as two SUVs pulled to the plane's stairway. A contingency of local police officers lined up as six more agents whisked President Harrison and a man with a metal briefcase up the stairs and onto the plane. Another agent climbed aboard; tonight there would be three Secret Service personnel accompanying the presidential family. The man with the briefcase was an agent code-named Quarterback. He was carrying the "nuclear football" that was always close to the President when he was out of his office. The case held the nuclear codes that allowed the President to order the implementation of nuclear weapons. Tonight during dinner, the agent stood behind a curtain ten feet from Harrison. It was the same every time the President traveled.

At 8:30 p.m. local time, 7:30 in Washington, Air Force One soared into the starry night, heading northwest toward the Gulf of Mexico. As it left Barbados, the Vice President's plane had already departed Honolulu after refueling for the long haul to Hong Kong. President Harrison walked through the sitting area, kissed his wife and girls, and said, "Okay, everyone. Ready for an adventure?" He went back to the plane's small office, where his Chief of Staff had Vice President Taylor on the phone.

Harry said, "All set, Marty?"

"Yes, sir, Mr. President. We left Honolulu forty-five minutes ago. We'll keep you advised."

"Same here, my friend. We'll say prayers on this end for Condor. You do the same for us. God knows we need prayers, and God willing I'll see you soon."

Twenty-five minutes later, at 9:17 p.m. Eastern time, the phone on the President's desk rang. Bob Parker picked it up, listened for a moment and handed the receiver to his boss. Harry heard the director of the National Security Agency say, "Mr. President, is Quarterback with you?"

This was always the first question in an emergency. And this was the first time Harry had ever been asked it. Knowing what was coming, Bob Parker had summoned the agent with the briefcase. He joined them in Harry's office.

"He's here."

"Thank you, sir. I am with the Defense Secretary in his office."

Neither of those men was part of the Condor team.

"I'm afraid I have some very bad news, Mr. President. Air Force Two disappeared from radar five minutes ago. Their last position was six hundred miles south of Honolulu over open seas. Secretary Vernon is dispatching a squadron from the 15th Wing at Hickham to begin a search where the plane was last picked up on radar."

Clark Vernon, the Secretary of Defense, took the phone. "I recommend going to DEFCON 3 now, Mr. President." Raising the level to DEFCON 3 meant security would be significantly heightened worldwide, putting the Air Force on alert for mobilization upon fifteen minutes' notice.

"That's approved, Mr. Secretary."

"And, sir, in the interest of national security . . . uh . . ." On completely unfamiliar ground, the usually stolid and unruffled Defense Secretary stammered for a moment.

The President interrupted. "Clark, get to the point. What do you want me to do?"

"I think you should divert to Naval Air Station Key West. We're sending a squadron of fighters to accompany you."

"That's approved."

"We'll be here all night, Mr. President. As soon as we know more, I'll be in touch."

Across the room the President glanced at a wall TV. He heard the frazzled CNN newscaster say, "We interrupt this program to bring you breaking news."

Harry turned on the intercom and pressed a button. The pilot answered immediately.

"Has Defense instructed you to divert to NAS Key West?"

"Yes, sir, I made the course change a moment ago. They've dispatched a squadron of F-22s to bring us in."

"How much time until the fighters get to us?"

"We're eleven hundred miles from Key West. If they leave now, they'll be here in forty-five minutes."

"Implement Condor. Repeat, implement Condor."

"Roger that, Mr. President. Implementing Condor."

BILL THOMPSON

CHAPTER TWENTY-FIVE

As soon as he heard the president's order the pilot disengaged the plane's autopilot and requested permission to descend to twenty-five thousand feet due to turbulence. ATC okayed his descent, but once the plane reached that altitude it kept going down and down. Then the pilot turned off the radio. The air traffic controller in Marathon, Florida, who was following Air Force One picked up the altitude change immediately and radioed the aircraft, but he got no response.

Roughly thirty minutes after Air Force Two vanished over the Pacific Ocean, the ATC stared in disbelief at his radar. He pressed a button to refresh the screen, and then he did it again. Nothing changed. What he was seeing was real. This was no drill. The Gulfstream was below ten thousand feet now and it was still dropping toward the ocean.

"Air Force One! Return to twenty-five thousand!" Nothing. Not a word came back from the men piloting the president.

He screamed to his supervisor across the room, "I've lost contact with Air Force One! It was below ten thousand feet and descending fast, and now they're not answering."

Suddenly the plane's transponder stopped working and the plane disappeared from the controller's screen. The man's supervisor reached his desk just in time to see the blip vanish.

The young controller screamed, "It's gone! Dear God! Commander, did you see it? Air Force One's off the screen!"

Except for the girls, everyone on board knew what was happening. Harry walked out of his office, glanced at the chief steward and said, "Implement Condor." Then he sat on a couch and motioned for his children to join him.

"We're going on a little adventure tonight," he told his girls calmly. He offered a simple explanation about what was going to happen but didn't tell them why. As he chatted quietly with his family, the crew members rushed to implement their parts of Operation Condor. Stewards locked down the food and beverage carts as the copilot was clicking switches, disabling the instruments that allowed tracking, just as his counterpart on Air Force Two had done a few minutes ago.

When the Gulfstream's altimeter read four hundred feet, the pilot turned on his landing lights. The powerful beams illuminated the churning sea so close below that it seemed he could touch it from here. He picked up a checklist, read the last item and said aloud, "Disable the flight recorder."

There was only this single item left. The flight recorder – the black box – was the component that allowed a missing aircraft to be located. It also held the recorder that captured every sound in the cockpit. The boxes on Air Force One and Two had been secretly modified last week at Andrews. The copilot flipped a toggle switch and disabled the black box.

The pilot thought about the next phase of Operation Condor. His part in this extraordinary mission was almost over, but the operation itself was really just beginning. Nothing in history had remotely approached what was unfolding tonight on both sides of the globe. He hadn't been told the purpose of this unprecedented, ultra-top-secret mission. Whatever was going on, it was important enough to forfeit the lives of the President and Vice President of the United States of America.

CHAPTER TWENTY-SIX

Present day

Belgrave Square is one of London's grandest and largest neighborhoods. In the 1800s it was home to dukes, earls and champions of industry. Today the homes of eastern European billionaires were nestled between embassies and ambassadorial residences of a dozen diverse countries, including Portugal, Ghana, Syria and Norway.

On the south side of a shady park in the middle, where Belgrave Place emptied into the square, stood a stately four-story building two doors down from the Embassy of Spain. A discreet brass plate below a doorbell identified its occupant as Hassan Group. This building had less traffic than most offices on the square, but the Hassans could rightfully claim a place here among their seriously wealthy neighbors.

Thirty-year-old Amina, known to her Western friends as Amy, managed her father's operations in London. Amin owned fifty companies stretching across the Middle East from the Mediterranean Sea to the Persian Gulf. A Syrian by birth, over the years her father had shrewdly become a friend and business partner to the ruling families of all the United Arab Emirates. From what the public could see, Hassan Group was one of the world's largest oil conglomerates. The more oil companies the company gobbled up, the more Amin Hassan seemed to want. He was in a unique position. His company was privately held, so it owed allegiance to no master except Amin and his partners. And his company had many, many more business interests than the ones the public could see. His conglomerate made billions more dollars in covert, illicit businesses than in oil. And they were a steady source of income. Good times or bad, people and governments wanted what Hassan Group offered behind closed doors.

His close friend and minority investor was Zayed al-Fulan, the wealthiest man in the United Arab Emirates, where Hassan Group was headquartered. Amin's Bentley limousine was often seen entering the gates of Zayed's palatial mansion, where Amin and his partner would have tea, dinner, cigars and profitable conversation. Zayed had no idea that Hassan Group dealt in such things as munitions, dirty bombs, plutonium and drugs. He knew only what Amin told him about – the vast oil, petrochemical, media and mining holdings that made Amin and his partner a half-billion US dollars each per year.

With the sharp decline in world oil prices in the last few years, Amin and his partner were in a unique position to acquire these companies. Zayed had cash and Amin had assets against which he could borrow billions. Together they could mount a takeover battle few companies in the stumbling petroleum industry could withstand.

ExxonMobil, the world's largest oil company, had seen its market capitalization drop sharply to under $350 billion. For less than eighty billion, Amin could gain effective control of the company, merge it into Hassan Group and create an even greater, more powerful petroleum conglomerate.

Amin's partner gave him a line of credit for fifty billion dollars, and he began to accumulate shares of Exxon, quickly reaching the level at which his company was required to disclose its holdings to the US Securities and Exchange Commission. It had been a bold and farsighted plan, but it met quick and decisive opposition both from the US Congress and the Federal Trade Commission. More alarming was the noise coming from the State Department, threatening an investigation of the secretive, private Arab company if Hassan continued his pursuit of Exxon. Abhorring publicity, his partner immediately insisted the takeover idea be dropped.

Amin capitulated. He sold the stock, but he was far from finished. He would bide his time and achieve his goal another way.

Armed with her MBA, Amin's only child had been handed the directorship of Hassan Group's London operation by her father upon her graduation. From the London office nearly three billion dollars of properties, companies and investments, five percent of the assets owned by Hassan worldwide, was managed by thirty professionals. Amina had nothing to do with any of that. People who answered to her father did the number crunching, and he made all the investment decisions personally. Although she never used the education she'd earned, Amy enjoyed what she did for her father's company. Her days were filled with lunches, dinners, charity events and socializing, all done to promote her family and its interests.

As an undergraduate at Penn, Amy majored in ancient history, and even in college she had begun to amass an enviable collection of artifacts. Today the two-thousand-square-foot office in which she sat, a room that encompassed most of the top floor of the Belgrave Square building, was itself a museum of priceless Greek, Roman and Arabian relics.

She waited for her American visitor behind a large desk, its top completely bare, sipping coffee from a small cup the Arab way. Brian Sadler, the famous owner of Bijan Rarities, had requested an appointment to discuss a subject he said he'd rather disclose in person. Although they hadn't met, she'd been more than once to Brian's gallery in the posh Mayfair area of London. Bijan always had fascinating artifacts, and she loved seeing them.

One thing about Brian's request to meet had made her agree immediately. Tickets to attend Bijan's twice-yearly televised auctions were harder to snag than an invitation to Buckingham Palace. As wealthy as her family was, she couldn't buy her way into a Bijan auction. No one could. There was one way, of course – she could have made a million-dollar purchase at his gallery. That might have gotten her an invitation. But that wasn't what this was about. She didn't want to *buy* a place at his exclusive table. She wanted him to *offer* her one.

She had seen the advertising for Sadler's upcoming auction called *The Wrath of Vesuvius*, and she was ready for him. She moved things here and there in the office, making sure her wonderful pieces from Pompeii and

Herculaneum were prominently displayed. When Brian Sadler left today, she'd have a seat at his next auction.

CHAPTER TWENTY-SEVEN

A white-gloved attendant served coffee as Amy and Brian sat at the conference table in her office.

"I hope you like the coffee," she said in unaccented English as he took a sip. "We brew it the Saudi way, with a little cardamom and saffron. It's strong, but it's my favorite."

"It's absolutely delicious, Miss Hassan," he replied sincerely. "But you're not Saudi, correct?"

"I was born in Dubai. I'm not Saudi, but I'm fiercely proud to be an Arab. And call me Amy, please. Now I want to know more about you, Mr. Sadler."

"Brian," he responded with a smile. She couldn't have been more than five or six years younger than he was, and her father was one of the world's wealthiest men. Dark and sultry, she was a truly stunning woman. She'd be a handful, he mused before dismissing the thought.

"There's not a lot to know about me," he began, knowing she would have done her homework; there was nothing he could say that she didn't already know. "I've been fortunate in growing Bijan Rarities to the modest success we're enjoying today."

She laughed. "Modest isn't exactly the word I would have used to describe Bijan. Broadcasting your auctions on the cable networks was a work of genius. Collectors are indebted to you for making antiquities interesting to the masses. You've allowed ordinary people around the world to have a glimpse into a world I love."

"Which brings me to the reason for my visit," he said, turning to a display case nearby. "May I take a closer look at these pieces?"

She used a small key to open the tall glass door. "Be my guest."

"May I examine this bronze?" he asked, pulling a set of white cotton gloves from his inside jacket pocket. She nodded and he took a three-inch statue from its shelf.

"Hercules, isn't it?"

"Yes, the founder of Herculaneum. It was discovered there in 1740. In those days, as you know, most things ended up in private collections, not museums. I'm fortunate to have acquired it during my university days in America."

"Are you aware of my upcoming auction of art and objects called *The Wrath of Vesuvius*?"

"Who isn't?" she replied with a laugh so fetching it made him smile too. "You do a grand job of marketing, as I said earlier. But I'm afraid the things in my collection are so dear to me that I could never part with even one of them."

"I understand completely and I don't blame you. I'd feel exactly the same way. Your pieces from Pompeii and Herculaneum are among the finest in any private collection I know of. I'd like to show the world how beautiful they are. With your permission I'd like to display them at the gallery before the auction. The evening of the broadcast I'm thinking of starting with an hour-long segment on the history of Vesuvius and the destruction of the cities. I envision your pieces being the primary part of that introductory segment. I'm also hoping that you will attend the event. It would be wonderful if you would provide commentary about your pieces. Whatever you decide, I'd be honored if you would join us for the auction."

What he wanted wasn't what she had expected, but it made a great deal of sense. Several ideas entered her mind at once, the primary one being that she'd accomplished her goal. No matter what, she was attending the auction.

"I accept your offer to attend, but I need to think about displaying the pieces in my collection. May I give you an answer by the end of the week?"

Brian assured her that was fine, and she said she wanted him to see one more piece.

"It's in a safe down the hall. Give me five minutes. Please look around and feel free to open the cases. One more thing before I go. Can you keep a secret?"

He said yes; she tossed him the key and left the room, closing the door behind her.

He walked from case to case, opening some and touching the sides of others to lean in closely. When he had finished, he walked to her desk for a moment and then returned to the conference table.

The attendant opened the door and Amina returned, gingerly carrying a two-foot candlestick. She placed it on the table in front of Brian as he sat open-mouthed.

"It takes a lot to take my breath away," he muttered at last. "Is this Cupid?"

"Yes. It's from –"

"It's from the House of the Genius in Herculaneum," he interrupted in a whisper. "This is incredible. So there were two?"

"There were. You know that this one's twin – the one the art world knows about – is in the National Archaeology Museum of Naples. They were discovered in 1830 by an archaeologist who turned one over to the government and slipped this one into his backpack. I'd heard rumors about it for years, but only two years ago I discovered it was real. A family in Verona didn't realize what they had. They sold a twelve-piece silver service, including the candlestick, to a dealer. Thank God I have a network of people around the world who call me first when they see interesting things. He contacted me, and here it is! Frankly I think mine's safer here in London than the other one is in Naples. If Vesuvius decides to spout again, Naples is going to end up in the ashes exactly like Pompeii did!"

"May I . . . I'm reluctant to ask, but may I hold it?"

"Of course you may. Be my guest!"

He cradled the object reverently in his hands, turning it around and around, admiring the detail.

Carefully placing it back on the conference table, he said, "It's one of the most beautiful things I've ever seen. If you decide to allow your pieces to be part of our broadcast, would you consider allowing the Cupid to be included? It would be the most stunning object I've ever displayed."

"I'm sorry. This one must always be a secret. It's my secret – and yours too now. I showed it to you today to give you a treat, since your love for antiquities and relics is legendary."

They wrapped up the conversation, and she rode the elevator down to the main floor with him, giving him a light air-kiss goodbye. He tried to hand her a card and she shook her head.

"I know how to contact you, Mr. Sadler. You'll hear from me shortly."

As he walked to the tube station at Hyde Park Corner, he reflected on his good fortune. There was little these days that fazed Brian. In the years that he'd owned Bijan, he'd had the opportunity to see – and to own – some of the world's truly singular rarities. But today the candlestick of Cupid had literally taken his breath away. That hadn't happened in a long, long time, and Brian considered himself extremely fortunate.

Although his visit to Hassan Group's London offices had been for an entirely different purpose, there had been an unexpected bonus when he viewed her collection. He was committed to making Amina Hassan his client. The rarities she owned were respected worldwide. Few people had the means to accumulate pieces of this quality. Bijan should be Amina's gallery of choice, and he would make that happen.

He'd also noticed that Amy was also a stunningly attractive woman. It was a little hard to miss. He felt a tinge of embarrassment as he thought of Nicole back in Dallas. But he let that go. This was business. Strictly business.

CHAPTER TWENTY-EIGHT

Amin Hassan sat at his desk, watching the video feed on his computer and taking an occasional satisfying puff from his cigar. It was four p.m. in Dubai and the blazing sun had raised the afternoon temperature to over a hundred degrees Fahrenheit, but the heavy draperies and constant air-conditioning kept his office almost chilly. There were a couple of lamps in the corners; otherwise the room was dark and full of shadows, as Amin always kept it.

With a click of his mouse, the picture changed. Where there had been a meeting on his screen, now there was a single individual, an Arab like Amin, sitting in front of a bank of computers.

"Zarif."

"Yes, sir," the man answered without turning around. He knew his boss could see anything and everything whenever he wished.

"Who is my daughter's visitor?"

Zarif Safwan, director of security for the Hassan Group, clicked the mouse on his own computer. He brought up the digital visitors' log from the first floor reception desk.

"His name is Brian Sadler. I believe he owns a gallery . . ."

"I know what he does," Hassan interrupted sharply. "Everyone knows." Without a word he switched back to the opulent office at Hassan Group's London base, where his daughter, Amina, and Sadler were having coffee. He turned up the volume; there was a slight echo because the camera was several feet away, but he could hear everything clearly.

He grew concerned as he watched the meeting unfold. In only a few minutes they'd dispensed with formalities and were on a first-name basis. That worried Amin, as did many other things about his daughter. To her way of thinking, her degree from Wharton guaranteed her a top position in the company. She wanted to help run the operation without earning her way in. She wanted to be entrusted with decisions, but her father didn't trust her judgment. She was a beautiful, young, impetuous Arab girl who often acted before she thought. Just look at today's meeting with Brian Sadler. Why was she meeting with the famous antiquities collector and television personality?

He took another long puff. Amin Hassan abhorred publicity. He thought he'd made that clear to his daughter. Perhaps there was a business purpose to this meeting. On the other hand, perhaps she was thinking with her heart again instead of her head.

Zarif would have to find out.

CHAPTER TWENTY-NINE

She put the candlestick back in the safe and went to her office. It wasn't the one where she'd met Brian Sadler – they called that the "receiving room." It was used for greeting visitors, displaying her vast collection, and entertaining her father's friends who visited London. Her working office was two doors down the hall and it was much smaller, more crowded and less ostentatious than the formal one. The public never saw hers.

She passed her assistant's desk on the way in and said, "Send Zarif in right away."

A few minutes later a swarthy man dressed in a black shirt and slacks stood before Amy's desk. Her father had personally picked Zarif Safwan as chief of security in the London office.

"Sweep the receiving room."

He nodded and walked out. Twice a day the entire fourth floor was routinely swept for audio and video devices. There was another sweep each time an outsider visited. Hassan Group was involved in many, many things more secretive than the management of properties and investments. Secrecy and security were ingrained in Amina Hassan. She'd been taught them since she was a child. She knew her father's business intimately – at least she thought she did – and Amin Hassan demanded secrecy about everything he did.

Zarif Safwan and his team were masters at their craft. Each of them had been a soldier, dedicated to Allah and the cause, but now fiercely loyal to Amina's father. Hassan paid them many times what ordinary security guards would earn because these were not ordinary men. These men would die for their boss. Others had given their lives when Hassan required it, and these men would willingly do it too.

Zarif swept the room where Amina and Brian had met. Before he reported back to her, he went to his office and dialed her father's cellphone. The old man was his boss, not this impertinent girl he'd known since she was a child. If there were orders to be given, he'd take them from the father, not the daughter.

He told Amin who the visitor was and that Amina had asked for a sweep after he left. "I found six devices," he reported tersely. They were all audio units, each around the size of an American quarter, and they were positioned randomly around her office. One was under the lip of the desk, another under the conference table where they had sat, and four more were in or around the display cases.

"I reviewed the video feed of his visit," he continued. "The man was good. He was very nonchalant, and without the sweeping equipment, I wouldn't have known that he planted them. Do you want me to remove them? And what shall we do with Mr. Sadler?"

"Do nothing. Leave his devices in place for now and we'll see what happens next. Tell my daughter you found nothing. Tell her everything is fine. And Zarif, watch her. Tell me if there's anything I should know."

"Of course, sir."

Amin Hassan opened a program on his computer and looked at live feeds from video cameras hidden in every room of the building. He switched over to the camera in her office, saw Amina's empty chair, glanced at his watch and knew she'd gone to lunch.

He'd always kept a close eye on Amina. She was a beautiful, passionate girl. The Arab blood in her veins fueled the fiery, unbridled daughter he loved, but he would never give her control over his business. She had no idea what he was involved in, the extent of his influence or the ends to which he would go to right a wrong against his family or his interests. His own Arab genes imbued power, ruthlessness and cruel retaliation toward those he believed were against him. He was one of the world's wealthiest and most powerful men. He'd gotten where he was by using his cunning and intellect, and that was the way it would continue to be.

When she returned from lunch, Zarif reported back to Amina. "Everything's fine. We found nothing. Is there anything else?"

"Yes. Keep this between us. There's no need to run to my father every time someone comes to visit. Do you understand?" She knew how the security chief operated, and she was determined to assert her position as his superior.

He nodded. "I understand perfectly, Miss Hassan."

Zarif reported that conversation to his boss as well.

———

On Friday Brian got the call he'd been anticipating.

"I've made a decision," she said. "Meet me for cocktails at six thirty at the Connaught Bar."

He felt another pang of remorse as he immediately accepted her invitation. Nicole was his fiancée, but she was at home in Dallas. *And it's not Amy I'm excited about anyway*, he assured himself. *It's simply business*, he said to himself one time too many. He *was* looking forward to spending time with Amy again. And hearing her decision, of course.

The walk from his gallery to the Connaught Hotel should have taken ten minutes, but on this Friday evening the streets were crowded with pedestrians browsing the stylish shop windows in Mayfair. He rushed in a few minutes late and saw her sipping a martini at the bar. She was dressed in a pinstriped pantsuit and jacket with a white shirt. Her jet-black hair flowed to her shoulders. She looked stunning.

Not as stunning as Nicole. But not bad.

He maneuvered through the crowded bar, leaned in and offered his cheek, but she put up her hand, turned his face into hers and gave him a kiss on the lips. He drew back in momentary surprise, smiled sheepishly and took the barstool next to her. A waiter appeared in seconds and whisked Brian's coat and case away to the cloakroom.

"Thanks for joining me. This is my Friday afternoon ritual. If it's been a good week, I have one martini. I allow myself two if my week's been really, really good, or really stressful, or if I'm thinking about being a little naughty!"

As they clicked glasses, she said, "I've decided to let you display my pieces at the gallery and during your broadcast. I'll provide commentary too if you wish." He smiled broadly and opened his mouth to reply, but she raised her hand to stop him. "I'm not quite finished. My decision comes with a stipulation."

"I'm sure our attorneys can work things out," he began.

"Of course they can. This isn't about contracts. Here's what I require. You owe me dinner. Tonight. Whatever plans you have, cancel them! We have a reservation at eight at Balthazar. Do you accept my condition?"

"Certainly!" *What else can I do? This is just business.* "I need to make a call and rearrange something, but I can't refuse the woman who holds the key to making my Vesuvius project an instant success!"

"Wonderful. Then finish your martini so we can have a second." She smiled slyly.

"Another martini? Has your week been really good or really stressful?"

She touched his sleeve lightly and whispered, "Maybe it simply means I'm being a bit naughty."

Danger, the little voice in his head said as he finished his drink and stood.

"I'll be back in a moment. Order me another!"

CHAPTER THIRTY

Brian sat in an overstuffed chair in the Connaught's quiet, refined lobby and called Nicole. Despite what he'd said, he didn't really have another engagement. He had a standing phone date with his fiancée every evening around seven his time. One of them frequently couldn't make the calls because of a conflict, but tonight his conscience wouldn't let him simply text that he had a last-minute meeting with a client. He had to talk to her now to make himself feel better about the dinner he'd just agreed to.

It was one p.m. in Dallas, and Nicole told him she was having lunch at an outdoor café on McKinney Avenue. He knew the place – it was only a couple of blocks from the building where she'd opened a solo law practice. She had recovered from the car crash that almost took her life two years ago but decided to leave behind the high-stakes, high-powered life of a white-collar criminal lawyer at one of the city's largest and most prestigious firms. It just wasn't worth it anymore. She had made millions of dollars and created a sterling reputation defending corporate executives charged with fraud, insider trading and the like. She could afford to step back, take more time for herself and explore with her fiancé, Brian Sadler, how marriage might actually work for them.

Although Nicole wore an engagement ring, they hadn't discussed a date. In the past twenty-four months their roles had switched one hundred and eighty degrees. Before the wreck, Nicole was the busy one. She worked long days and long nights handling high-profile clients, winning nearly a hundred percent of the cases but having almost no personal life. Now Brian's hectic schedule, constant international travel and increasing notoriety made him the one who was always busy, always gone and always tied up with one client or another.

When Brian had proposed, his intentions had been noble. He would move to Dallas, marry Nicole and build his new Texas gallery to augment his well-established operation in London. But something unexpected happened. He couldn't have imagined the popularity of the television broadcasts. Now Bijan Rarities had far more business than one man should have handled, but so far he wasn't willing to share the decisions involving multimillion-dollar purchases and sales with anyone else. As he worked harder and harder, Nicole realized her newfound freedom from the corporate yoke came with a price. Now it was she who was alone much of the time. It was difficult for her as her body and mind continued to mend from the near-fatal car crash. Occasionally she yearned for those days when she was a power lawyer on top of her game. Usually those thoughts came during the lonely nights when she was home and Brian was in Calcutta or Marrakesh or Zurich.

"I need to make this quick," he began. "A dinner came up at the last minute with a client who's agreed to display some unique artifacts for the Vesuvius show."

She certainly understood. How many times had she herself cut a conversation short because *she* was the one going to drinks or dinner with a client? She hadn't considered then how it must have felt to him, but she understood it now. She loved him and trusted him, but it was a big world out there. She'd seen it first-hand, but now the shoe was on the other foot.

"I won't keep you. Go on and do what you need to do. Just tell me this client isn't a beautiful woman whose motives for my fiancé are totally immoral!"

Brian hesitated, wishing he hadn't mentioned the Vesuvius exhibit. As soon as they started marketing Amy's pieces as part of the show, Nicole would know exactly who had joined him for dinner tonight. He'd better get this over with.

Apparently he hesitated a moment too long.

Her voice was tinged with a little sadness. "It's okay, sweetie. I have no right –"

"You have every right," he responded urgently. "Nicole, I love you. I miss you and I wish I were there with you. The dinner's with Amina Hassan. Look her up. She has an unrivaled collection of things from Pompeii, and I've successfully arranged to display them at the gallery."

"Great, baby. Call me tonight when you're done if you want," she said. "You don't have to. If it's late and you're tired . . ."

"You're on, sweetie. I'll call you when things wrap up and I'm back at the flat."

"Good luck tonight. I love you."

"I love you too. I promise I'll call you."

BILL THOMPSON

CHAPTER THIRTY-ONE

The conversation at dinner was stimulating and easy. It was as though they'd known each other for years. They talked about archaeology, acquiring ancient things, and the challenge in privately accumulating artifacts that arguably should be on public display. Both had faced criticism from museums for their roles in keeping priceless relics in private hands. But the museums could be criticized too. Thousands more pieces were stored in basements than were on display in the viewing rooms of the world's great museums. Thousands of beautiful, interesting, thought-provoking things would lie in dusty boxes for decades, maybe forever, unseen and forgotten.

Brian glanced at the check and tossed out his credit card. The champagne she'd ordered was the finest the restaurant offered, and the food here had been both wonderful and pricey. The bill for the two of them was over four hundred pounds sterling – almost six hundred dollars – but as much as it had cost, it was far short of the most expensive tab he'd ever picked up. Expense-account entertainment was a fact of life in his business. With the profits Bijan Rarities racked up each year, a six-hundred-dollar meal was nothing.

As they walked to the curb, a driver tipped his hat and opened the door of a Bentley sedan.

"Can I offer you a nightcap at my place? I have a few more things I could show you that I think you'd enjoy!"

After the martinis and champagne, Brian's brain struggled to decide if she was talking about her artifacts or something else. He glanced at his watch – it was after midnight – and remembered his promise to Nicole.

"I'd better call it a night." With a grin he added, "This was an unexpected dinner, you know, and I'd better get to bed if I'm going to be productive in the morning!"

I have a bed, she almost said before deciding against it. They hugged and she gave him a kiss. This time she couldn't miss how he concertedly kept his cheek turned to her lips, avoiding the real kiss she'd managed earlier.

This is how it always goes, she thought as the driver took her home. *Whether it's artifacts or men, I always want the ones that are the hardest to get. I always get the most satisfaction from the most difficult acquisitions.* She smiled. This had just begun. There was plenty of time.

There's no need to carry my briefcase home, Brian thought as her sedan pulled away. He decided to walk back to his office, drop it off and then take a cab home. He texted Nicole to let her know dinner was over and he'd call shortly. He began walking through the winding streets of Mayfair toward Old Bond Street.

He walked through Berkeley Square, where the streetlamps cast eerie shadows on the empty sidewalks. He cut across to the east side and was heading down Berkeley Street when he heard footsteps behind him.

Brian turned and saw a man in the darkness coming up quickly. He raised his briefcase to fend him off, but the stranger hit his arm with something hard, maybe a pipe. The case fell to the sidewalk and Brian's arm hung uselessly at his side.

He yelled in pain and cried, "If it's money you want . . ."

The man merely smiled and shook his head.

Then everything went dark.

CHAPTER THIRTY-TWO

"He's bleeding!"

There were sirens somewhere in the distance.

"Can you hear me?"

Someone was shaking him, making his arm hurt.

Brian opened his eyes and saw a well-dressed man and woman kneeling on the sidewalk beside him. The singsong wail of the siren suddenly grew much louder, and it made his head pound like hammers clanging on metal. An ambulance pulled to the curb, its flashing red and blue lights making him dizzy. Two paramedics hopped out and asked how he felt.

"I think my arm's broken," he said, holding it up. "He must have hit me in the head too. It hurts like hell!"

The woman said, "Yes, he's bleeding right there. Look." She pointed to the back of his head where Brian's hair was matted with blood.

A police car screeched to a stop as more pedestrians gathered to see what was going on in this usually quiet neighborhood. "Give them room to work," the officer barked to passersby who had crowded in close to watch.

Within a few minutes Brian had garnered enough strength to sit up against a light pole. He gave a statement, saying he'd been assaulted by a man who had a stick or piece of pipe. The officer pulled out a notepad and pen. He took Brian's personal information down; then he asked what the man had taken. Brian looked through his pockets, saw his case lying nearby on the sidewalk and said nothing was missing. He still had his watch, wallet and even his gold cufflinks.

"That's odd," the policeman said as the paramedics worked on Brian. One bandaged his head while the other gingerly massaged his arm. Brian winced in pain as the EMT put pressure on the area.

"Your arm's broken," he told Brian, who wasn't surprised.

The cop was still taking notes. "Have you ever seen the man before? It's obvious this wasn't a robbery. Did he say anything?"

"Everything's hazy. He . . . I think he smiled. But I don't think he said anything."

"What do you think this was about? Any recent problems with anyone?"

Brian honestly replied that he had no idea. He'd been at dinner with a client and was walking back to his office to drop off his briefcase before going home.

"What do you do for a living, Mr. Sadler?"

"I own a gallery a few blocks from here. Bijan Rarities."

"I knew it!" the female half of the couple who had found him said. "I recognized you, but it's so dark I didn't put it together. You're Brian Sadler!" She turned to the officer. "He's famous! He's on television all the time!"

That was the last straw. About to collapse, Brian smiled weakly and said to the cop, "I'm happy to cooperate, but can we continue all this in the morning? I need to get some rest."

The paramedic said, "You need to go to the hospital. You have to get your arm dealt with, and you need to be checked for a possible concussion."

It was nearly two when Brian finally got to bed. His arm was in a cast and he'd been given an injection to ease the pain. He also had prescription painkillers in case he needed them. He had to get some sleep – the policeman was coming to the gallery at eleven to continue the interview.

Brian stripped off his clothes. He'd have loved a shower, but dealing with the cast on his arm would be difficult under good circumstances and impossible now when he felt like a walking zombie. He crawled into bed, mentally and physically exhausted.

At four in the morning he heard a ding on his phone.

Shit! He'd forgotten all about Nicole. And she had been very, very patient, making no attempt to contact him even though he'd told her the dinner was over. But now it was late – very late – and he hadn't called. He looked at her message.

"Are you alive?"

Shit!

Groggy from the medication and his snap out of a deep sleep, he called her.

"Hey, I'm so sorry. After the dinner was finished, I decided to walk back to the gallery and drop off my briefcase. Somebody assaulted me along the way."

"My God! Are you all right?"

He explained what little he knew about what happened and that his arm was in a cast. "The guy hit me with a pipe, I think. My head hurts like hell and they gave me a shot. I came home and fell into bed. I'm so sorry for forgetting to call."

Her voice was full of concern. "Are you kidding? Don't worry about it. I'm just glad you're okay. Was your client with you when it happened?"

He was grateful to be able to answer truthfully that her driver had picked her up at the restaurant and he declined a ride.

"Can we talk more tomorrow? I've got to get some sleep," he said wearily. "The police will be at the gallery at eleven and I have to rest."

"Go to bed. Call me when you can. I love you."

He was asleep before they disconnected.

BILL THOMPSON

CHAPTER THIRTY-THREE

The officer fired questions at Brian.

Who was the person you had dinner with? Was she married? Had you been out with her previously? Could this be retaliation by a jealous boyfriend? What was the purpose of your dinner? Are you sure the attacker said nothing to you?

Brian answered every question and finally said, "Personally I'm grateful for your interest in my case, but I'm wondering why you've taken so much time on it. There must be a hundred assaults a night in London."

"Likely even more," the policeman conceded, "but yours got my attention. In the first place, attacks in Mayfair are rare. It's one of London's most upscale neighborhoods; even after midnight the streets are mostly well lit and there is usually pedestrian traffic nearby. You were attacked in Berkeley Square two doors down from a Rolls Royce dealership, on a dark part of the sidewalk. It wasn't random; the man took absolutely nothing, but you say he smiled. This was no robbery – from what you've told me, he didn't take a thing. I'm thinking he was delivering a message."

He told Brian that the high-end auto dealership had six security cameras in its showroom and covering the sidewalks in front. If it was in range, the attack might have been captured on video. He was working on that angle and hoped something would turn up. Meanwhile, he asked Brian to call if there was anything more he recalled.

At noon, six a.m. in Dallas, Brian called Nicole. He repeated what had happened in Berkeley Square last night and the questions the officer had asked today. The lawyer in her homed in on what she considered most important – the attacker might have been delivering a message.

"Are you sure he didn't say anything?"

"I don't think so. Everything happened so fast, and he hit me in the head as soon as I saw him."

"Tell me again the girl you had dinner with. What was her name again – something Hassan?"

"Amina Hassan. She runs the London office of her father's investment group." He could hear the click of a keyboard. Nicole was looking it up.

"She's beautiful. I guess you noticed that too," she said jokingly. "Is she married?"

"The cop asked me that too. She's single and nothing was going on. Nothing. It was as simple as I told you. She asked me to meet her for a drink at the Connaught so she could tell me her decision on exhibiting some artifacts she owns. Then she invited me for dinner to talk more about it. We discussed all the things you'd expect – private collections versus museums, the pieces she's accumulated, and how the display at Bijan might work. Even if she had a jealous boyfriend, there was absolutely nothing that happened."

She believed him, but there were niggling questions. She and Brian talked almost every evening. She had a pretty good idea how his days were going, and she knew of nothing he was doing that should have precipitated an attack.

"For whatever reason, all this has something to do with Amina Hassan. Do you think I'm right about that?"

He knew that was a possibility, but he didn't tell her why her involvement actually might make perfect sense.

Later Brian sat in his office, thinking more about last night. He was almost certain what was behind the attack. He'd been on a mission when he went to Amy Hassan's office – a mission for the United States government. Although he hadn't been told why, the CIA had asked him to plant listening devices in her office. In his position as owner of Bijan Rarities, he could easily get an appointment with a wealthy collector who never publicly displayed her treasures.

Once he saw what she had, he was fascinated, but he also completed the mission. He planted six tiny bugs while she was away getting the Cupid candlestick. Had someone – perhaps Amy herself – discovered them? If so, she was a masterful actor. She seemed perfectly at ease, and it certainly hadn't stopped her from agreeing to let him display her priceless relics, going to dinner with him and even inviting him to her place for a nightcap.

Had his mission to Amy's office been the reason he ended up with a broken arm, or was this purely a coincidence? What else could it be? If that was what it was, why did Amy appear no different than the last time he'd seen her?

Unsure what to do next, he called the man who'd asked him to put the devices in Amina Hassan's office.

BILL THOMPSON

CHAPTER THIRTY-FOUR

The director listened as Brian described his attack. He didn't believe in coincidence. In his years at the CIA, he'd learned that most seemingly coincidental things turned out to be no coincidence at all.

By now Case realized the office where Amina had met Brian wasn't her actual workplace. She spent almost no time there; usually the room was completely quiet. In fact, the devices had picked up just two conversations since Brian left. Each had been casual talk between Amy and another person. One conversation had been in Arabic and the other in French. From the discussion, it appeared both of her guests were friends of Amy's father who were in London on holiday and who had simply stopped by to say hello.

Case assumed the listening devices hadn't been found so far. They were still operating perfectly, albeit infrequently. Brian had done exactly what he'd been asked to do, and it wasn't his fault the outcome had been less than what the CIA had hoped for. But something was better than nothing.

At the end, Brian asked if Case was going to contact the London authorities.

"No, not directly. I can ask someone from the embassy to touch base with them for new information, but a call from my office would raise a lot of questions about who Brian Sadler actually is and why the CIA is interested in a routine assault."

"I hadn't thought of that. Oh, one more thing – the officer told me that the Rolls-Royce dealership has video cameras. Do you want me to ask what he found out?"

Case did, and a few hours later Brian advised the video feed did include a clear shot of a man dressed head to toe in black, wearing gloves and a ski mask. He was carrying a crowbar and stayed in the shadows.

"I'm on camera too," he added. "When I crossed the square and started down Berkeley Street, he was ten feet away from me, standing in the north corner of the building in the dark. As I walked along the sidewalk in front of the dealership where it's well lit, he moved out to the street where it's not. When I was in the shadows again, he came up behind me fast."

"Did the cop offer any opinions?"

"He thinks the same thing I do. It couldn't be a robbery because he didn't take anything, nor was he scared away before he could steal my stuff. It sounded like there was no one nearby until that couple found me. So once we rule out robbery, what else could it be? A random act of violence by a guy dressed in black holding a crowbar? What was he – a mental patient? It just doesn't make sense."

Case also thought it didn't make sense unless it had something to do with Amina Hassan. But what? Was it retaliation by a jealous lover? There'd be no way to find that out except by asking Amina herself.

"Where do things stand with Miss Hassan?"

"I was going to ask you the same thing," Brian replied. "When I agreed to meet with her and plant the bugs, I didn't realize the extent of the collection she has. She's accumulated some truly remarkable pieces, including something so unique I didn't know it existed. She's agreed to let me display some of them before my next auction. It's going to be awkward if I suddenly act like I'm not interested anymore. So I'll fire the question back – should I continue building a professional relationship with her, or do you think there's a risk in doing that?"

Case knew exactly what he wanted from Brian. It was always risky putting civilians in a potentially volatile situation, but there was nothing to indicate there was any risk of danger in his discussions with Amina. There was the attack, but was it connected? There was no way to know.

Her father was a different story entirely. Amin was truly dangerous, a man the CIA believed was sponsoring terrorism and who had likely ordered the murders of over a hundred people. Case wanted to know everything he could about the Hassans, and Brian could help immensely.

"I see no problem moving ahead on a professional level," he answered. "You're a savvy businessman, Mr. Sadler, or else you wouldn't have gotten where you are today. You know how to keep your eyes and ears open, not only to help out your country, but personally. Just be aware of what's going on around you. Oh, and maybe stay out of dark squares at midnight."

Brian laughed halfheartedly, his hopes buoyed by affirmation from the director himself that he should continue meeting with Amy. He had already decided to do one thing differently going forward in his relationship with the fiery Arab girl. He had to stop this flirtatious behavior and he knew just how to do it.

BILL THOMPSON

CHAPTER THIRTY-FIVE

After his call to Case yesterday, Brian had spent an hour on FaceTime with Nicole. Although he knew her remark about his beautiful client had been in jest, he sensed the jealousy. God knew he'd felt it himself often enough. When she had been a star attorney in Dallas's most prestigious firm, she was always out until all hours with one client or another. He felt a tinge of resentment every time she was late returning a call or didn't call back at all or was too busy to talk right then.

Now the tables were turned, and Nicole was both recovering from her wreck and working solely for herself. Brian was determined to give her no reason to doubt him. He had to admit Amy had gotten to him for a moment. She was stunning, daring and aggressive, and she'd surprised him with a real kiss. But that was as far as it was going. Next time he and his new client met for lunch, Nicole would be with them.

"I want you to come over next week if I can arrange a meeting with Amy Hassan," he'd said. "I want you to get to know each other. You're already working on the contract she'll be signing, so this will be a business meeting between my lawyer and my client."

"Feeling guilty?" He could hear the smile in her voice. There wasn't much Nicole missed after all these years.

"Not at all. Nothing to feel guilty about!" He hoped that sounded as flippant as he wanted it to be.

She agreed to fly over from Wednesday until Sunday and Brian said he'd arrange a lunch with Amy. He hoped her schedule would allow it; now that Nicole had said she would come, he was really excited about seeing her. He wanted to keep the evenings free for cozy dinners.

He called Amy. "How about joining me at the Langham a week from Friday at one, and I'll fill you in on developments so far. I'm bringing my attorney to present a draft of the contract. And lunch is on me since you're my client now!" Brian didn't tell her about the attack or that his arm would be in a cast the next time they saw each other.

Amy accepted without hesitation after glancing at her calendar and deciding lunch with Brian was far superior to the glorious hands of her excellent masseuse. She'd move that standing weekly appointment to another day.

Brian and Nicole arrived at The Langham Hotel half an hour ahead of their one p.m. reservation and sipped wine in the Artesian Bar. Brian was here often and he introduced the bartender to his fiancée, which earned her a free congratulatory drink. Soon Brian waved and Nicole turned to see a dark-haired woman in a red suit walk into the bar.

"Amy, good to see you." He tried unsuccessfully for an air-kiss, but she was far too clever for him.

"This must be your attorney." She offered her hand. "Amina Hassan."

"This is Nicole Farber. She is my attorney, but in fact, she's also my fiancée."

Amy's eyes flashed for a second. "You kept her a secret when we had dinner the other night!"

Thank God I told Nicole about that.

"And what have you done to yourself? Why is your arm in a cast?"

"First things first! Shall we have a glass of wine here before we move into the dining room? Let's get you a drink and I'll fill you in."

She took the bar stool next to Nicole and ordered a Kir Royale. Then Brian told her what happened after he left her the other night.

"Oh my gosh!" Her voice and her eyes were sincere. "What do you think it was? Was it a mugging? Or a robbery?"

"The guy didn't take anything. He broke my arm with a crowbar, and then I guess he hit me in the head with it too. I was out cold on the sidewalk until some tourists came by and found me. The police think it's pretty brazen, since it happened in Berkeley Square, where there could have been tourists coming around the corner at any second, but I guess attacks can happen anywhere."

"I'm so sorry, Brian! Is there anything I can do?"

"I have to ask something although I'm sure this attack had nothing to do with you. Is there any chance someone you're seeing could have been jealous?"

She laughed. "Sorry! I know this situation isn't funny to you, but there's nobody I know who likes me enough to fight for me!"

As she said it, one tiny thought crept into her mind. Actually there *was* one person who was capable of violence like this, a person who actually *would* fight for her. Her father. But he didn't even know she'd met Brian. And why would he have ordered such an attack anyway? *No, it wasn't him,* she assured herself as she turned to visit with Nicole.

BILL THOMPSON

CHAPTER THIRTY-SIX

They lingered over a last round of Pouilly-Fuisse in the Artesian Bar where they'd started. They had taken their time over lunch, wine and coffee as the females discussed each other's pasts, their likes and dislikes and their mutual love for London.

Brian had thought they would hit it off. Both were driven individuals with dynamic personalities and a zest for living. Now that Nicole knew Amy, it made his life a lot easier since he would be spending time with her over the next several months before the broadcast.

He called for the check, and Amy said with a smile, "I hate to interject business into our otherwise perfect afternoon, but do you have a contract for me to review?"

Brian laughed. He'd forgotten about it completely. Nicole brought out an envelope and handed it across the table.

"I'm sure you've seen a non-sale consignment agreement," Nicole said. "This one is very typical."

"I haven't, actually. I've never agreed to let my pieces be displayed. Brian was so subtle and persuasive that I just couldn't say no!"

"He can be that way." Nicole smiled. "It took a while, but I finally learned how to say no."

Brian smirked, "Not very often!" That brought a laugh from the ladies.

Amy said her attorney would get back to Nicole soon. She asked, "Now that business is done, I want to know how long you'll be in London. Let's get together again before you leave."

"I'm heading back the day after tomorrow. This one's a short trip."

Amy asked them for dinner Saturday evening at her club, but they kept their promise to have dinners alone. Nicole said they were busy, but she put her hand on Brian's knee and said, "Sweetie, can we do lunch tomorrow?"

That worked fine for everyone. "It'll be my treat," Amy said. "Shall we say 12:30 and may we go casual? I'm usually in jeans on Saturdays. There's a great little place just off Leicester Square called Cork and Bottle. They have nice wine and food and a great atmosphere. I think you'll enjoy it."

They spent a wonderful, relaxing afternoon strolling around Soho and Covent Garden. By the time Nicole left on Sunday morning, the two had become fast friends with promises that Amy would come to Dallas and that Brian and Nicole would someday visit her family home in Dubai.

As he tracked Nicole's plane departing from Heathrow, the man who had been following Amy the entire time emailed his report.

CHAPTER THIRTY-SEVEN

Amin Hassan now had a comprehensive dossier on the man who had planted the bugs. Everyone knew Brian Sadler – the famous gallery owner was hard to miss if one was interested in antiquities and relics. Amy had made a deal with him to display her artifacts from Pompeii and Herculaneum. At first her father could have cared less about that – those were hers to do with as she wished.

The nagging question was why he had installed listening devices. Was this the way Sadler did business, cheating and eavesdropping on his clients? That made no sense at all. There was something else to this. Maybe Sadler hadn't been interested in Amy's pieces at all. Maybe the entire purpose of his appointment was to get her out of the room long enough to plant devices in an office he presumed was hers.

He thought it was likely that someone – perhaps an American intelligence agency – enlisted Sadler to gain access to Amy's office under the pretext of borrowing her relics for an upcoming auction. That was what he wanted to know more about.

A few days later Amin Hassan learned a startling fact about Brian Sadler. His college roommate and lifelong best friend was Harry Harrison, the former President of the United States.

His best friend is the man killed by the Falcons of Islam, and now he turns up in my London office, planting devices.

Suddenly Amin understood. This was no coincidence. Sadler's visit, his sudden interest in Amy's artifacts, the listening devices – the American government had orchestrated everything. More disturbing was the fact that his daughter was becoming personal friends with Sadler and his fiancée-slash-attorney. The urgency of this situation suddenly escalated a hundredfold. There was no time to waste.

Once again he called the man who'd solved his problems for years. Zarif had been a loyal and trusted servant, and he asked no questions about his boss's instructions. He'd executed orders over and over again, never leaving a clue that Hassan Group was behind the often-violent acts.

"It has to be an accident and it has to be soon."

"Of course, Mr. Hassan. Leave everything to me."

Amin called his daughter next. "I'm putting Zarif on a project, my dear. He'll be out of the office for a few days, maybe a week. Is there anything he's working on for you that we need to move to someone else?"

Her father hardly needed Amina's input; he knew exactly what Zarif was doing every minute of every day. Amina didn't particularly approve of her father's methods, but she had to give him credit. Things always turned out well for Hassan Group when Zarif went on one of his "projects." The problem always went away. Zarif was dangerous. She knew that, but she also was certain he would never hurt her. Her father would kill Zarif if he did. Regardless, it paid to be careful.

Putting Zarif on a project meant something was wrong that Amin wanted him to fix. From Amy's standpoint, the one thing that had consumed her time the past two weeks was her involvement with Brian and Nicole. She'd come to enjoy their company during the brief time they'd been together, and now she was already planning that trip to Dallas they'd discussed. She'd be leaving in a couple of weeks. She was becoming close to them. Warning bells went off in her mind. What was Zarif up to?

"I'm good, Father. I hope you are too. Everything's under control here. Where's Zarif off to this time?"

"Out of town," he said noncommittally as always. They said their goodbyes, and she walked down the hall to Zarif's office. His door was always locked, but she had a master key that opened every room in the building. She put it in the lock and tried to turn it. Nothing happened.

Suddenly the door opened and the security chief said curtly, "May I help you, Miss Hassan?"

She pulled the key out of the lock. "Why doesn't my key work? I'm supposed to have access to every door. You know that."

"I have no idea," he said evenly. "Perhaps it's a malfunction. I'll work on it."

"When? I hear you're going out of town." She glanced at the desk behind him. On top lay an open manila folder stuffed with papers. The top sheet was a picture. She stepped further into the office toward the desk, and he spun around, quickly closing the file.

"What do you want, Amy?"

Amy? Don't call me by my nickname, you bastard!

"I was just wondering where you're going. Is my father sending you off again to make something right that's wrong?"

"I suppose you'll have to talk to your father about that. Now if there's nothing else, I have work to do."

She walked out and he closed the door behind her. Had she seen the file? Probably not.

But she had. She'd seen the picture on top of the file – Brian Sadler's photograph.

BILL THOMPSON

CHAPTER THIRTY-EIGHT

Amin Hassan, his daughter Amina, and Zarif Safwan had been on the CIA's watch list for three years. Amin was a known sympathizer and clandestine supporter of terrorist organizations in the Middle East. Zarif was his security chief and enforcer and the agency kept a close eye on his activities. His passport was flagged in case he traveled to the States, but he wouldn't be stopped anywhere in the process. Instead, the CIA would monitor his activities. But for the three years he'd been under observation, Zarif had never come to the United States.

Moments ago the director was awakened by a call from the night desk at Langley. Zarif had just purchased a ticket online to travel from London to DFW International Airport. Three days from now he'd arrive in Dallas, the home of Brian Sadler and Nicole Farber. Although it was possible Safwan had other plans, it was much more likely he was coming for them.

Case thought it even more curious that Amina Hassan herself was apparently becoming personal friends with the couple. She'd been with Brian and Nicole twice while they were in London, and now she had a ticket too. She was coming to Dallas in ten days, presumably to see the couple. Case wondered what Zarif's trip had to do with Amina's. It was likely they were connected, but the CIA couldn't assume that Zarif would stay put until Amina arrived a week later. They had to move quickly.

He took a huge risk in keeping President Parkes out of the loop about Safwan and the agency's interest in his upcoming visit to the United States. But what the hell? Case's time as director was short; the new President would soon replace him with a crony who had no backbone. It was happening every week, and with every new appointment it was more and more clear to everyone inside the Beltway that experience and leadership didn't matter anymore. Yes-men of the Democratic persuasion were the new order of the day in the Parkes administration.

So the President knew nothing about Brian Sadler, the Hassans or Zarif Safwan. Ever since that meeting in the Situation Room – ever since the President had told his people to ignore the Falcons of Islam – Case had deliberately kept him out of the loop. But there was a far more important reason that Parkes knew nothing – Operation Condor.

The CIA director made a phone call, explained the situation unfolding with Zarif Safwan, and he was given instructions on how to proceed.

Sitting in his home office in his pajamas, Case glanced at his watch. As much as he regretted what he had to do next, there was no alternative. It was after midnight in Dallas. He was about to disrupt two people's lives and make them very angry. Everything would be fine eventually, but in the short term it was going to be difficult.

The shrill ring of Brian's phone woke them both from a deep sleep.

"Listen closely," Case said after identifying himself. "There's something happening that you and Nicole Farber are suddenly part of. I'm going to apologize only once that I can't tell you anything more, but you and Miss Farber have to come with my agents. Now. They'll pick you up in front of your building in an hour."

"What?" Brian responded as he became more alert. "What do you mean? I can't just leave the gallery on a moment's notice. And Nicole? What does she have to do with this?"

Nicole sat up in bed and pulled the covers to her chest. His words were scaring her.

"Who is it?" she whispered.

"Hold on a moment," Brian said, turning to Nicole. "It's the director of the CIA. Some agents are picking us up in an hour."

"To go where?"

He put the phone on speaker and then said to Case, "We're not going anywhere. I've done what you asked so far, but Nicole and I have lives. Besides that, Nicole has nothing to do with any of this. If there was something that could help Harry and Jennifer and the girls, I'd go to the ends of the earth to do it. So would she. But they're dead. You guys can take it from here. I'm tired of all this."

"I was hoping it wouldn't come to this. This isn't a request, Mr. Sadler. You are both in grave danger. The two of you must come with my men in fifty-two minutes. Voluntarily or involuntarily – it's up to you. This is a matter of national security. And trust me, it *will* help us learn more about what happened to President Harrison and his family."

Given her background in criminal defense, a thousand thoughts flew through Nicole's mind. Were they being detained? It didn't sound like it, although they were certainly going somewhere one way or another – voluntarily or against their will.

"This is Nicole, Director Case. I'm an attorney. Under what authority are you ordering us to go with your men? Where and why are we going? Are we under arrest?"

"You are not under arrest, but if you refuse to come voluntarily, I will have you placed in the temporary custody of the agency. I can't tell you where you're going. All I can promise is that this will help in the loss of your friends. I regret doing it this way, but everything will be clear soon."

Brian didn't say a word as Case told them to plan for two weeks away from home, to pack casual clothes and expect very warm weather.

"Is this some kind of damned vacation?" Nicole shot back.

"Not in the least, Miss Farber. I'm sorry . . ."

"Yeah, we got that part."

"One last thing. Ninety minutes from now you won't have access to your phones for an extended period of time. Please make whatever arrangements you need for two weeks out of the office, and do it now."

"This is absolutely crazy," Brian exploded. "It's the middle of the night, for God's sake! If you think we're doing this –"

Case interrupted Brian calmly. Dear God, he wished this weren't how it was, even though he knew they'd be on board a hundred percent by this time tomorrow.

"I've told you this is a matter of national security. You have to go, period. Your help has been of immense value so far, and we need you now more than ever. My men will see you downstairs in . . . forty-seven minutes. If you're not there, they will come and get you."

"What about Nicole? Why's she included?"

But the phone was dead. Case had hung up.

Don Case felt like a heel. This guy had done nothing but cooperate. He was a civilian who happened to have been best friends with President Harrison, and they'd put him right in the middle of all this. He wished he could have been honest. It would have made things so much easier. What little he had told Brian and Nicole was true, but he hadn't told them much. The biggest thing they couldn't be told was that this sudden trip was to hide them from a murderer – Zarif Safwan.

Brian was torn between patriotism and his fiancée's welfare. Ever since the car wreck Nicole had been a fragile person. She was recovering slowly and steadily, but she was certainly not as strong as she once had been. His agreement to help the CIA was one thing, but including Nicole was another thing entirely.

No phones for a long time? Pack for warm weather? Away for two weeks?

"We're not going," he told Nicole flatly.

"You're wasting time. We *are* going. As much as I don't like it, he has the authority to do what he's doing. Obama signed a law in 2011 that gives the CIA wide powers in the fight against terrorism, even inside our borders." She got up and pulled a suitcase from the closet. "You'd better get ready."

"We're not terrorists. Surely our government can't threaten ordinary citizens and take them away against their will. Is that what the world is coming to?"

"That's not the point. Give it up. He can do what he says if we refuse to go. I just want you to do one thing. Do you have his direct number?"

"Yes."

"Call him back right now. Make sure that was really him and that we're not being handed over to kidnappers or something."

"Are you crazy? Kidnappers?"

"Crazy? Crazy? What part of all of this isn't? Just call and confirm so we don't get into a car with a couple of strangers and disappear forever."

He made the call and they began throwing clothes into suitcases. Thirty minutes later they took the elevator to the lobby. Waiting for them was a man with an earbud winding up from his shirt collar in typical government-agent fashion.

"Small change in plans," he said, ushering them toward the back and helping with their suitcases. "We're going out through the service doors."

Good thing I had him call the CIA guy, Nicole thought as they were whisked through narrow halls toward the rear entrance of the building. *Otherwise I'd be scared as hell right now.*

"Why are we going out through the back?"

"Those are my orders, ma'am. We need to hurry."

We need to hurry? What the hell's going on? Now she *was* getting scared.

A dark sedan with heavily tinted windows was idling by the trash dumpsters. As they sped away, the agent said, "Mr. Sadler and Miss Farber, tonight we'll be requiring your cooperation in the interest of national security. I apologize for the inconvenience, but I assure you all this is essential. You may use your cellphones until we reach Love Field. At that point I'll collect them and you'll get them back at a later time. If you have a laptop or a tablet – anything with GPS – we'll disable the location services features so that you may use them on the plane."

He handed them heavily tinted sunglasses like the ones people wear when they have their eyes dilated. "In a few minutes we'll ask you to put these on."

Suddenly Nicole had had enough. She lost her temper. "I'm getting a little tired of this 'in the interest of national security' shit you all throw around so easily! You already said we're going to Love Field. We don't need to hide our eyes. We know where it is."

"I'm sorry. Once we're at the airport, we'll ask you to put the glasses on for a few minutes while we take you onto the airport grounds. There are governmental facilities at Love that the public isn't aware of. For now, please feel free to use your phones."

"Thank you so much," Nicole muttered sarcastically.

Brian called his assistant Cory Spencer in the London gallery, where it was early morning. He brought him up to speed on a couple of urgent projects and said he was off for a couple of weeks on a secret mission he'd explain later. Cory wasn't surprised – he knew his boss would travel anywhere, anytime to see something exciting or unique. This wasn't the first time Brian had taken a sudden under-the-radar trip.

Nicole left a voicemail for her paralegal, telling her she and Brian had decided to take a last-minute fling outside the country. It sounded hokey and nothing like her, but it would have to do. A couple of court dates might have to be changed, but she had a lawyer buddy who'd make an appearance on her behalf if necessary. The other things she was working on were on the laptop with her.

As best they could in the limited time left, they firmed up things for two weeks away from the office.

They were on Lemmon Avenue now, heading along the east side of Love Field, where dozens of private aircraft were hangared. Several flight operations firms were also located on this side of the airport.

"Please put on the glasses and let me have your phones," the driver instructed.

With the dark shades on, they couldn't see a thing. They felt the car stop for a moment – probably at a security gate – then continue. When the car stopped again, nothing happened for a minute or so; then he said, "You may remove them now."

They were parked inside a private aircraft hangar and its giant door was closing behind them. A sleek Lear 70 business jet was the only plane in the cavernous building. The men ushered them on board, passed over their carry-ons and stowed their suitcases in a compartment at the back. All the window shades were lowered; when Brian reached to open the one next to him, the agent sitting opposite said, "Sorry, sir. The shades have to remain down for the entire flight."

They're going to extraordinary measures to keep us from even knowing what direction we're headed.

Within minutes the plane began moving, then made a U-turn and stopped as two pilots in the cockpit went through their final preflight checks. The plane's engines powered up, and seconds later the jet soared into the moonlit sky. Brian checked his watch; it was 2:28 a.m.

"How long will the flight take?"

"Around four and a half hours."

Long flight. Brian wondered how fast a Lear flew. Maybe five hundred miles an hour? He wasn't sure, but if that was in the ballpark, their destination was over two thousand miles from Dallas. He made a mental calculation – they could fly to Venezuela or Nova Scotia or Vancouver, British Columbia. He had no idea what to expect; he'd never experienced anything remotely similar to this clandestine operation. Not only didn't he know where they were going, he didn't even know why it was happening.

Nicole asked, "Is it okay to use my laptop and iPad?"

"Certainly. May I please see them for a moment? Yours too, Mr. Sadler." He checked for GPS, made some adjustments and returned them.

"I apologize again for the inconvenience. I've been told you will understand the reason for the secrecy once we reach our destination. I assure you this is a matter of national security."

Nicole was getting irritated. "Can you please just knock it off? I'm getting a little tired of national security."

Half an hour into the flight one of the agents went to a tiny galley area at the back of the plane. Soon they smelled the aroma of coffee brewing, and they both ordered a cup. He also offered sodas, wine, beer and water, and said he'd mix up a Bloody Mary if they liked.

Three hours after departure they had breakfast – a box containing an apple, a hard-boiled egg and a ham sandwich. As unappetizing as it seemed at first, they were hungry and devoured everything along with more coffee.

Four hours and twenty minutes after they left Dallas, Brian's ears began popping as the plane began a steady descent. The shades were still closed, so they felt rather than saw the plane's tires touch down.

"Are we doing the dark glasses again?"

"No, sir. You're free to open the window shades now. I can't tell you anything – that'll be up to the people we hand you over to – but we appreciate your cooperation during the flight."

They looked out the windows as the plane's engines powered down. They were on a paved runway next to a sandy beach that ran down to clear blue water stretching endlessly away. The sun was just peeping up over the horizon. There was no other land in sight.

The agent opened the door and lowered the stairway, and a man in shorts and a T-shirt came onboard and stuck out his hand. There was a pistol in a holster on his waist; it looked out of place with his beach attire.

"Good morning, folks! I'm Special Agent Jackson Pope, CIA. I'll be taking over from here. Thanks, guys," he said to the two agents on the plane. "Have a safe flight home."

They looked around – there was lush vegetation everywhere but no buildings. Their clothes that had been comfortable in the middle of the night in Dallas were hot and sticky now. Nicole rolled up her sleeves and Brian took off his sweater.

As soon as the bags were offloaded, the door was pulled shut and the plane taxied to the end of the runway, then turned. Its engines whined louder and louder; then the pilot released the brakes and the jet screamed down the runway. They'd have to refuel somewhere along the way back, Brian thought idly as he watched the Lear heading away through wispy clouds.

They walked to an open-top Jeep Wrangler with no doors. As they drove away, they saw tall mountains covered in dense vegetation not far away.

"Where are we?"

"Only a little while longer," the CIA agent said with a smile. "I'm not authorized to speak with you about the mission. You won't be in the dark much longer now."

The mission?

The agent drove for several miles down a narrow dirt road that wound through lush tropical vegetation.

"We were told to pack for warm weather," Brian remarked. "Glad we took the advice. It's hot as hell here."

"It's apparently always like this. Great weather if you're from the northeast like I am!"

They drove up and up into the mountains until they reached a massive fence with black iron gates held open by two armed men who waved their vehicle through. Brian noticed security cameras at the gates and there were more along the lane they were on. Suddenly the jungle ended at a broad expanse of lush green grass and an attractive ranch-style house, a rambling white one-story nestled into the side of a hill. There were broad patios with umbrellas and pool furniture that overlooked the ocean far below.

Nicole commented dryly, "Maybe I should have packed a swimsuit."

"No problem. I think you'll find everything you'll need is here."

Everything I'll need? For what? We're actually going swimming? I'm damn sure not doing it! This is no vacation. We're virtual prisoners, after all, "in the interest of national security."

The Jeep pulled up in front of the house. Another armed man in shorts came through the front door. Pope said, "I'll handle your bags. This is Agent Moore. He'll take you from here and I'll see you inside."

They could feel a warm sea breeze and smell the salty tang of the ocean. The place was gorgeous, with

163

flowers and palm trees everywhere. If this was a private residence, Nicole thought for a second, then it belonged to someone with very deep pockets.

The agent offered a handshake and said, "Wesley Moore, United States Secret Service. Good afternoon and welcome. I hope your flight went well. Come in, please."

Brian glanced at Nicole, a question on his face. *Secret service? Here? Why?*

He led them through the front entrance of the massive house. In the sudden transition from glaring sunlight to dark shadows, their eyes had to adjust for a moment. Someone was walking down a long hallway toward them, but Brian couldn't make out who it was.

Then he heard a familiar voice. "Welcome, you two. Thanks for coming."

What? How could this be? What the hell is he doing here? What's going on?

Former senator Henry Harrison walked up and hugged Nicole. Then he took Brian's hands in his own and squeezed them tightly. "Thanks for your friendship, Brian. I'm glad you're here, both of you. We're *all* glad. I apologize in advance for everything, but now it'll all make perfect sense."

Brian was totally confused. "Senator? But you're supposed to be . . . are we in the Mediterranean?"

He laughed. "No. That was a fast jet you were on, but it wasn't *that* fast! Come on in and let's explain things."

The former President's father led them down the hallway. A pleasant breeze wafted through huge double doors at the far end. Past them was what appeared to be an expansive, screened-in veranda. They could see the ocean out in the distance as they walked through the wide-open doors.

Out on the porch there were smiles, laughter, squeals of youthful delight and warm, sincere greetings from a small group of people who had been anticipating their arrival.

Nicole broke into a wide grin, but Brian looked around in disbelief.

What's happening? This can't be true!

He felt himself teetering unsteadily, and suddenly he collapsed to the floor in a dead faint.

BILL THOMPSON

CHAPTER THIRTY-NINE

Brian woke to a hodgepodge of concerned faces – familiar faces – gathered around him as he lay on the tile floor. Nicole was kneeling beside him. She saw his eyelids flutter open and said, "He's awake!"

There was another voice. "Brian! Are you okay?"

He recognized it immediately. But how could it be?

"Harry? Where am I? You're . . . you're dead, aren't you?"

There was laughter.

"Not quite yet," the First Lady quipped. "Come on, Nicole, help me get him up off the floor. We should have expected the surprise would give you guys a shock. I just didn't think someone would hit the deck!"

He and Nicole sat on a long couch on the veranda, and a man dressed in shorts and a T-shirt served them tea. Suddenly the President's girls Lizzie and Kate rushed over and plopped themselves between Nicole and Brian, snuggling up to them.

Kate kissed him on the cheek and said, "Hi, Brian! They didn't tell us you and Nicole were coming! I hope you guys will swim with us! We have a great big pool. We're having a secret adventure, and now you're part of it too!"

Brian looked at Harry. "I'd say adventure is an understatement. Boy, I have a lot to figure out here. I don't think I've ever been so happy to see people before. Especially since Nicole and I were in Oklahoma City for your . . ." He paused. Maybe the kids didn't know people had attended their funerals.

"Yeah, that's the part I regret most," Harry admitted. "Especially having to put Mom and Dad through that part." He glanced at his mother, who shook her finger at him disapprovingly. "Once we explain everything, you'll see why all this had to happen."

So even Harry's parents didn't know. What the hell was this all about?

He looked around the room. He was surprised to see the Vice President and Secretary of State. He'd never met either but here they were, which meant that the 747 hadn't crashed either.

Nicole saw a dozen people indoors having lunch at a long table. She asked Jennifer who they were.

"That's both crews and our Secret Service agents. There are twenty-five of us, plus Special Agent Pope, who was here when we arrived. I'm sure you heard that number a thousand times on the news. Twenty-five Americans were killed in the two crashes."

"So there weren't crashes at all? What happened to the planes?"

Harry replied, "I want your questions answered as much as you do, but it's better to start from the beginning. I'll let my Chief of Staff give you the details this afternoon, and you can ask me anything you want afterwards. First, how about lunch? We have sandwiches and all the trimmings."

They walked inside and Harry introduced their new guests to the others. "This is my best friend," he said with a tear in his eye as he put his arm around Brian's shoulders. "Just like all the people back home who love you guys, both of these people thought we were dead. I'm so sorry it has to be this way for all of you. What we're doing is for the good of our country. You all know that already."

Brian and Nicole could see everyone was on board with whatever was going on here. They laughed among themselves and appeared very comfortable with each other and their surroundings. Brian, Nicole, Harry and Jennifer filled their plates from a sideboard loaded with food, picked up beers and went outside to eat. They caught up during lunch; then Harry turned them over to Bob Parker.

They signed the same confidentiality document every person here had executed, the one with federal prison as its penalty for violation. The lawyer in Nicole wanted to read it, but she knew it was wasted energy. There was no negotiating anything at this point.

Parker started by saying that all of this, from the disappearance of the planes to the secret location here, was part of a mission called Operation Condor. As they listened to how things had unfolded, Brian was astounded at the boldness of the terrorists. Nothing even approaching this had ever been carried out before. By all appearances two planes were down, the top two leaders plus a cabinet secretary were dead, and the United States was in fear once again.

As remarkable as the jihadist operation had been, as earth shattering as the disappearance of Air Force One and Two, the other side of the coin was far more incredible and audacious. The countermeasures dreamed up by a small secret cadre of United States government officials were brilliant. Bob Parker said Operation Condor would someday be called one of history's most daring missions.

He explained that they were on a private island a few hundred miles from the US Virgin Islands. Its owner, a billionaire from England, had rented it lock, stock and barrel to a CIA shell entity a year ago. The island had a paved airstrip, the main house, a dozen outbuildings, and everything they needed to be self-sufficient for months.

"But Vice President Taylor and the Secretary of State are here too. Is the 747 here somewhere?"

"No. Some things just wouldn't work. Right now the 747's on an uninhabited four-square-mile island in the Pacific called Palmyra Atoll, thousands of miles from anywhere. It's sitting inside a rusty hangar from the Second World War. That's where it landed after the terrorists thought they detonated the bomb. Everyone from that plane came here on a private jet the CIA sent. They'll deal with getting the 747 back when this is all over."

He said that the Gulfstream – Air Force One – was still parked at the end of the runway where they had landed earlier today.

Nicole was surprised. "I never saw it."

"Good. That means the guys have done their jobs well. It's covered with mesh netting and jungle camouflage, and it blends in perfectly with the vegetation. You'd never see it from the air. Don – the CIA director – sent a couple of recon planes over the island, and everything looks perfectly normal. We look like guests on a private island enjoying a vacation."

"How long do you think you all can stay hidden here before someone finds out?"

"Probably not that long. Word's bound to leak with an operation this complex. Every one of us had to endure the pain of putting friends through funerals that weren't real and suffering grief and mourning for people who weren't actually dead, including the President of the United States and his entire family. Until President Harrison brought his father and mother here, even they didn't know. It was killing them, he knew, so it was killing him too. He made that decision and Director Case agreed. But with that said, the more people who are here, the more chance there is of someone figuring things out. If a sailboat or a large yacht happened to stop here, they'd run into armed men patrolling the shores and they'd be told to leave. I'm sure guards and privacy are common occurrences with very wealthy individuals, but we're trying to be careful not to create a situation that could bring attention to us."

"What about the Internet?"

"The house has Internet and satellite TV. The television helps pass the time, but connectivity doesn't matter. We have no one to contact because we're all dead. None of us has a device that can send messages anyway. We turned in our cellphones when we got here, and they're locked up so no one accidentally makes a mistake. All of us have modified Kindles. People can read anything they downloaded before they came, but they can't connect to Wi-Fi. We have every comfort here except the comforts of home. The crew and security people were selected for the mission specifically because they have no immediate family to grieve for them. But we all have close friends. That's the hardest part, but it'll be worth it once the CIA figures this out."

Brian asked why the two of them were suddenly being brought in on the secret.

"That happened because some events are unfolding that involve you. Both of you. President Harrison issued the order to bring you here for your safety."

That alarmed Nicole. "What events are unfolding? What are you talking about?"

"That's something for you to discuss with the President. For now, let me continue the story. In addition to the twenty-five of us who were on the planes, there are only three other people who knew what was going to happen. Three people in DC know we're alive now, hiding somewhere in an undisclosed location. Those people are CIA Director Don Case, the chief justice of the Supreme Court, and Michelle Isham, the Majority Leader of the Senate. That's important for you to know. Our entire mission, including all of us sitting here today on a private island, happened so the CIA could find out who wanted to kill the President and the Vice President, and why."

"But now everyone knows, correct? The Falcons of Islam took credit. Are you saying it wasn't them?"

"It was the Falcons, but that's not the information President Harrison and the CIA are looking for. They want to know who within the United States government is involved."

"There are traitors within *our* government? Is that what you're saying?"

"I'm not authorized to discuss that aspect, but you may certainly ask President Harrison. He can explain more, I'm sure."

Months before, intelligence services had picked up chatter from Syria that indicated a secret initiative had begun. Although there were snippets here and there about operatives inside the Great Satan, there was nothing concrete or specific. The information was cataloged and crosschecked against new intelligence as it came in.

Since the reopening of a suburban DC mosque after 9/11, a worker there had provided the CIA with solid information on terrorist activities in the United States. Two of the mosque's members, who used the names Ali and Mo, had spoken once about recruiting an American citizen. Ali and Mo were affiliated with the jihadist group known as the Nusra Front or al-Qaeda in Syria, one of the world's deadliest terrorist organizations.

The CIA mole didn't know the American's name or much about him. As far as he knew, the man had never been to the mosque. The operative recently heard that Mohammed al-Joulani, leader of the Nusra Front, had contacted Ali and Mo. He didn't know the reason.

A few days later a portion of a phone call from Syria to the mosque was recorded and sent for analysis. It was a short clip in Arabic; the caller advised that a man had the package. The CIA had no idea what it meant, but it could involve the two terrorists.

Joulani and the American Muslims had been extraordinarily cautious, but the mole in the mosque kept his eyes and ears open. He heard about a meeting that would be in a park in suburban Baltimore. Ali and Mo would be there.

The CIA rushed into action, positioning men and women, young and old, joggers and bench-sitters, all over the park. A couple of days later the meeting took place. Spotters hidden in dense foliage snapped photos of three Arab men sitting on a secluded park bench and talking in whispers for twenty minutes. They knew the Syrians Ali and Mo, but the third man was their target today. They wanted to know who he was.

They followed as the man drove to a salvage yard. An hour later operatives at Langley were analyzing everything they could find about Yusuf "Joe" Kaya, a first-generation American who owned a chain of junkyards. They briefed the director, who was keeping a close eye on this critical breakthrough.

Parker explained Joe Kaya's background; then he paused and asked if they wanted a cup of coffee and a restroom break.

Ten minutes later the briefing resumed. Within hours the CIA had copies of Kaya's personal and business tax returns. They knew everything about his education and service at the embassy in Baghdad, and they knew he was a convert to Catholicism who never missed Mass on Sunday.

Joe Kaya seemed to be an ordinary American. But, as these agents knew well, that could be the most dangerous kind of all. If he was a sleeper terrorist embedded in American society, a man born and raised in the USA, he could be the perfect agent for jihad.

Director Case communicated with President Harrison daily, Parker said. When Harrison was told about Kaya, he brought in the Vice President and Secretary Clancy. Everyone – the CIA in Washington and the supposedly dead leaders here – had the same questions. Who was he? Why was he meeting with known supporters of terrorism? The Syrian caller had said there was a man who had a package. Was that Kaya, and what was the package?

They couldn't move in yet. For now, agents would keep the three individuals under constant surveillance.

It took the CIA very little time to link Kaya with two high-ranking noncommissioned officers in the United States Air Force. More importantly, these weren't just any career military men – each held a sensitive position requiring a top-secret security clearance.

One was Command Chief Master Sergeant James Perkins, the highest-ranking NCO at Andrews Field, from which most of the flights carrying the nation's leaders departed. Perkins ran the show at Andrews and was considered a highly capable individual. He was a decorated twenty-year veteran and his service record was without a blemish.

The other was forty-one-year-old Master Sergeant Jeremy Lail. Also a twenty-year veteran, he was the senior line operator at Andrews and reported directly to Perkins. Part of his job was to inspect the planes just before takeoff and put his signature on the final checklist. Without Lail's sign-off, a plane wouldn't depart, period. Like his boss, Jeremy's service record showed no issues.

Brian interrupted to ask about the timeframe. They knew who Jeremy Lail was, of course. His name was as familiar to Americans as that of another traitor – Oklahoma City bomber Timothy McVeigh. The story Parker was telling them today was a prelude to events that had already reached a partial conclusion. Master Sergeant Lail had fled the USA after the planes disappeared, and Syrian terrorists filmed his beheading.

Correct, Parker confirmed. The CIA was quietly gathering information without raising suspicion. Agents talked to friends of friends and found out that Kaya, Perkins and Lail played cards at Jeremy's house every other Saturday night. To the uninformed, it was as American as tailgating. Seven people, at least three of whom were bachelors, got together for some beer, some lighthearted conversation and a friendly game of poker. One night Ali from the mosque had come along too.

People in law enforcement couldn't afford to jump to conclusions. When dealing with terrorism in the United States, the CIA considered every possibility, no matter how much it might stretch the imagination. Finally they started connecting the dots.

Names of the players were displayed on a whiteboard in a conference room at Langley. At the top was Mohammad al-Joulani, a known terrorist and leader of the dangerous al-Nusra Front in Syria. He had contacted two men nicknamed Ali and Mo, who attended a mosque outside Washington.

Joe Kaya, an American salvage yard owner who was the son of Iraqi immigrants, had met with Ali and Mo – not at a Starbucks or a bar, but on a bench in a quiet park in Baltimore. Were they simply nature lovers? Did they enjoy the outdoors? Or were they ensuring no one saw them get together?

The story got more interesting with the addition of Joe's poker buddies Jim Perkins and Jeremy Lail. By now the CIA was certain one or both of them was a traitor. Director Case ordered extensive background checks and learned that Lail considered Kaya his best friend and mentor. Kaya was giving the senior line operator at Andrews lots of advice and counsel.

Jim Perkins checked out with no red flags; the agency would keep his name on their list for now, but they were beginning to home in on the other NCO at the base. The FBI and CIA put new checks in place that Lail didn't know about. While the sergeant was diverted to other duties, dogs and men with sophisticated equipment swept every inch of every plane that the sergeant had signed off on. They got nowhere for a few weeks, but they kept the checks going.

During those few weeks, a plan came together to nab the perpetrators, whoever they were and wherever this plot led. It was code-named Operation Condor and it came straight from the President himself.

The three of them had been talking for two hours. After a short break Bob said, "This next part was told to me verbatim by Don Case. I'm going to repeat it to you the best I can. I have to admit it gave me cold chills."

Not long ago, Case had been in a meeting at the Oval Office. President Harrison had brought several of his key advisors together to help finalize his game plan for the upcoming Barbados meeting of the Organization of Central American and Caribbean States, or OCACS.

As others were talking, the CIA chief stared at the briefing sheet that had been handed out. He looked at the dates of President Harrison's trip to Barbados. Something caught his attention, something he couldn't put his finger on. Then it came to him.

He shouted, "Mr. President!"

The deputy chief of the Drug Enforcement Administration was answering a question from President Harrison and he stopped abruptly, miffed at the interruption.

Harrison glanced over, surprised at the normally reserved CIA director's outburst. "Don? Do you have something to add?"

"Sorry, sir. I was just looking at the dates of your trip. Aren't the Vice President and Secretary Clancy away at the same time?"

"Yes. They're going to Hong Kong to meet the President of the PRC. What's your point?"

Case's heart was beating wildly now. "Which plane are they taking?"

Unsure what was happening, Harry Harrison replied, "Where are you going with this? What does it have to do with this meeting?"

"Stay with me a moment on this, Mr. President. Are they taking the 747?"

"That's my understanding, yes. It makes sense because it's long range –"

Case interrupted again. "And which plane are you taking? Which plane will be Air Force One for that trip?"

Harrison was known for his friendly, outgoing demeanor, but this had gone about far enough. He was beginning to get a little irritated. "I don't know. One of the smaller jets, I guess. Don, are you feeling okay?"

All of a sudden Donovan Case knew exactly what was going to happen.

This meeting wasn't the place to discuss it. He and Harrison were the only two in the room who knew about Operation Condor.

"Sorry, sir. I've got something to go over with you when we break up."

Case told Bob that the next thirty minutes were the longest in his life. He had squirmed and fidgeted in his seat until he and the President were alone at last.

Once everyone else had left, Harrison said, "Let's hear it. What was so important you had to interrupt the meeting? This had better be good."

"It's about Condor, sir. I think they're going to bomb both planes. I think they're going to surpass everything they did on 9/11 by killing the President and the Vice President at the same time!"

Harrison sat in silence for what seemed to Don like an eternity.

"It would be a brilliant plan, wouldn't it? But how could they possibly accomplish it? The planes are at

Andrews Field, where the security is tighter than anywhere else in the country. Is this guy Kaya involved?"

"That's what we have to find out. I've got to get started now, sir. It's only a week until the Vice President leaves. I'll keep you advised."

Parker paused. "Quite a story, don't you think?"

Brian took a deep breath. He was captivated – this was like something out of a novel, but it was real. Nicole was sitting with arms folded, shaking her head. How could a plot of this magnitude be pulled off? She couldn't wait for the ending to this crazy saga.

Just then there was a rap on the door and Harry came in.

"Are you guys about to wrap it up? You've been in here holed up for hours, and if I know my friend Brian Sadler, it's cocktail time!"

Parker said, "Yes, sir. Folks, I'm happy to resume tomorrow morning."

Brian glanced at his watch. It was, in fact, cocktail hour, and he wanted only one thing more than a drink with the Harrisons. He wanted the rest of the story. He turned to Nicole.

She said, "We can't stop now! That's like walking out of a movie before the ending!"

Everyone laughed. Bob said, "Twenty minutes, Mr. President. I'll have them out then for sure!"

Harrison nodded with a smile and closed the door.

"As you've undoubtedly surmised, Director Case was right. I won't go into details of all the surveillance that was used to watch the people involved, but the CIA learned within days that Kaya facilitated a man who'd worked at Andrews for two years. Joe gave Jeremy the fanciful bucket-list selfie-photo story, and Jeremy made it happen, not once but twice. That night when agents took the bomb dogs aboard Air Force Two, they found a sophisticated device the size of a paperback book attached with Velcro under the flight engineer's seat. It had a timer that could be started remotely using the plane's Wi-Fi. I don't know what was inside. They removed it and took it to be detonated.

When the bomb went off, it blew a hole in the ground five feet deep."

Parker explained that the entire scenario was repeated two days later when the Gulfstream, now Air Force One, was outfitted with an identical device. This one was in a closet just outside the cockpit. It exploded with the same force as the first one. The planes would have been decimated.

"What happened to the man who planted them?"

"He resigned his job the morning after he planted the second bomb. He's on everybody's watch list, but he's gone. The CIA thinks he either left the country, maybe by car to Canada, or he was killed by the people he worked for."

Nicole wondered how the CIA knew exactly when to implement Operation Condor. "The terrorists, presuming that's who they were, started the timers remotely. How did the CIA know when that would happen? How could they know exactly when to make the planes disappear? It could have happened anytime after the planes took off, correct?"

"Yes, and they were ready for anything. However, given where they were both going, the CIA believed the most likely scenario would be to detonate the bombs over water. Air Force Two would be taken down on its outbound flight, they thought, and Air Force One the same day on its return flight from Barbados. There were a dozen contingency plans, and the avionics on both planes had been modified so the pilots could disable everything that allowed tracking, even the black boxes. As long as they flew very, very low, they wouldn't be detected by radar. There were thoughts about having the planes land at abandoned airfields inside the US or somewhere else along their routes. Palmyra Atoll and this island were the ideal spots, and it worked perfectly.

"Agents had the timers from both bombs. They watched them constantly. Once they started, they would count down for two hours, then the bombs were supposed to explode. The timer for Air Force Two started shortly before the refueling stop in Hawaii. Director Case immediately notified President Harrison and the pilot, and the first phase of Operation Condor started.

"As the timer ticked down to zero, the copilot on Air Force Two shut off all the instruments and the pilot took the plane down until they were a few hundred feet above the waves. They landed at Palmyra Atoll half an hour later. Two CIA agents with supplies for a month's stay had gone in a week before. The place was perfect; it had an adequate runway built in 1941 – that place had been a Naval Air Station until the end of the war. B-17 Flying Fortress bombers were stationed there for possible use against the Japanese, and there were a couple of hangars, one fortunately large enough to accommodate the 747.

"Once everyone had gone through the drill and Air Force Two had disappeared, they knew exactly what to expect. In fact, it had been much easier with the small Gulfstream. The CIA had leased the tycoon's private island months before and they'd used it for several secret meetings with Cuban officials over the normalization of relations. No one was there now, so it was perfect. They decided that the Gulfstream would appear to crash into the Caribbean while actually flying here. A day later they took a seat from the plane and dumped it in the water. The CIA was directing the search for wreckage and, conveniently, there it was. A seat with the Presidential logo. Confirmation that Air Force One was gone."

The Chief of Staff stopped. "I promised to have you out in twenty minutes and I'm already late. You know the story up to today. We're waiting to see what happens next. Agents are tracking money movements and intel worldwide, and the Falcons of Islam have claimed responsibility. Jeremy Lail's dead, which is actually too bad. It would have been helpful if the CIA could have interviewed him to see if he and the man who planted the bombs were working together, or if Lail simply thought the guy just wanted to see the cockpits. That's a little far-fetched for me, but it could have happened. Regardless, Lail knew someone had been on the planes and he signed off anyway. He was unquestionably involved."

They thanked Bob for the briefing and commented on how brilliant Operation Condor really was. It was perhaps the boldest covert act in history, and so far no one suspected anything.

"One more question," Brian said as they walked onto the porch to join the others. "I know President Parkes can be . . . well, difficult. Plus he's a Democrat and no friend of Harry's and Vice President Taylor's. Was it hard to get him to sign off on the mission?"

"That's not something I'm authorized to discuss," Parker replied affably. "You'll have to ask your friend the President that question."

Brian made a mental note. Right now the things he wanted most were close at hand. He and Nicole pulled up chairs, joined their friends and ordered drinks. Nicole opted for white wine.

"This may be too much to ask, but can you do an extra-dry XO Vodka martini?" Brian asked the steward.

Harry shot out a reply. "Are you asking if we knew you were coming? Of course we did! So of course we can arrange an XO Vodka martini! Kelly, fix my friend here his favorite drink!"

CHAPTER FORTY

The sun became a giant orange ball as it slowly slipped into the ocean. When it was gone, the darkness was immediate and intense.

Brian and Nicole joined in a game of Monopoly with the children, something Harry said had become a routine every evening since they arrived. When it was over, Harry's dad said, "We're on babysitting duty tonight. There's nothing better than grandchildren. You two had better get started or you may never know what I'm talking about!"

"Henry!" his wife said in mock disgust. "Now you leave Brian and Nicole alone!"

Their grandparents accompanied the girls to their bedroom as Henry, Jennifer, Brian and Nicole walked outside to a candlelit table on the veranda. Everyone else stayed indoors to allow the old friends time to reconnect.

"Thank God this place has a state-of-the-art exercise room, because we eat well here," Harry said as they were served a beautifully prepared grilled fish filet, rice with beans, and a medley of fruit. "Air Force One's chef is a master – thank goodness he's here. Everything on your plate is from this island or the sea around it.

"Somebody ends up going fishing every day or so. There's a boathouse down at the shore with a couple of nice boats, and the guys and gals usually catch enough for everyone. Jen and I aren't allowed to go, of course. We're a long way from civilization, but it might cause a stir if someone saw the dead President out on a fishing trip!"

On that note, Jennifer apologized again for putting them through the agony of funerals. "I can only imagine what I'd have felt had it been yours," she said, tears welling up in her eyes. "Hopefully everything Bob told you explains why we're doing this. This is so bizarre, but we believe it has to be done for the sake of our country."

"It's an amazing story," Nicole agreed, "and Bob gave us a lot of information. But he said only Harry could answer some of our questions."

"Now's your chance," the former President said. "Ask away!"

"If there's something you can't answer, we'll understand. I was sick of the words *national security* when they were bringing us down here against our will, but now that I'm here, I understand that national security's what this is all about. So here goes. Harry, you were willing to allow this to happen – to lose the presidency – for the good of the country. But how can it be good for the country to let a buffoon like Parkes get into office?"

"Good question, and trust me, Parkes is far worse than a buffoon. Here's the logic. He's already running for President. The Democratic convention's in less than four months and the election is three months after that. He's probably going to get the nomination since his only remaining opponent is a political lightweight. The nominal danger the country might be in as a result of his being President these few months is offset by the chance to watch and see what he's up to. The CIA wants to know what Cham Parkes is all about. In my opinion, the people have to know that too. I think it would blow people's minds if they knew what his agenda really was. I don't often speak badly of other people, but this is a fact. Parkes is a liar and a criminal. Hopefully all we're going through will help us catch him red-handed."

In all the years he'd known Harry, Brian had never heard his friend speak badly about another person. He was passionate about this, no doubt.

Brian said, "When I asked how hard it was to get President Parkes to sign off on this mission, Bob said to ask you. From what you just said, I'm beginning to think Parkes doesn't know about Operation Condor, but how is that possible? Bob told us only three people in DC know you're alive. He didn't name Parkes, but he has to know, right? He's the President."

"Only those three know. Don Case is the most important one. He keeps me informed on everything Parkes is doing, in particular how the President's addressing – or to be more accurate, *ignoring* – the threats made by the Falcons of Islam. I'm worried that the President's going to fire Don as CIA director. If he does, we lose our eyes and ears behind closed doors. I just hope all this will be over before it comes to that."

Brian couldn't make sense of it. "So the sitting President of the United States doesn't know . . ."

Harry paused to gather his thoughts. "According to the officers who were with him, Cham said some very odd things as Operation Condor was unfolding. When they ran into his office to secure him, he was very calm and said something like, 'It's been a long time coming.' As crazy as this was – he was being taken out under a Code Red, the highest alarm we have – but he was peaceful, like he knew what was going on."

Harry paused a moment and then spoke more quietly. "Cham Parkes doesn't know about this because Don and I think he's involved in the plot to kill the Vice President and me. He may be the major player. We also think that's why he's ignoring the Falcons of Islam and their threats."

"Holy shit! A sitting American President may be involved with terrorists? I can't believe it!"

"It's so unthinkable it makes all the deceit, all the grieving mourners and all the plotting totally worth it. We have to learn what's going on and we have to stop it."

They ate in silence for a few minutes, and then Nicole smiled. "When the world learns that all of you are actually alive – especially when Cham Parkes and his buddies find out – there's going to be a massive, collective *uh-oh* from a lot of people."

"You're being too polite," Harry responded with a laugh. "I was thinking more of an *oh, shit!*"

The steward removed their plates and they ordered coffees all around. "We also have some excellent brandy, courtesy of our host," Harry advised. "Will you join me?"

Since the wreck Nicole had been careful around alcohol, given her regimen of medications. She and Jennifer passed, but Brian opted in.

"Okay, Harry, here's my question. Were you all just missing us a lot? Is that why you had the spooks whisk us away in the middle of the night off to this desert island? Or was it the 'events that were unfolding' that Bob said to ask you about?"

"I figured you'd get around to this eventually," he replied, raising his brandy glass for a clink with Brian's. "You mean you weren't ready for a little vacation?"

"The part about bringing clothes for warm weather pissed Nicole off a little," Brian admitted. "She wasn't too excited about a vacation with the CIA."

Nicole shrugged as Harry and Jennifer laughed.

"Okay, here's the part you don't know. You know that little task you did for the Agency? Unfortunately that appears to have created a problem."

Nicole jumped in. "What task did you do?"

"She doesn't know?"

"Your father and Don Case both told me not to tell her."

Nicole's voice quivered, betraying the anger she felt. "Harry, I love you guys, but I'm getting tired – and frankly a little scared – of what you all got Brian involved in. So let's hear it. What have you and Brian done that makes us part of all this Condor thing?"

"Let me try to explain. First, for the record, I have to remind you about the confidentiality agreement. This is ultra-top-secret information. Only a few people know what I'm about to tell you."

Even Brian hadn't known the reason why he'd been recruited to put listening devices in Amina Hassan's office, so this was news to him. Harry said that Amina's billionaire father wasn't only involved in the things you read about in *Forbes* magazine. The CIA had kept an eye on the Hassan Group for years because of its suspected involvement in the funding of Middle Eastern terror groups, including the Falcons of Islam.

It had been Don's idea to bug Hassan's London office. The company's Dubai headquarters would have been best, but there was no way to make it happen. A general wariness in Dubai concerning Americans, the airtight security in Hassan's building, and a company policy that no outsiders were ever allowed to venture above the first-floor conference rooms – all these things made it impossible to penetrate Hassan Group there.

Compared to Dubai, London would be a cakewalk, Case thought. Hassan's daughter was a socialite who entertained friends and business associates of her father's in the office almost every day. Although the four-story building in Belgrave Square was under the watchful eye of Hassan's enforcer Zarif Safwan, it was also much more accessible by the public. Unlike Dubai, Amina entertained visitors often in her fourth-floor office.

Harry continued. "The fact that you and I were friends had nothing to do with the decision to recruit you. It was Amina's collection of antiquities coupled with your international prominence in the field of rarities that made it all work. It seemed simple at the time. I was already here, consumed with Operation Condor. I know you can't understand this, but when I was in the White House and had a hundred advisors at my beck and call, decisions were a lot easier to make than they are now. Now I have a handful of people I can bounce ideas off – all good, don't get me wrong – but it's just Don, Marty, Aaron, Bob and me. CIA, the VP, the Secretary of State and my Chief of Staff. Granted, the decisions I have to make now are one percent of what they used to be, but the ones now are more important than any I ever made back at home.

"So yes, I gave Don permission to discuss the plan with you – to recruit you, if I'm being honest. Yes, I asked my dad to call you, to convince you to cooperate. But I promise you, Brian – and you too, Nicole – if I'd realized where we would be right now, I wouldn't have done it."

Nicole yawned and glanced at her watch. It had been a long, long day and she was sinking fast. But this night couldn't end without the answers.

"So where exactly *are* we right now, Harry?"

"You two and Amina Hassan have developed a personal relationship, which I have no fault with. Brian, we used you in the beginning to get into her office. You played the part perfectly, but obviously you also were intrigued with her collection. That made things even more realistic."

"No kidding. In fact, she has something priceless –"

"Stop!" Nicole said harshly. "I'm sorry, sweetie, but we have to stay on the subject. I'm about to crash. Keep going, Harry."

"You became friends; she spent time with Nicole when she visited London –"

The CIA watched our every move, Nicole thought bitterly.

"– and now she's planning a trip to Dallas in a few days."

"Damn! I forgot all about that! We didn't cancel that trip, Brian. Harry, I need to call her!"

"Tomorrow. Don will meet with you tomorrow on how to handle that."

In her frazzled state she took Harry's response as flippant. She realized she was losing it, mostly because she was exhausted from lack of sleep and the stress of everything that had happened today.

She stood up and said evenly, "I need to call it a night. I have to hear the rest, but I'm getting angrier by the minute. I need to get some sleep and maybe I'll feel better in the morning. Let me just say this. We can make our own decisions on how to handle our personal lives. We're not spies or government agents. We're just people. I can call Amy and cancel the trip myself. Oh, I forgot. Actually I can't. You guys took away my phone."

Jennifer jumped up and hugged Nicole tightly. Saddened by the halfhearted hug back, she said, "None of us has phones anymore. It's just too dangerous. Except for Harry, that is, and his is an encrypted satellite phone. They'll let you call Amy tomorrow." She glanced at Harry, who merely stared back impassively. "I know you're frustrated, and I'm so, so sorry you're in the middle of this."

Nicole hugged her a little closer. "So am I. You can't imagine. But thank God you're all alive. That's the most important thing of all, and that makes everything else okay." She kissed her good friend on the cheek and said goodnight.

She and Brian walked through the house, waved at a small group who were eating popcorn and watching TV, and went to their bedroom.

BILL THOMPSON

CHAPTER FORTY-ONE

Sleeping naked the way they always did, Nicole snuggled down in the soft duvet next to Brian and listened to the sound of waves crashing against the shore. A light wind stirred the curtains on the French doors that were open all night, and the morning sunlight bathed their private patio in a warm glow.

She felt him stirring and whispered, "Ready to get up and get moving?" She reached out and ran her hand up and down his body. "Uh-oh, Something's already up and moving!"

"Something's been missing you!"

They pushed off the covers and made love slowly, easily and comfortably, enjoying something that made their lives seem normal again. Afterwards they lay in each other's arms for a few minutes and then they dressed and went to the exercise room.

The room was obviously a popular place. There were six people working out when they arrived and others came in later. Nicole recognized two as Secret Service agents and figured the rest were crew members.

Fox News was on a wall-mounted TV so they caught up on things as they worked out. This morning the talk was all about the race for the White House. The President and his opponent had faced off in a debate in Maine two nights ago. The commentator criticized both candidates, dubbing one Mister Meanie and the other Mister Weenie.

On the Republican side, the battle had become more complicated when the incumbent and presumptive nominee Harry Harrison, died on Air Force One. The newscaster pointed out a strange twist of fate in all this. Harrison had been serving the remaining term of his predecessor John Chapman, who himself had disappeared in an ancient tomb in Mexico two years before. With Harrison gone, there were two men and a woman vying for the nomination. A majority of delegates were already committed to Harrison, so no one could win on the first ballot. It looked as though there would be a battle on the convention floor.

Nothing made news people happier than a fight, Brian commented to Nicole as they exercised.

There was more news. At a press conference yesterday, Parkes had announced the replacement of the cabinet secretaries for Interior, Energy and Commerce. Those weren't the positions Brian would have expected him to fill first, but the rest would come soon enough. By the time Parkes started replacing the ones that mattered to Operation Condor – Homeland Security, Defense, Treasury and the attorney general – Brian hoped for Harry's sake this mission would be over.

What about the two Supreme Court vacancies, a reporter had asked the President. *All in good time* had been his response.

Forty-five minutes later Brian and Nicole strolled through the living room, where Fox News was also on. A reporter was asking the President when he would choose a new Secretary of State, since Aaron Clancy had also perished on Air Force Two with the Vice President. *How bizarre is this,* Brian thought as he waved good morning to a dead man. On TV, the new President's response was noncommittal; in his usual curt manner he said he'd make an announcement when he was good and ready. Clancy laughed out loud and said if Parkes would wait a little longer, maybe he'd apply to get his old job back.

They went to a sideboard loaded with breakfast food. Wes Moore, the CIA agent whom they'd met yesterday, told them it was like this every day. "We're all going to be as big as a house if we have to stay here much longer. The chef does a great job on all this food!"

They got coffee and a plate of fruit and went out onto the patio. Jennifer and Harry weren't there, but Marty Taylor, the former Vice President, invited them to join him. The weather was gorgeous; Marty said except for brief showers most afternoons, it had been like this every day.

"Harry's working on a few things in his office this morning, and I haven't seen Jennifer so far. We're all getting a little soft around here," he admitted. "I've never slept until nine in my life, but it's not so bad. I'm not the kind of guy who can read books and watch movies for very long. I never was very good at vacations, and this one's already beginning to take its toll. I'm itching to get back into things."

He and Nicole understood the comments about sleeping late. They were normally early to bed and early to rise, and neither dealt well with downtime. They were overachievers and driven individuals, although Nicole had been forced to learn how to slow down after the wreck.

They wondered how the Vice President expected to get back to work. They didn't know him well enough to inquire, but for him there wasn't any job to go back to. There was a new Vice President now, the churlish Louis Breaux. Maybe Taylor was planning to become a consultant to the government like so many other former politicians did. Or maybe he had something else in mind.

"I can't recall if you have children, Mr. Vice President," Nicole said. "I was wondering how the ones here who have families are dealing with their not knowing."

"Call me Marty, please," he said. "I was married twice and never had kids. The only one of us here besides Harry and Jennifer who has close family is Aaron. He has a daughter who's in her forties, I think, and lives in LA. She's single and has no kids."

"This had to be hard on her."

"I think Aaron's involvement was the hardest decision about this mission, but there wasn't any way around it. The Secretary of State had to go to China. Our trip had been announced for weeks and everything had to appear to be normal – just business as usual. He had to be along. He agreed, and that was that.

"We didn't know until a couple of days before our trip that Operation Condor was going to happen now. The day the guy planted a bomb on our plane was the day Aaron and I learned we would end up here instead of in

Hong Kong. It's strange knowing the day you're going to die," he added wistfully.

Brian was interested to know more about Palmyra Atoll, the World War II airstrip in a remote area of the Pacific where the 747 still sat. Marty said it was surprising how well they'd gotten along for the two days they were there.

"The CIA agent who arrived ahead of us brought rations and bottled water, but we had plenty on the plane. The President's chef kept everybody satisfied until they brought us here."

As they were finishing breakfast, Agent Moore came to the table and asked if they would mind coming with him so Nicole could take a call from Director Case. She and Brian followed him down a long side hallway to a pair of tall double doors. They entered a large, bright room with a pool table in the center and a row of twelve-foot windows along the back. From a desk in front of the windows, Harry waved them over. He was on speakerphone with the CIA director.

"Don, I have Brian and Nicole with me. Guys, I asked Don to chat with you before Nicole speaks with Amina Hassan so we can all be on the same page. I know we're interfering in your private affairs, and I apologize for that, but this mission has to come before everything else. We've invested too much in Condor to be unprepared on any part of it, no matter how insignificant."

Nicole nodded. "I understand, and I apologize for losing my temper last night. I was tired and I'm completely ready to cooperate in any way you tell me."

Case suggested that she feign illness as the reason for canceling Amina's upcoming visit to Dallas this weekend. "You went through a traumatic event that still affects your everyday life," he reasoned, "and anyone should understand that you may suddenly decide you're simply not up to it."

"I couldn't agree more," Nicole replied. "That's exactly what I was going to propose."

They hung up and waited while Case's people created a phone call that appeared to originate from Nicole's cellphone in Dallas, in case Amy Hassan's security men could track it. Obviously Nicole would be calling from home if she were ill.

The phone rang on Harry's desk and he clicked the speaker. Director Case was also on the line from DC. He'd be listening, as would the President and Brian.

"I've preprogrammed Amy's number," Case said. "Are you ready?"

Five minutes later it was done. Nicole had apologized for the late notice, coughed and snorted appropriately, and Amy said she understood completely.

During the call, Amy wondered if she should say anything about what was bothering her, then decided she owed it to her friends.

"Nicole, before you go, I want to tell you something. My father is a very powerful man. He likes to keep an eye on me – I guess he still thinks of me as his little girl. He has a security man who works for him named Zarif Safwan. I saw a picture of Brian in Zarif's office and now Zarif's off on a trip. I don't know where he went, but I want to let you both know. My father may be wondering why Brian was so interested in my collection, but he hasn't asked me that directly. Sometimes he sends Zarif to poke around. It's just a heads-up, really. Nothing to be concerned about, I'm sure." Amy wished she really believed that.

When the call ended, Harry said he was glad Amy had revealed the information about her father. Her actions didn't seem like those of a person who was involved in the plot.

"What she revealed just then is exactly why you and Nicole are here. If you all have time right now, let's continue our discussion from last night. In a few minutes you'll understand what's going on with Zarif Safwan."

Nicole grinned as she sat down. "We have all the time in the world. Since we're your prisoners, we'll do whatever you tell us to do!"

That made Harry laugh out loud.

"I told you about the government's concern over Hassan Group," he began. "We believe Amin Hassan has one primary agenda, and that's to dominate the world market for oil. Brian, I know you read about his attempt to take control of ExxonMobil not long ago. Hassan's largest minority partner is one of the wealthiest men in the United Arab Emirates. As soon as the SEC found out Hassan Group owned nearly fifteen percent of Exxon, the red flags went up. The FTC got involved and so did several members of Congress – all Republicans, I might add. Cham Parkes and his buddies didn't see anything wrong with Hassan's takeover at all.

"I assembled the cabinet Secretaries and we created a strategy that ultimately made Amin back down. Aaron got the State Department to announce that if Hassan Group continued to hold its shares in Exxon, they would launch an investigation. It's always been an incredibly private company and State said it was it in the interest of national security to find out exactly who was trying to take over the world's largest petroleum operation and why."

He stopped for a drink of water. "Well, that worked perfectly. The short-lived takeover attempt came to a screeching halt, and Hassan Group sold its shares for a modest profit. In case you're wondering what really caused the about-face, our ambassador to the UAE learned that Zayed al-Fulan, Hassan's wealthy partner, was livid at Amin's actions. He was making a stock play that would allow the Americans to legally investigate Hassan Group. The partner pulled the plug on Amin's plan.

"All of us are betting Hassan's not done yet. With oil prices so low, Exxon's a bargain now. Something over fifty billion dollars would give him control, and his partner has that much in petty cash. Biggest news? The one major obstacle he faced – *me* – is no longer an issue."

Brian raised his eyebrows in astonishment. "You think he's tied in with Parkes?"

"Personally I'd bet the farm on it. It's going to be much harder to find out things if Don's replaced at the agency, but there are still plenty of people in Washington who'll fight to the end to keep Hassan from getting what he wants. What's interesting is to watch the cabinet appointments Cham's making first. He's not dealing with Defense or Homeland Security. He doesn't have to now. Marty and I are dead. So's the Secretary of State. Look at which ones he started with. Interior, Commerce and Energy. Do you see what he's doing?"

"I do now that I've heard your story. I never thought about it before. Those are the three posts that oversee the oil business, international trade and all of that. Cham Parkes is getting things lined up to approve Amin Hassan's next move. Is that how you see it?"

"Absolutely. One interesting thing is that Parkes has kept his personal cellphone active since he became President. That's not illegal, but I can tell you from experience it's not protocol. I gave mine up because I didn't want even a hint of impropriety. Every call of mine went through the White House switchboard. Cham doesn't know that the CIA began covertly monitoring his phone activity the minute Operation Condor began. Want to hazard a guess who called Cham within minutes after he became President?"

Nicole jumped in. "I guess Amin Hassan!"

"Yep. His was the only call Parkes took that afternoon on his private cellphone, a phone that allows him to talk without going through the White House Communications Center. The call lasted two minutes and the agency couldn't monitor what they said. Was Amin giving congratulations? Was he just saying hello to an old friend? In my personal opinion, if the President of the United States takes one single call minutes after his inauguration, from a man whose burning goal is to take over the world's largest oil company, and this man is suspected of sponsoring terrorist organizations . . . see where I'm going here? Whatever the call was about, it doesn't make old Chambliss T. Parkes look good. Oh, and how about the convenience of two Supreme Court justices dying just after Parkes becomes President. Now he can appoint two justices right up front or just leave the court alone, swaying four-to-three on the liberal side."

"This is getting wilder by the minute," Brian said. "Do you guys really think Parkes was involved in murder?"

"There's nothing about Cham Parkes that's good for America, that's all I know. I hesitate to accuse a man of anything when I'm not sure, but all this is becoming a little too coincidental for the CIA's taste."

"So what does this have to do with me? You said there's a part of this story that involves me and that it has to do with what Amy just told Nicole. Do they know I planted the devices?"

"No one knows that for certain. The bugs are still there and they're still operating, but that room isn't her office. Did you see any other areas while you were there?"

"Only the hallways and that room. I did notice that her desk was bare and the place was set up more like a showroom than a functioning office."

"It's a reception area for guests, we think. Don says they've learned nothing of value from the devices, but what has us worried is Zarif Safwan."

"The guy Amy mentioned to Nicole. Hassan's security chief."

Harry shook his head. "He's far more than that. He's done Amin Hassan's dirty work for years. He's been arrested a dozen times, but he's never been charged. That's Hassan money at work, the CIA thinks. Don thinks he's a key player in Amin's drug and munitions deals and in moving funds to terrorist groups. All three of them – Amin, his daughter and Zarif Safwan – are on the CIA watch list. Zarif hasn't been to the USA in years, but he bought a ticket just hours before I authorized Don to bring you two here."

"I still don't understand . . ."

"Safwan's coming to Dallas, Brian. He arrives there tomorrow. He's not coming to see the Cowboys play football. The CIA believes he's coming for you and Nicole. If that's what's happening, he's operating under orders either from Amina or her father. She pretended not to know where he was going, but the CIA doesn't know who's involved."

"He's coming for us?" Nicole shouted. "What does that mean? Amy wouldn't hurt us!"

Harry answered, looking intently at Brian. "It's more likely her father. Here's my personal take, and Don agrees with me. I think that Safwan found the bugs you planted and Amin left them in place to throw us off. They don't know who sent you or why, but you can bet they've done a lot of background work on you. Hassan Group has unbelievable resources, and Amin usually gets what he wants. The easiest thing for people to find out is the connection you and I have. Amin does a background check on Brian Sadler and finds out he's best friends with the President, who's just mysteriously disappeared in the loss of Air Force One. Suddenly it's no mystery in Amin Hassan's eyes why you were picked to bug his daughter's office. You're an antiquities dealer, so you and Amina already have a connection that'll get you inside her office. Plus, you're secretly working for the American government. That's not only true, it's a logical connection anyone might assume if they found the bugs."

He paused a moment. "I don't think Amina knows about the bugs, and after our conversation with her, I think she doesn't know about the rest of this. She plays no active role in management even though Zarif keeps her under surveillance twenty-four hours a day. She's basically her father's hostess, wining and dining his celebrity and royalty pals as they blow through London on their way to one island paradise or another to unwind. I said that the CIA's had all three of them on its radar for several years. During that time Amin has always called the shots and Zarif has always carried out his orders."

"So you really think Amina doesn't know I planted the bugs?"

"Right, but again, that's just my opinion. I say she believes you came because you want to display her ancient relics. Fortunately for us, you actually were intrigued by what she has, so that made your visit even more realistic.

Next, you were attacked on the street just after having dinner with her. Don thinks that was a warning. Maybe it was Zarif acting on his own. It's a known fact that he doesn't like Amina. He's been seen scolding and berating her in public. I think he resents her being presumptive head of the London operation, even though he answers to her father.

"Here's the bottom line, from where I see things. Zarif finds the bugs and tells Amin. Either Amin or Zarif decides to have you beaten up, but that doesn't make you go away. In fact, just the opposite happens. Amin sees his daughter becoming personal friends first with you, and then you, Nicole. She hangs out with you all in London; then she buys a ticket to come visit you in Dallas. That was the last straw. Amin orders his hit man to pay a visit to Dallas first."

Harry told them there was only a little of the story left to tell. When Safwan bought his ticket, it was time to pull Brian and Nicole out of harm's way, and both were brought here to the island. "As much as we love having you here, I hope this visit doesn't last. We can't keep this a secret for long."

That was something Brian had been wondering himself. "What has to happen in order for you to go public and announce that everyone's still alive? Man, that's going to be the most amazing revelation in history!"

"Just keep an eye on the President," Harry replied. "Exxon is the key to everything. I'm looking for an executive order or an amendment buried in some unrelated piece of legislation or a subtle change in the nation's energy policy. Something's going to happen really soon because Hassan's not a patient man. He's waited long enough and he's been spurned already. It won't happen again because his man's in power now. Before long, a little change here or there will allow Hassan Group, a private foreign company headed by a man who funds terrorism, to swoop in and buy control of ExxonMobil. It'll happen so fast nobody will see it coming. The second he gets the okay to dominate world oil is the moment we'll make our move."

CHAPTER FORTY-TWO

Cham Parkes and Lou Breaux sat in the Oval Office, where the Vice President had become something of a regular every evening around five. He and the President drank Scotch on the rocks while Parkes filled the room with smoke from another of his stinky cigars. Lou wasn't complaining, of course. Thanks to Cham, he was headed straight toward Easy Street for the rest of his life.

"The cabinet appointments went well," Breaux commented in his New Orleans drawl. "The press didn't have much to say about them, and it sounds like the Senate isn't interested in picking a fight with you, at least so far!"

"It's perfect timing," the President replied with a grin. "We're in the middle of a presidential election and that's all anybody's focused on. The folks on the Hill are spending all their time scrambling around trying to choose the Republican nominee now that Harry's out of the picture. I couldn't have planned it better if I'd done it myself!" He grinned smugly in the knowledge that, in fact, everything had been planned perfectly. Breaux would never know that, of course. All Lou had to do now was shut up and go along for the ride. So far he was doing exactly what he was told, and that was good.

The new cabinet appointees, two from Parkes's home state of Texas and one from Breaux's native Louisiana, would face Senate confirmation, but in the meantime the positions would be vacant. Parkes was banking on the fact that it was in the Republican-controlled Senate's best interest to get things moving, especially in this election year when constituents were particularly observant of blatant attempts toward obstructionism.

The Senate Majority Leader, one of the three in Washington who knew that Harry Harrison was still alive, had promised Parkes the confirmations would go smoothly. And they would. That was all part of Operation Condor, after all.

Five days later Parkes had three new cabinet Secretaries.

Back on the island, Brian and Nicole commented at lunch how they wished they'd thrown in swimsuits, and an attendant appeared moments later, carrying two. "Hopefully these will fit. These were already here – our landlord apparently had thought of his guests' every need. There are a dozen other sizes if these don't work."

They swam for a while and then Nicole went inside for a nap while Brian did some work on the upcoming Vesuvius auction. He found it strange to be doing "normal" things on his laptop while he was sitting in the middle of what was undoubtedly the most complex and unsettling operation in history.

As cocktail hour approached, everyone gathered on the veranda as usual. Harry played backgammon with one of the crew members from Air Force One while a lively game of low-stakes Texas Hold'em was underway at a table by the pool. The players – two female flight attendants, the two pilots, two Secret Service agents and one former Vice President of the United States – whooped and protested as one of the ladies won nine dollars, the largest pot of the afternoon.

What strange bedfellows all this has created, Nicole thought with a smile as she watched the camaraderie.

Harry waved them over to a table where he and Jennifer sat with Harry's mother and dad. They were by the railing where it was quieter and breezier than where everyone else was.

"The usual?" asked the same steward who'd served them last night, and soon they were raising glasses in a toast.

All day long Fox News had been turned on but muted in the living room. Since there was nothing new to report about the missing airplanes, tonight's news was focused on one subject – the upcoming conventions. Just like everyone back home, the people on the island talked about how crazy things were. Brian wanted to ask Harry a question, but he was reluctant to bring it up. Fortunately Harry's father asked before he could.

Henry asked, "Do you figure all this will be over in time for you to step back in? How would the convention work if you came back into the picture?"

"I was just talking to Bob about that today." Harry had asked him to research a situation that had never been considered. A candidate for the presidency had swept all early voting states and already had enough delegates to be the nominee. That candidate suddenly disappeared. He then miraculously reappeared before the convention. Could he step back in as though he had never left?

One reason for letting the chief justice in on Operation Condor had been to make certain that Harry wasn't officially declared deceased. That was key to Harry's eventual return. Even though Parkes had said Harry Harrison was dead, his words carried no legal weight. The chief justice had smoothed the way for Parkes to take Harry's place; that was all part of the plan.

There was no precedent for any of this, and Harry wanted to keep his options open while the CIA worked to expose Cham Parkes as the traitor he appeared to be. The highest judge in the land might be able to keep the issue – and the former President – legally alive sufficiently long for things to get back to normal.

Harry answered his father. "Dad, this has to be over before the convention. That's three months from now, and there's no way we can keep things quiet that long. Everything has to happen fast, and I'm planning to accept the nomination at the convention. You'll be there – all of you will!"

That was good news to everyone at the table. Harry sounded confident and upbeat, and they all needed that kind of optimism right now.

BILL THOMPSON

CHAPTER FORTY-THREE

"They're gone."

"What do you mean they're gone? Where are they?"

"They're simply not here, Mr. Hassan. The man who is in charge of Sadler's gallery in London is here, apparently running things in his boss's absence. I called for an appointment with Sadler, and I was told he was on a buying trip and he might be out for two weeks."

"And the girl?"

"She has a small law office – it's just her and one legal assistant – also a female, who said her boss is out of town. I asked for an appointment next week and she seemed unsure about when Miss Farber would be back."

Amin cursed loudly and slammed his fist on the desk in his dark office. "He's hidden them!"

Zarif knew when to back off. He usually was privy to just about everything, but this time he had no idea who was hiding them. Now didn't seem to be a good time to ask.

"What would you like me to do, sir?"

"Stay in Dallas until you hear from me."

Zarif had come in yesterday. Although a Syrian by birth, he was a naturalized citizen of the United Kingdom and he had a British passport. He therefore didn't need a visa to enter the US. He'd come through arrivals without incident and was staying in an apartment in a Dallas suburb called Plano. One of Amin's contacts, another Syrian in Dallas, had offered the flat. Zarif settled in. He'd watch TV and order in pizza until his boss gave him orders. He lit a cigarette and sat back on the couch to watch the latest Batman movie.

Six people were in the Oval Office, discussing North Korea's increasing tests of nuclear missiles. President Parkes listened, but as usual his mind was on other things. That new assistant he'd seen in the hall this morning was quite a beauty, he mused about a girl who could be his granddaughter. Maybe he'd invite her in for a private tour of the Oval Office. *Worked for old Bill Clinton.* That made him smile.

From across the room on his desk, his cellphone suddenly rang. He stood and said, "Keep talking. I'll be right back."

He saw the caller ID and hit decline. Just as he sat back down, the phone rang again.

He declined the call again and stuck the phone in his pocket. Twice more during the meeting it vibrated steadily, and twice more he ignored it.

When he was alone at last, he looked at the screen and saw a text. "Call me now."

Nobody gives me orders. Not even you. He sat back, lit a cigar and waited. It didn't take long.

When the phone rang again, he answered.

"What part of 'don't call me on this phone again' wasn't clear?"

Amin was livid. His Arab blood was boiling at the disrespect Parkes was demonstrating. He held his temper and kept his words even.

"What have you done with them?"

"What the hell are you talking about?"

"Brian Sadler and his girlfriend. Where are they?"

Parkes knew Brian Sadler's name. He was from Austin, just down the road from Dallas, and he'd met Nicole Farber once at an event hosted by Randall Carter, Nicole's former boss at the prestigious Dallas law firm.

Parkes was losing his temper too. "I don't know what you're talking about. How dare you accuse me of anything!"

"Are you playing games with me, *Mister President*?"

That was enough. "Goddammit, you stupid A-rab, pull your head out of your ass and listen to me. I don't know anything about Brian Sadler or his girlfriend. Now don't ever call me on this phone again. You hear?" He clicked the phone off.

As he lay in bed that evening, he heard the ding of an incoming text. He glanced at the phone. It was from that damned Amin Hassan. Son of a bitch!

Check your financial affairs closely.

He couldn't sleep after that. He wondered what the cryptic message meant. Not long after midnight something crept into his mind. What if the bastard . . . but no. He couldn't have done that. *Could he?*

Cham sat straight up in bed, turned on the light and grabbed his phone. His wife muttered groggily, "Is everything all right?"

"Go back to bed. I have to do something."

He entered a URL address. It was the website of a bank, but there was no other bank website like this one. There was no name, no advertising, no colorful home page, no offers of mortgages or CDs. There was simply a blank white screen with two boxes. He entered a user ID and password and went to a new page. This one displayed only a number, exactly as he expected. What he didn't expect was the number he saw. USD $1.00.

A nervous shiver went down his spine and he began to perspire as he entered everything once more. Was it a mistake? This simply couldn't be! With growing dread, he began to understand exactly what was going on here.

This afternoon his account had been $9,999,999 higher than it was now.

That bastard withdrew the ten million bucks he wired me. Amin had left a dollar so Cham would know exactly what happened.

He pulled on a robe, stuck the phone in his pocket, turned off the light and opened the bedroom door. The Secret Service agent in the hall jumped to attention, startled. It was nearly two and Parkes had never done this before.

"May I help you, Mr. President?"

"No," he snapped. "I can't sleep. You stay here. I'm capable of walking around by myself."

He went to the empty Lincoln bedroom down the hall, shut the door and turned on a floor lamp. He called

Amin's number. It went straight to voicemail. As he listened to the message, Cham could almost feel Hassan's glee as he recorded it.

"Don't call me again on this phone."

"You slimy bastard," Parkes snarled out loud. "You son of a bitch! You're going to pay for this!"

There was no more sleep for the President that night. He tossed and turned, alternating between anger, fear and gritty determination. It was almost daybreak when he decided on a course of action. As rich and powerful as Amin Hassan was, he was no match against the President of the United States of America.

Cham was alone in his office the next morning when the cellphone rang. There would be no anger, no frustration and no fear on his side of the conversation today.

"What do you want?"

"I hope your investments are doing well."

"You've made a big mistake, Amin. I've got more money than I can use anyway. Yours was important because we made a deal. I promised to help you achieve a goal if you'd help me become President. The ten million was your idea, but I deserved it. You performed, and I'm already fulfilling my side of the bargain. Now you've reneged like a cheating weasel. Do you have weasels in your sand dune of a shithole country? I don't know how in hell you managed to get the money back out of my account, but it's immaterial now. The deal's off, my friend."

Amin didn't flinch and his voice never wavered. "That money I wired you? Getting it back was simple. You chose an offshore bank that I happen to own! Wasn't that convenient?"

Parkes realized how simple it had been. Hassan merely instructed some bank manager to undo the wire transfer. *What Amin did would be illegal as hell if the money weren't there illegally to start with,* he reflected as Amin continued.

"The deal's *not* off. It's going to continue exactly as we planned it or everything you've ever worked for in your life will be gone in an instant. Don't trifle with me, *Mister President*. You have no idea who you're up against. Now, I'm going to ask you one last time where Brian Sadler is."

Parkes wasn't afraid. Amin needed him at this point more than the other way around. And as long as he got the ten million back, Cham was willing to finish the deal.

He said, "I have two things to say, so listen to me. First, I have no idea what you're talking about, and second, put the money back. Now. Today. Then and only then will our deal happen. If you don't do as I say, I'll unleash the full power of the United States government against you and your entire sleazy operation. I may go down too, but I damn sure promise you'll rot in prison for the rest of your life, and that'll be satisfaction enough for me, regardless of where I end up."

It took every ounce of restraint in Amin Hassan's body not to reply in kind. Finesse was the key word now. But Amin swore to Allah that Cham Parkes would pay with his life for disrespecting him. He spoke quietly and calmly.

"Of course. Anything for an old friend."

BILL THOMPSON

CHAPTER FORTY-FOUR

Don Case wasn't invited to the President's strategy meeting this morning. It was just Harry and the Vice President. It happened this way now and then when Harrison had fast decisions to make before bringing in the others.

Case was entering notes from yesterday afternoon's session with Harry and the crew when his assistant rang.

"A. J. Minter and Representative Platt are here to see you," she said. "He doesn't have an appointment, but he said they would only take a moment of your time."

Minter? President Parkes's Chief of Staff? What is he doing here?

"Are they right there with you?"

"Yes, sir. Shall I bring them in?"

She was clearly flustered by this breach of protocol. No one showed up unannounced and asked to see a person at this level in government. Even congressmen and presidential assistants called for an appointment.

Don closed his laptop and said, "Of course. Show them in."

Minter came in first, followed by Eric Platt, a Democratic congressman from . . . where? Case couldn't recall. He'd never met the man, but you recognized the faces when you'd been in Washington awhile. When your agency was beholden to Congress for funding, you made sure you didn't ignore even the ones you didn't know personally.

The Chief of Staff was his usual jolly self, Case thought wryly as he watched the slump-shouldered man shuffle in with the representative in tow.

"Good morning, gentlemen. To what do I owe the honor of this visit?"

Minter said, "You know Representative Platt, I think."

Case shook the man's hand. "I'm not sure we've met, but of course I know who you are, sir. The agency appreciates everything you folks up on the Hill do for us."

In his usual awkward manner, Minter hemmed and hawed, gazed at the floor and said, "Uh, you can go back to whatever you're doing, Mr. Case. I just wanted to show Representative Platt the office for a minute . . ."

Don suddenly realized what was going on, but he was determined not to make this easy for either of them. If Platt was taking a tour of the director's office, accompanied by the President's lackey, it could mean only one thing.

He played dumb. "I'm not sure I understand, Mr. Minter. You two are on a tour?"

Minter was so flustered at this point it would have been laughable in other circumstances. As happened so often, the President had put him in an extremely uncomfortable situation, one that the Chief of Staff had no idea how to handle. He stammered a moment and Platt stepped in.

"I'm sorry, Director Case. I was under the impression you knew why we were here."

"He doesn't know," Minter mumbled under his breath. "The President hasn't told him."

"I'm so sorry, Director. There's obviously a serious miscommunication here and I apologize for the inconvenience. We'll get back with you later."

Now Don twisted the screw. Platt was a good guy and he was caught in the middle, but the director was going to have a little fun with the situation. He had nothing to lose at this point.

"No, no! You've come all the way over here. By all means, look around. I insist! Do you need a tape measure or anything? I'm here to help. Some of this furniture's mine personally, by the way. Do you want me to show you which pieces?"

Platt was turning red with embarrassment and Minter looked like a whipped dog.

The representative said sharply, "A.J., let's go. Director Case has work to do and so do I."

When he was alone, Don couldn't help but laugh, even though this was deadly serious. He called the island and Harry answered immediately – any news from the CIA at this juncture could be critical.

"We'd better get into high gear, sir. They just paraded my replacement through my office."

BILL THOMPSON

CHAPTER FORTY-FIVE

A. J. Minter didn't have any friends.

He couldn't remember having even one in his entire life. Maybe that was his fault. God knows his mother had said enough times he'd never have any friends if he didn't get out and meet people.

Then again, his mother had said a lot of things.

Children are to be seen, not heard. A.J., let's play the quiet game. See how long you can go without interrupting. If you don't have anything to say, don't say anything. Can't you ever stop talking?

Every time he came home from school, bursting to tell her what had happened today, she said one of those things. *I'm busy right now. Don't talk. Can't you see I'm doing something important?*

At last he got it. He quit trying, and he stopped talking to other people too. He hung his head a lot and boys bullied him, calling him a sissy. He was smart – really smart – and he made top grades, but he never, ever had any friends.

Some people felt sorry for A.J. His high school counselor couldn't remember ever seeing a more awkward boy, and he took pity on the intelligent kid who had no social skills. He'd gotten a flyer announcing that two students could go to Washington, just an hour away, and serve as pages in the United States Senate for a week. It might be good for the boy, the counselor thought as he wrote A.J.'s name and one other on the nomination sheet and sent it in. When A.J. was chosen and his mother agreed to let him go, no one was more surprised than the boy was. He figured she just wanted him out of the house so things would be quiet. But he decided that now, for once in his life, he was going to step out. And he did it.

He and a girl from his class who'd never spoken to him rode the bus to Washington. They stayed in a hotel with a hundred other pages who worked in the United States Capitol building for a week. He'd never been there and he was absolutely blown away. He was randomly assigned to Representative Cham Parkes from Texas, and he spent a week mostly running errands and doing whatever the congressman told him to do. Parkes wasn't very nice to people, A.J. noticed, but at least he talked to the boy. It was the most exciting thing he had ever done in his entire life, and he vowed to work there someday.

A.J. won a scholarship to the University of Virginia, majoring in political science and graduating with honors. He returned to Washington to do the one thing that had piqued his interest. He wanted to work in the Capitol, and he went straight to the only man he knew – Representative Parkes, who hired him as a staffer.

A decade later, here he was, still a glorified page but now Chief of Staff. He was still running errands and getting ordered around by the man who had been Speaker and now was President. It was exciting, A.J. had to admit, but his boss really was a jerk.

Tonight he faced a dilemma. He'd listened and overheard things time and again that were underhanded, sneaky and sometimes just plain wrong, but he'd never overheard anything like what had happened today.

He had felt downright dirty yesterday when he and Representative Platt had walked into Director Case's office. He knew Parkes was shoving Case's replacement down his throat, announcing his impending termination the dirty way – Parkes's way – but A.J. wished he'd had no part of it. Platt didn't like it either – he was a nice guy and he was deeply embarrassed by what had happened. It was simply wrong.

For the first time in years, he decided to do something that was good, proper and right instead of being pushed around by other people. He picked up his home phone. He would never dare to make this call at the office.

"There's a call from A. J. Minter at the White House, sir."

Case glanced at his watch – it was nearly eight. He was surprised that Minter worked as late as he did, and after yesterday's office visit, he wondered what was next.

"This is Don Case. What can I do for you?"

"We need to meet. I have something to say, and I don't know anyone else to talk to. It's something so big we have to find a secret place to meet, someplace President Parkes can't know about."

They met after dark in the parking lot of a Walmart not far from where Minter lived. He appeared extremely nervous and went straight to the point.

The President had taken a call from Amin Hassan, he told Case. "I had dropped off some cups in the pantry next to the Oval Office, and he didn't know I was there. I didn't intend to eavesdrop, but I couldn't help overhearing. It was wrong, but what the President's doing is wrong too. I didn't know who else to call, and after the embarrassing thing in your office yesterday, I thought of you. I know you're no friend of the President, and right now I'd be afraid to tell this to anyone who is. But someone has to know. This just isn't right, Director Case. It's bad for our country."

You don't know the half of it, Case thought.

Minter had only heard one side of the conversation, but he related how Parkes had called Hassan a slimy bastard, how they'd talked about ten million dollars Parkes got and how he was already working to fulfill his part of a bargain. Case grew more and more astounded – and concerned – as he listened.

Finally he told Minter to go home and keep everything to himself. He promised to be back in touch as quickly as he could.

"Hurry," A.J. advised. "The President's not going to keep you around much longer. I can stall it a day or two maybe once he gives the order. But it'll be really soon. Just hurry."

As he drove home, Don Case, director of the CIA, a man who was typically unflappable in a crisis, literally shook like a leaf.

This was it! Holy Mother of God!

Case went back to Langley. His men had hacked Cham Parkes's cellphone. They could see the calls but had no idea what was said. They knew Cham Parkes had called Amin Hassan during the night and that Hassan had called him back this morning. That last call was the one A. J. Minter was talking about. Case looked at the record – there it was, date and time noted. He picked up the secure, encrypted phone. This was the mother of all smoking guns and he had to tell his boss immediately.

CHAPTER FORTY-SIX

Brian wasn't sure what was going on this morning, but it certainly wasn't business as usual around here. He and Nicole were having breakfast on the patio with Henry and Julia when Agent Moore walked from table to table, whispering in the ears of three people – the Vice President, Secretary of State and the Chief of Staff. Each exited the room immediately, leaving his breakfast unfinished. For the past hour they had been with the President behind closed doors.

Nicole commented, "I wonder what's up?"

Henry replied, "I can only hope it's a breakthrough. We need something to get the ball rolling."

In Harry's office at the other end of the house, the attendees listened to Director Case on speakerphone, explaining what he'd told Harry last night. Case said what Minter had revealed. The men around Harry's desk agreed there was no way Parkes could get out of this one. His words left no room for misunderstanding. He was in something dark – something criminal.

The team was upbeat even though this was the most serious situation the United States had ever faced. There had been instances of betrayal from within but never at the top. And never involving such a heinous individual as Amin Hassan.

The Speaker of the House had obviously made a pact with the Syrian billionaire. In exchange for Hassan's paving the way for Parkes to become President – which could only happen by getting rid of any obstacles – Parkes would receive ten million dollars and fulfill "his side of the bargain." That part wasn't spelled out, but everyone in the room knew what Hassan wanted. He wanted to dominate the oil business worldwide, starting with ExxonMobil. He'd been blocked once in that quest, but he was making sure it didn't happen the next time he tried.

With a puppet in the White House, Amin could achieve his goal. The President and Vice President had been eliminated. Two conservative Supreme Court justices were dead, leaving the court leaning to the left. There were three new cabinet Secretaries, each in a position to help Hassan. With Parkes and Lou Breaux running the country, it was a classic case of the foxes in the henhouse, except this time there was a fearsome specter behind the scenes. There was a man who financed the Falcons of Islam, the terror group who had taunted Americans, saying they had sleepers – non-Muslim terrorists – hidden inside the US already. They were planning to attack the country from within, and the President of the United States was right in the middle of it.

In the interest of grabbing power and fortune, Chambliss T. Parkes had literally made a deal with the devil. He had to be stopped. The men in this room, all of whom were presumed dead by the American people, had to create a plan. They had absolutely no time to waste. If Parkes replaced the CIA director, their plan to stop Parkes would end. Don Case was their conduit of information, and they had to move quickly before he was shut down.

Brian and Nicole were swimming with Jennifer and the girls when Harry and his team walked out onto the veranda. They joined him at a table and he said, "Sorry I was tied up this morning. We have a major development and we've been discussing strategy with Don." No one could miss how serious he sounded.

"Are we leaving, Daddy?" Lizzie asked. "Are we going home now?"

"Not yet, honey. We're going to stay a little while longer."

"Oh, boy!" Kate said, clapping her hands. "I love it here! I don't ever want to go home!"

Their mother laughed and commented, "Ah, the sweet innocence of youth!"

Nicole nodded her head. It was nice to see the girls so happy.

Brian asked, "Not meaning to pry, but are you optimistic about this major development? I'm hoping it was a positive one."

"It was positive and it's huge. I wish I could discuss it with you, but for the moment we're keeping this one under wraps. I will say this – it's not going to be easy, and there are some huge obstacles, the primary one being that we have a very short timeframe to make some really big things happen." He took Jennifer's hand. "I'll be tied up in meetings, the first one starting right after lunch. This may go on for a while."

She squeezed his hand. "You've been a basket case since we got here, Harry. You've been pretending things are okay for the sake of everyone else, when all of this is weighing hard on you. Cham Parkes is dangerous – every decent American knows that. Whatever needs to be done, go do it. Your team's the best and I have faith in all of you. I'd rather have our country's future in your hands than anyone else's."

Brian and Nicole nodded in agreement.

They went through the buffet line and brought soup and fish sandwiches out to their table. Clearly deep in thought, Harry ate in silence as the adults chatted and the girls laughed at each other's jokes. As soon as he finished, Harry excused himself. They didn't see the team again that day. Later Jennifer explained that the four of them were having a working dinner in the office.

The next morning President Parkes announced his choice for attorney general. The position required Senate confirmation, but in an unprecedented side note, Parkes said the current AG, an appointee of Harry Harrison's, would be leaving office immediately.

"I'm sure you've heard about Parkes's AG appointment," Brian said when Harry joined them at the breakfast table. "I saw it on the news a few minutes ago."

"He can't do what he's doing. Not legally, I mean. I spoke to Michelle this morning. She's livid, as we all are."

Michelle Isham was the Senate Majority Leader and one of the three in Washington who knew Harry was alive. She was a Midwesterner – an Iowa girl – who was in her fourth term in the Senate. The attorney general had called her last night and said he was being forced out. Parkes had told him to submit his resignation this morning and the AG had complied.

Isham told Harry that the AG had simply given up. "I'm not serving under that asshole. They can all go to hell. Life's too short," he had said in defeat.

Harry told Michelle it would have been better for the cause if the AG had stayed and fought, but he understood. Although she wasn't in the loop on the newest development, Isham knew time was short. Something had to happen to stop all this, and it had to be soon.

"Back to work," Harry said, pushing back his chair. Just then his mother and father came outside, and Harry stopped to kiss her cheek. "See you guys by lunchtime, God willing."

CHAPTER FORTY-SEVEN

That morning Brian and Nicole took bicycles and traversed an eleven-mile trail that ran along the island's shoreline. It was a beautiful day and a great ride. When they returned, they went to the veranda and were pleased to see Harry and his kids in the pool. The President looked happy, Brian thought. Maybe things were going well.

Things *were* going well, Harry believed. He and Marty had spent two hours alone this morning. They had worked out a plan. It was good, but implementation would be the difficult part. It was tough when so few people were in on the secret. Most people thought Cham Parkes was someone they had to live with, at least through the Democratic convention in August and most likely for four years after that. Only the people on the island and the three in DC could be enlisted to help.

This afternoon they'd bring Aaron and Bob back into the office, get Don Case on the line and finalize things. Time was so short that they agreed to work straight through until what they had dubbed Operation Clawback was finished and ready to go.

Time seriously *was* running out for all of them. If they didn't have Don as CIA director, Harry would have to let more people in on the secret or the mission couldn't be accomplished. Even one more person who knew Air Force One and Two really hadn't crashed was one more person who could blow the entire thing wide open.

If Cham Parkes – or worse, if Amin Hassan – found out they were alive, Harry feared for the future of the country itself. If the Falcons of Islam really did have a band of sleeper terrorists across America and if they struck at once, it could mean the end of the United States. And President Parkes would have been an instrument of the jihadists to make it all happen.

It was a strange crew who sat around Harry's desk on the island this afternoon. Three dead men – the President, the Vice President and the Secretary of State –

conferred with three very live individuals who sat around a conference table in Director Case's office. The always-secure phones had been checked once again before the meeting started. This would be the call to end all calls.

The team took a huge risk by choosing Case's office. The Senate Majority Leader and the chief justice were very familiar faces in Washington, and it would be hard to meet anywhere in secret. Inside the Beltway someone was always watching – looking for a news story or a tidbit of information that a foreign government could use. Finding a place and getting the players there was an obstacle; Harry finally told them to use the director's office. Case had a private elevator that ran directly from the underground parking garage to his office, and it had carried many individuals who were here for meetings nearly as sensitive as this one.

President Parkes learned about the meeting from the CIA agent who'd driven the chief justice out to Langley. That man owed his job to a recommendation from then-Speaker Parkes six years ago. The agent was fiercely loyal to the new President, and he was eager to repay his debt.

All Cham knew was that the chief justice had gone to CIA headquarters for a secret meeting with the director. That was enough to make him wonder what the hell was going on out there at Langley.

CHAPTER FORTY-EIGHT

Vincent Valgardo sat in his office on the fiftieth floor of the building on Park Avenue that was emblazoned with the company's name. Valgardo Capital was the world's third largest private investment bank. It held billions in stocks and bonds of corporations, and it was the largest shareholder in ExxonMobil.

Valgardo had met Harry Harrison when they attended Harvard Law School. He hadn't known the future President well, but they had remained casual friends over the years. Vincent contributed modestly to Harry's campaigns, and they exchanged pleasantries now and then when they bumped into each other at meetings or dinners. Valgardo played both sides of the political aisle; he wanted to keep Valgardo Capital's interests in front of lawmakers, regardless of their affiliations.

His executive secretary advised Senator Michelle Isham was on the line. That was nothing special; he was accustomed to calls from politicians. The Political Action Committee he'd set up had funded hundreds of them over the years. Had he contributed to the Senate Majority Leader's campaign? He couldn't recall.

"Good morning, Senator Isham. How are things in our nation's capital?"

She quickly dispensed with the pleasantries. As they talked, his assistant opened the office door, alarm on her face. "It's the CIA!" she whispered, trying not to interrupt his call. "An agent's standing right here and he insists on seeing you now!"

"One second, Senator," he said. "Your man's here." Valgardo waved to his secretary. "It's fine. Bring him in."

Isham had advised him that a CIA agent would arrive momentarily with a confidentiality agreement. If he chose to sign, she would explain the reason for her call, saying only that it was a matter of national security that involved Valgardo. No, she assured him, there was nothing wrong. In fact, the government was asking for his help.

Vincent listened as the agent told him the penalty for violating a federal security confidentiality agreement; then he signed it with a flourish.

The agent spoke to Senator Isham for a moment, confirmed the agreement had been executed, and left.

Now she told Valgardo a critically important, top-secret piece of information. She asked him to sweep his office for listening devices every day, reminded him of the agreement he'd just signed, and hung up.

He sat back, trying to get his mind around the shocking revelation he'd just heard. Five minutes later his private line rang.

"Don't say my name. Do you know who this is?"

"Yes, sir. I just spoke to Senator Isham."

"I know. Whenever we speak, don't say my name aloud, just in case. I'm going to tell you an incredible story that is dangerous, completely true, and the consequences of which could bring down the United States. Then I'm going to ask you to do something you're not going to want to do, in order to help your country. You're the only person who can help us in one critical thing that has to happen."

Harry Harrison and his old law school classmate talked for thirty minutes. The corporate titan learned about Air Force One and Two and he learned about Operation Clawback, although Harrison never used that name. He heard a little about Cham Parkes and Amin Hassan. Vincent became more astounded with every revelation, and by the end of the call he was totally on board.

"I consider myself a loyal American," he told Harry, and by God, of course he'd help in any way he could.

Operation Clawback was officially underway.

The next morning Michelle Isham sat in the President's office. She was the ranking Republican in the Senate, and Cham Parkes was easily her least favorite person in Washington. She was certain he felt exactly the same toward her. Today she had a job to do and she was going to make it work. She forced a smile as he spoke curtly, like always.

"You asked for this meeting. What do you want?"

"I'm prepared to change a position I took earlier, and I wanted to discuss it with you personally."

"And what would that be, darlin'?" he said condescendingly. He frankly didn't give a damn about this woman or her positions.

Deep inside she was seething and she hoped her face wasn't flushed. Parkes was famous for belittling women, and this wasn't the first time she'd seen him in action. She had work to do today and she wouldn't allow his behavior to impede her. She kept her tight smile and responded, "If we can reach an agreement on a few things I have on my agenda, I'm willing to support Amin Hassan's bid to take over ExxonMobil."

You could have knocked Cham Parkes out of his chair with a feather. He tried to mask his excitement. "What do you want from me?"

She was ready with a list of things that were important enough to seem worthy of a trade, and he readily agreed to every one, as Harry and the others on the island had known he would. There was nothing bigger than the Hassan-Exxon deal for Cham Parkes.

They talked about how she would lobby her fellow Republicans in the Senate and deliver the votes for any reasonable bill the House sent over that allowed Hassan to make his move.

"It's going to be close," she advised. "You have to deliver every single Democrat or it won't come to a vote." Besides voting for it herself, she had to sway nineteen Republicans. As much infighting as had happened the last time Amin tried this, Cham couldn't imagine how she'd deliver nineteen Republicans, but she was offering a deal and he jumped on it.

That afternoon Cham called the Vice President over early for cocktails. It was time for a celebration. His opponents were finally seeing the light. They were getting used to life after death. They didn't have Harry Harrison to mollycoddle them now. Now people were coming around. Michelle was only the first of a long line he'd be seeing, hat in hand, wanting to make peace. Cham was sure of that.

Life was good. And so was this aged single-malt Scotch they were sipping.

He'd checked the bank account this morning. The ten million was back. He called the law firm in Panama he'd used before and by noon they'd created a new bank account, time zones away from the bank Amin Hassan owned. Before the close of the day his money was safe and sound in a new account free from thieving hands.

It was a good thing Amin had done what he promised. But then why wouldn't he, the President thought. *He's afraid of me. They all are.*

Tomorrow President Parkes would throw his Arab friend a bone. A big bone called Exxon. That would finish his part of the bargain and get this asshole out of his life.

CHAPTER FORTY-NINE

The team had a challenging task. There was no time to work with the Federal Trade Commission and the Securities and Exchange Commission to change their position on Hassan's takeover of Exxon. It had to happen another way. Although it was a daunting task, the quickest way to allow Hassan to move on the company was to get a bill through Congress.

Democrats controlled the House, and Harry expected to see a bill passed before the end of this week. The President would move quickly before Majority Leader Isham changed her mind.

The big problem was the Senate. There were sixty Republicans, and it took sixty votes to bring the House bill to the floor for a vote. Parkes had promised to deliver all forty Democrats. Michelle would vote in favor. The issue was how to convince nineteen other Republicans, each of them bitterly opposed to the Exxon sale, to vote yes. She would have to make it happen without telling them the whole story.

It was critical now that no one else know Harry was still alive. If word got out, everything they were doing would come crashing down. The future of the country depended on Operation Clawback's success.

What Isham *could* do was to let these Senators in on a *different* secret – the close and clandestine partnership between the US President and the Syrian billionaire.

Twenty Republican senators were up for reelection this fall. Those would be left alone. There was going to be enough fury from constituents over the sudden reversal of opinion, and the ones up for reelection didn't need this added damage. Instead, they could liberally bash their fellow Senators who'd switched to the dark side.

The team pored over the names of the remaining forty, half of whom would have to switch their votes and support an issue they detested. Never mind that the sale would quickly be undone – the people back home would already have formed their opinions. The good news was that if everything worked the way the team hoped, Americans would quickly understand why all this deception and subterfuge had been required.

By the end of the day they had their list, and Majority Leader Isham began making calls. The next morning she, CIA Director Case and nineteen Republican Senators met in a secure conference room in the basement of the Capitol. She had asked the Capitol Police to sweep the room and she required the attendees to leave phones and briefcases outside.

After reminding the group of the need for absolute confidentiality, Isham and Case presented the facts of Cham Parkes's secret agreement with Amin Hassan. They tied Hassan to the Falcons of Islam and demonstrated other jihadist groups his largesse had benefitted. Without revealing how they knew, they disclosed President Parkes's angry discussion with Hassan after the latter withdrew ten million dollars he'd wired Parkes immediately after his inauguration as President. The money was back in his secret account now. Otherwise Cham Parkes wouldn't be back on good terms with the Arab.

Through the Falcons of Islam, Hassan was clearly tied to the disappearance of the two planes and the deaths of Harrison, Taylor and the others. Parkes was tied to Hassan and therefore he was complicit too. Case also pointed out how convenient it was for the President that two Supreme Court justices were suddenly out of the picture.

The Majority Leader told them she had met with the President yesterday and agreed to back Hassan's takeover of ExxonMobil. She explained how it would all come down, exactly what would happen, and that despite how bad it would look on the surface, all this would work in the interest of the nation and to put Chambliss T. Parkes in prison for the rest of his life. The Exxon deal would be unwound – Hassan would never end up with control, she assured them.

"They'll crucify me back home," the Senator from Tennessee commented. "I'll bet I've gotten five hundred calls and letters about Exxon, all against the deal. Nobody wants to see the world's largest oil company in the hands of Amin Hassan."

"Short term, you're absolutely right," Michelle replied. "You have two years before you stand for election again. Long before that happens, what you did today will be hailed as courageous and patriotic."

"I can't tell you yes on this, Michelle. I'm going to have to give it some thought."

This was what Harry's team had feared most. If any of them wouldn't play, then others had to be brought in. Nineteen was already too many for a secret this big; adding more could spell disaster. Michelle had a huge job right now – a job she was qualified for as Majority Leader, but a tough one.

"There's no time for giving it thought," she replied calmly. "We've explained the gravity of the situation and we've entrusted the knowledge of this project to you. I have to know – and I have to know now – if you're willing to help me save our nation. I want to see a show of hands of who's in."

Seventeen men and women raised their hands. She needed the other two, and she knew what she might have to resort to in order to accomplish it.

Promising to stay in close communication and keep everyone constantly updated, Isham thanked everyone for their support and asked Case and the seventeen supporters to leave the room.

She sat at the long conference table with two senators, a man and a woman. Both were relatively new to Congress and she empathized with their plight. Reversing position on an issue as sensitive to constituents as this would be political suicide if things didn't work perfectly. They simply weren't willing to chance losing everything they'd worked for, to support a bizarre scheme to take down the President.

"I have to have you on board," she told them earnestly. "I can't afford to bring even one more person in on what's happening. This is the most important issue of national security you will ever be involved in. There's far more here than what I've told you. I've barely scratched the surface with the secrets you learned today. We have to fight for this country, to avenge the loss of our two leaders, the Secretary of State, the President's family and the others on those planes. I promise you that what I'm asking you to do is the right thing, the honorable thing and the patriotic thing. Even if we don't bring Cham Parkes down – we will, believe me – but even if we don't, there'll be a revelation to the American people that will cause mass celebrations across our country. I can't tell you what it is, but I've never told you anything that wasn't true. You must join me. You absolutely have to. For our country, there's no choice."

She paused for a breath. She hoped they'd understand. She didn't want to force the issue, but she was prepared to withdraw the support of the party from these two individuals. No more help from the Republican National Committee and its PACs loaded with campaign funds. No more endorsements from national leaders. It would be the kiss of death, and she hated even thinking about using that threat. She wasn't even certain she could deliver it, but it would sound ominous regardless. These were decent individuals who'd done nothing wrong. In fact, they were standing by their principles. But that wasn't acceptable now.

"So are you with me?"

Thirty seconds of dead silence seemed like an hour to Michelle. Then the woman raised her hand.

"I'm in."

"What the hell," the other senator said with a shaky laugh. "I was looking for a job when I got this one. Count me in too." His hand went into the air.

CHAPTER FIFTY

On this gorgeous spring morning, Vincent Valgardo decided to walk over for his appointment with President Parkes. The Willard Hotel was virtually across the street from the White House; taking a cab made no sense at all.

Before daybreak he'd gone for the jog he managed almost every day, rain or shine, regardless of where in the world he was. This morning when he ran past the United States Capitol building he felt a shiver of nervousness about his meeting. Valgardo had met everyone from heads of state to the Pope. As CEO and majority shareholder of one of the world's largest investment banks, he was comfortable in any surrounding, self-assured and on top of his game.

His nervousness wasn't a result of fear. It was a shiver of anticipation and pride. As he ran past the Capitol, draped in scaffolding for its ongoing renovation, he thought it symbolic of what he was going to do today. He was going to serve his country and stand up for what was good and just and right. He was excited.

President Parkes motioned him to a chair by the fireplace and took another beside it. They engaged in a few minutes of small talk about politics and the state of the financial markets and then Parkes got to the point.

"I've called you here to ask for your help," he began cordially. "I'm sure you know my feelings about the Exxon merger with Hassan Group that fell apart some time back when Harry Harrison was President. The Republicans have always fought me over this issue, and for the life of me, I can't figure out why. I like it. I think it's good for America and good for Exxon. And, I might add, good for Valgardo Capital, since you own nearly fifteen percent of the stock."

Vincent played his role perfectly. He listened politely but said nothing.

"I've made some major progress in the last day or so. Majority Leader Isham finally agrees with me that she was wrong. The House will send a bill over today, and Isham's going to get it passed."

"Really?" he replied, genuinely surprised. Isham hadn't revealed that this was part of the plan. As he listened, he wondered how on earth she could deliver twenty votes, given the vehement and unanimous Republican opposition to the merger not that long ago.

Full of himself as usual, Cham leaned back, tipping his two-hundred-year-old Chippendale chair precariously onto its two spindly back legs. "Yep, really. The girls are always the easiest to convince. They know when to let a man do the thinking, you know what I mean? She got a few tidbits from me in the deal, but Hassan Group gets the green light to begin accumulating Exxon stock again. That's good for them and good for America."

Bullshit if it is! Valgardo thought, recalling what Harry had told him about Parkes's personal agenda. "And how can I help, Mr. President?"

"I'd like your company to lead the support for Hassan's accumulation of Exxon stock. With your fifteen percent on his side, he gains control with less cash outlay."

Never in a lifetime would Vincent Valgardo have imagined he'd be agreeing to this deal. It wasn't good for America at all. Only Harry's explanation of what was going on made him tell Parkes he'd think about it. He was going to do it, of course. Harry had already asked him and Vincent had agreed. But this had to look genuine. He couldn't jump on the bandwagon immediately. It had to appear that he gave it serious consideration before agreeing.

"Presuming my people decide that it's a good idea for us to join Mr. Hassan, and that's a large presumption at the moment, may I in turn count on your future support for policies Valgardo Capital considers important for America and our company?"

"Of course! That's what politics is all about, Mr. Valgardo. It's about quid pro quos."

Maybe your idea of politics is. What happened to doing what's best for the people?

As his private jet flew back to New York, Vincent thought about the major, first-class shit storm that would blow in when he announced Valgardo Capital was going to help a billionaire Syrian take over a US oil company. He had Harry's word this wasn't going to last long and that everyone would know the truth when it was over. He desperately hoped the former President was right.

BILL THOMPSON

CHAPTER FIFTY-ONE

"Tell me there's a reason for this! Tell me, Michelle! Why in hell would you turn on us?"

At eighty-three, Samuel Pennington was the oldest member of the Senate. He led the pack that had stormed into the Majority Leader's office. There must have been twenty of them. As much as she'd been expecting this, the thing that hurt most was how disappointed they looked. She'd planned for fury, expletives, and screaming voices, but it hurt her deeply to see the people she led now ashamed of their leader.

"You joined forces with that asshole! You made a deal with him and didn't even have the common courtesy to ask us what we thought!"

"Some have said they'll join with me. I have enough votes . . ."

"Yes, Michelle," Pennington said, the tone of resignation in his old, shaky voice almost too painful to hear. "You're a great leader. You've made a choice and you brought some of us along with you. We all know it's the ones who aren't standing for election this year. At least you had the decency to spare those who were."

Another woman, the senior senator from Idaho and a close friend of Michelle's, spoke up, calling Isham by her nickname. When she used the word, it made the Majority Leader cry.

"We're angry, Shells. We're hurt, too. I don't know what you were thinking. How come even I didn't know you were so gung ho about the Exxon merger? You never acted like it. Now you've arranged a block to outvote all of us, who've been your friends and who voted you in as Majority Leader. My constituents don't want this, and they're damn sure going to know I don't want it either. Once the vote on the Exxon debacle is over, we want you out of here. Out of this office, out of your leadership position and, if I had my say, out of the Senate. Either you resign as Majority Leader or we remove you – it's your choice. You're an embarrassment to the office. You're as bad as the President is. And that's just about the worst thing I can think of saying about anyone." She was crying as she and the rest of them left, slamming the door behind them.

Michelle didn't leave her office for the rest of the day. Around four she decided to go home. As she was packing her briefcase, her cellphone rang. It was Harry, asking how the day went. They both knew today would be the day of confrontation.

"It went pretty well," she said with a weak chuckle. "They all came to see me. One of them had a noose, but I guess they decided not to use it."

"I'm so sorry. I wish it could be different."

"I'm sorry too. When Sam Pennington, a man I've revered and been in awe of since I came here, tells me I'm a traitor, selling out my fellow senators, what can I say? He's right. He's absolutely right, Harry." She'd kept things bottled up all day, but now she began to sob bitterly.

"They want me to step down or they'll vote me out. That'll happen in the next few days, right after the Exxon vote, they said. So unfortunately your Operation Clawback will be too late to save my job."

"If there were anything I could do to change all this, I would."

"You can. I have to tell them about you and Marty and the Secretary of State. They can keep a secret. They've done it for years right here in Congress. You can't leave me out here all alone like this on my own. At least you people down there have each other. I don't have anyone. Except for nineteen of my colleagues, each of whom is now considered as big a hypocritical Judas as I am, I'm all alone. And those nineteen are sworn to secrecy. They can't tell the others why they suddenly changed their minds. We're as bad as Cham Parkes, Harry. In the public's eyes, we're the same lying cheats he is. I never thought about this part of it when you asked me to help. I don't know if I can do this anymore."

He soothed her, assuring her things would look up soon. With the passage of a little time, tempers would cool and reason would win out. It wouldn't be clear until the mission was accomplished, but it was worth sacrificing things you considered important.

"Michelle, I know you're devastated at the temporary loss of face with your good friends. But think of this. I put my own father and mother through the funerals of Jennifer and me and their only two grandchildren. Don't you think that actually tore my heart out? I cried for two days. I grieved with real pain shooting through every inch of my being. But it had to happen. I knew it and they knew it too, once they joined us here. Please stick with me."

At last she agreed. She gave Harry her word and promised to call tomorrow. She went home, put on pajamas and sat in her living room with all the lights off. She had divorced long ago and her daughter was grown and living in Pennsylvania. There was no one here but her. There was no one *anywhere* but her anymore. Those feelings – those awful feelings from this afternoon – crept back over her like dirt covering a coffin.

She felt a powerful anxiety attack coming on and found the Xanax in her medicine cabinet, thanking God her doctor had just renewed her prescription. She had these attacks now and then. She hadn't had one in a long time, but this was a hell of a good day for one, she thought bitterly. She took two tablets, poured herself a glass of wine and turned on the television. The President had wasted no time in announcing that the House was reconsidering the ExxonMobil deal with Hassan Group of Dubai. He revealed he had also spoken with the CEO of Valgardo Group, Exxon's largest shareholder, who was supporting Hassan's position.

"I have the country's best interests in my thoughts every moment of every day," Parkes said with a Cheshire-cat smile. "My friends in Congress who opposed this deal the last time must now rethink their positions. Amin Hassan, the chairman of Hassan Group, has promised major investment in American oilfields, so at last we can reduce our dependency on foreign oil. This merger is critical for the future of our country. Most Americans agree with me –

they favor the strong alliance that will be created. I'm confident the House will pass the Exxon bill tomorrow and send it to the Senate."

She cringed as she saw her own picture fill the screen. With a confident smirk, Parkes continued, "Senate Majority Leader Isham told me today that she has the votes necessary to pass this legislation. The Republicans – at least the farsighted ones – will be joining us to make this happen."

The President pointed his finger at the camera. "When this bill reaches my desk, my fellow Americans, I promise you I will sign it, and we will create the world's strongest oil conglomerate, boosting US oil production, increasing jobs and our economy. God bless you all."

She barely listened. The part about a stronger economy and increasing domestic oil production was a damned lie. It was never going to happen. She knew it, Parkes knew it and so did all her friends in the Senate, even the ones who had promised to vote for the bill. It made her nauseous.

Mercifully, she fell asleep at last. She dreamed she was a zebra being stalked by lions. She dodged this way and that, into and out of the trees, until a man stepped out of the jungle directly in front of her. It was Chambliss Parkes and he held a hunting rifle. He pointed the gun at a huge lion running toward her, but then he swung it around and shot her instead. As the last of her life drained away, he stood over her with that awful feline smile on his face.

CHAPTER FIFTY-TWO

Michelle Isham had fulfilled her duty. She overcame the vehement fury of forty Republican Senators whom she had respected and enjoyed working with. She held firm, demanding a vote and breathing a sigh of relief when every single one – all nineteen in her coalition – voted as they had been told to vote. She and forty Democrats also voted yes and the bill passed sixty to forty. A Middle Eastern oil conglomerate – Hassan Group of Dubai – was given the green light to purchase ExxonMobil stock.

The bill and a quick ruling by the new Parkes-appointed attorney general thwarted previous efforts by the Federal Trade Commission and the Securities and Exchange Commission in advance. Moments after the President signed the legislation, the AG told the agencies to back off. This was now the law and he gave it his full support.

The three new cabinet Secretaries, all Parkes appointees, had vigorously endorsed the legislation, calling it a visionary move that would strengthen America and stabilize oil prices at a much higher level.

As Michelle Isham watched all this drama, she was both physically ill and mentally exhausted. No one understood more clearly than she that what she had done was absolutely necessary. Harry Harrison was the leader she respected most in Washington, and she had accomplished what he told her was required. What she did would help to bring down a criminal enterprise that reached to the Oval Office. History would show that she was a hero who had done something extraordinary with great personal sacrifice.

That was all good, but she couldn't get past the short term. Although she'd secretly done a noble thing, to the public it looked as though she was a turncoat. She was a Republican, a vehement enemy of Cham Parkes, suddenly supporting his bill just like his appointees who did what they were told. For some time to come she had lost her reputation, her friends and her own sense of self-esteem. This afternoon her colleagues would vote her out as Majority Leader. Who could blame them? She would have voted with them if someone else had done what she did.

She went home around noon, shut the drapes in her bedroom, crawled into bed and pulled the covers up around her face. She was one of the strongest women in America, she had been *Time* magazine's Person of the Year in 2015, and now she was shaking like a leaf.

I'm not strong, she said to herself. *I make everyone think I'm strong, but I'm not. I'm weak and I've done something that makes me a fool in front of everyone. How can I live with myself?*

The Xanax bottle was still on her nightstand. She shook out two tablets and held them in her hand.

It felt to Michelle as though she was in a parallel world, watching herself and knowing what she was going to do next, even though she didn't know for sure that she was going to do it.

She put the two pills back into the bottle and went to the bathroom for a glass of water. She put it next to her bed, lifted the Xanax bottle and poured forty-six pills into her mouth. She almost gagged, but she was successful. With the help of the water she managed to get them all down.

Soon she fell asleep. This time there were no dreams.

This time there was nothing at all.

CHAPTER FIFTY-THREE

Harry had one last request for Brian. Having no idea what was coming, he sat in Harry's office with the team who planned to take down Amin Hassan.

Brian had offered to help more than once, but so far there'd been nothing he could add to the mission. The group had decided there was one thing that would seal Hassan's fate once and for all. They wanted him locked away for the rest of his life. They had the goods on his illegal deals with a sitting President, but they wanted the rest. They wanted him gone, just like they believed Cham Parkes would be gone.

Harry approached the subject cautiously. Once again he was going to ask his best friend to step into a potentially dangerous situation for the good of his country. He and Jennifer loved this couple, and Harry had agonized over what was next.

"I'm just going to lay it on the table," he began somberly. "I'd like to sugarcoat this somehow, but I don't see how to call this anything but what it is. We need your help. You're sitting here with your arm in a cast from the last help you gave us, and that doesn't make this discussion any easier. What I can promise you as your friend, not your President but your friend, is that trained operatives will have your back every moment of every day, every step you take."

"Damn, Harry. I'm in! You've made this sound so enticing I can't wait to sign up!"

The men around the table grinned, although this was no laughing matter for any of them, especially Brian.

Harry had decided not to mince words. This was a tough request, and he wouldn't blame Brian one bit for telling all of them to go to hell. He explained the plan.

"We want to send you back to Dallas, put you out in public and use you as bait. That's about as clear as I can make it." He looked at Marty and the others. "Do any of you want to say anything before I continue?"

He explained the plan. "Zarif Safwan is Hassan's security guy in London and the man who's done Amin's dirty work for years. He knows where the bodies are literally buried, and we want to take him into custody. He's a killer who was trained by Syrian terrorists, fiercely loyal to his boss and willing to die if a job required it. We can't simply arrest him because he hasn't committed a crime. If I were President, the CIA could pick him up, interrogate him and see what he knows. Parkes will never stand for that because he'll do whatever his buddy Amin Hassan tells him to do.

"Taking Zarif into custody isn't the answer anyway. First, he's gone deep underground – we don't know where he is, but we don't believe he's left the States. We think Hassan is keeping him in Dallas until the boss figures out where you are. Second, he knows the USA can't hold someone indefinitely without charging him or her. He'd simply stay quiet until we had to let him go. Once he was free, I guarantee we'd never get another chance."

Brian saw where this was going. "You want me to go back, appear in public and draw him out."

Everyone nodded.

"What about Nicole? I absolutely will not let her be involved in this."

"Neither will I," Harry said sincerely. "She'll stay here with us until your mission is over."

"What kind of protection will I have?"

"You'll have a joint team of FBI and CIA professionals around the clock, eight men to a shift. They'll be with you every moment, but they'll be out of sight. Every evening you'll give us your next day's itinerary minute by minute and you'll have to stick to it. Wherever you are, undercover agents will be with you. A lot of them."

"Anything else?"

Harry looked at the others. No one spoke, so he said, "That's about it until we get to the details."

Brian stood and pushed his chair back. "I have to talk to Nicole."

When he was gone, Marty said, "I think that went as well as it could have."

Shaking his head, Harry replied, "I just hate this. God, you don't know how I'd feel if this went wrong. I just hope we're doing the right thing, coaxing a civilian – my best friend – into doing the government's dirty work."

"It's the only choice we have."

Once Brian was on board, the first item on the list was to let his killer know he was back in town. Brian made a call to the executive producer at Fox and Friends in New York and said he had a major announcement about his upcoming Vesuvius auction.

He was instantly granted a three-minute slot on Thursday's show. Fans always looked forward to Brian's commentary, and the hype began immediately. The world knew that in two days he'd be on with Steve, Ainsley and Brian. He wouldn't be in New York; he'd be at the Fox affiliate in Dallas, airing via a live feed. Security would be increased both in the Big Apple and the Big D since no one knew where Zarif Safwan was.

The next afternoon a private jet landed at Love Field and Brian Sadler was home. A private sedan dropped him at the Ritz-Carlton Residences.

"Good afternoon, Mr. Sadler."

Brian nodded at the lobby doorman and realized he'd never seen him before.

He wondered if this was his first encounter with an undercover officer.

"Are you new? Where's Rafael?"

"Off on vacation, sir. I'll be working days until he returns."

"How'd you know my name?"

"Everyone knows you, Mr. Sadler," the man said with a wink.

———

"He's back."

"I saw that," Amin replied, still seething over his daughter's decision to display her relics. Hadn't she learned

243

anything from him about keeping a low profile? That damned Fox show this morning had plastered Amina's name and picture on televisions around the world. Brian Sadler boasted about displaying her priceless artifacts at his upcoming auction. What made Amin madder was how Brian had teased the audience, using Amina as a pawn to get publicity for himself and his gallery.

"Get rid of him and do it quickly. Don't fail me this time. Don't let him slip through your hands again, Zarif. Do you understand?"

"Clearly."

On Brian's drive from the Fox studios to his gallery, he tried to spot CIA agents following, but he saw nothing out of the ordinary. He knew they were there – at least he hoped they were.

The only picture of Zarif Safwan the agency had was a passport photo taken five years ago. Brian looked at Safwan's swarthy complexion and jet-black hair. If the guy was as good as Harry's team said, Brian would never see him coming. The double-edged sword in all this was that Brian really didn't have to do anything. He just had to go about his daily routine, precisely following the itinerary he and the agency had agreed upon for each day. If anything happened, the men assigned to protect him would take over.

At least that was the plan.

Bijan Rarities' Dallas gallery occupied the ground floor of an office building in Uptown. He pulled into a parking garage next door, saw two attendants at the entrance who'd never been there before, and drove to his reserved space. Two women, deep in animated conversation, fell in behind him as he walked on the sidewalk to the gallery. They kept going when he turned and went inside.

Probably FBI, he thought. Now he was beginning to think that everybody was an agent. That would be nice if it were true.

Brian spent the morning in conference with Cory Spencer, his associate who ran the London gallery and who had filled in while Brian was away. Cory would return to England tomorrow on the afternoon flight.

Adhering to his schedule, at exactly 11:45 Brian walked outside and went down the sidewalk. He frequently ate lunch at his desk, but the CIA wanted him more visible, so he strolled two blocks to a Mexican restaurant with a huge covered patio. He was craving Tex-Mex after those few days on the island. Although he was apprehensive every minute, he found himself really enjoying the routine of a margarita, chips and salsa, and an enchilada plate.

Most of the tables around him were full. He saw couples, foursomes, single men and single women, casual diners, business diners – all kinds. How many of them were agents? Who knew?

After an uneventful lunch, Brian spent the afternoon catching up on a hundred things that had accumulated while he was away. When he heard a tiny ding, he looked at his watch. It was already nearly six and the gallery would be closing soon. He had to be in his car by 6:05 to drive eight blocks back to the condo, and then he was scheduled to have a drink alone in the Lobby Bar of the hotel next door at 6:30.

So far this day was just like any other day in his routine. *There's nothing out of the ordinary,* he thought as he sipped a martini and chatted with the bartender, whom he'd known for several years. The bar was packed as usual and he'd been lucky to get a barstool next to a nicely dressed young couple engaged in conversation. She turned and smiled as he sat down, then went back to talking with her boyfriend.

"I saw you on TV this morning," the bartender said. "I just want to say I'm glad you decided to open a gallery here in Dallas. It's putting this part of town on the map. I'm sure you're aware that a lot of your out-of-town customers stay here. The Ritz is your kind of place, after all. Since I know you, it's interesting to hear these people sit at the bar and talk about you and Bijan. I never say anything; I just listen.

"I hope it's not all bad," Brian quipped. "Don't tell me if it is. I'm not sure my ego could take it!"

"Never. In fact, just the opposite . . ."

Suddenly there was the muffled thump of an explosion somewhere across the lobby, maybe a hundred feet from the bar. White smoke began to rise and people began screaming. A dozen hotel staffers rushed in that direction as Brian watched a man stride purposefully across the lobby toward the bar. At the moment Brian noticed the rifle he carried, the man began firing. The girl seated next to Brian had seen it too. She yelled, "SHOOTER!" and her male friend dropped to the floor on one knee, a pistol in his hand. The girl leaped on Brian, pulling him backwards off his barstool and onto the floor. By now her filmy dress was bunched around her waist and she drew a small pistol from a thigh holster as she shielded Brian with her body. He couldn't see a thing in the terror of the moment, but he would later recall having felt no fear but only thinking how good she smelled.

Two shots rang out. He heard glass breaking and thought it might be the huge mirror behind the bar. He hoped his bartender friend was safe back there.

From somewhere in the bar he heard a man shout, "Take him alive! Take him alive!" Then there were more shots.

Although it was over in seconds, it seemed to him like five minutes before someone in the lobby yelled, "All clear!"

The female agent who'd been on top of him extricated herself and stood up. He sat up and she stuck out her hand. "Special Agent Sara Malloy, FBI. Sorry about that, Mr. Sadler."

Don't mention it.

Brian looked through the bar door into the lobby. It seemed like everyone there was holding pistols. There was a small crowd gathered in the middle, presumably where the attacker was lying. Now that things were over, he began to shake as he realized the enormity of what had just gone down. This was it. The guy had been after him.

"What happened?"

"I think the shooter tossed a smoke grenade across the lobby to draw attention away from him. This was your guy; I'd bet my career on it. He was coming straight to the bar. There are agents everywhere in here, some ours and some CIA. Right now we need to get you out of here. Once the cops arrive, they'll lock this place down tight. We don't need them talking to you."

"I know the back way," he started to say as she shook her head.

"So do we. No talking. Just keep up." Malloy took a position on one side of Brian, and the man who'd posed as her boyfriend was on the other. They walked slowly away, unnoticed amid the chaos. She pulled out her phone and made a call as they wound through service hallways beginning to fill with terrified employees who were also trying to get to the back doors.

By now they were in the midst of a dozen people pushing and shoving. In seconds everyone poured out into a parking garage. The workers ran for the street as a four-door sedan pulled out of a parking slot and stopped next to them. They had undoubtedly been caught on security cameras but snatching Brian out of danger was the only priority for Agent Malloy and her partner. They'd deal with the Dallas police and discussions about jurisdiction later.

"Go! Just get out of here!" she ordered the driver.

In front of the Ritz-Carlton, a Dallas police car pulled under the porte cochere, and two officers rushed into the hotel with their weapons drawn. They saw a dizzying sight – there were at least ten people holding handguns.

"Hands in the air! Everyone drop the weapons! Now!" the officers screamed, hoping against hope these were the good guys and they weren't walking into an ambush.

"CIA!" a man in shorts and a polo shirt shouted as he dropped his weapon. He held his hands up and said, "Hold your fire! I'm going for my badge!" He slowly put his hand in his pocket and drew out a shield and ID. Except for the ones guarding the perpetrator, who didn't move a muscle, everyone else did the same.

The officers relaxed a little and asked the agent, "What's going on?"

"Shots fired! There's the shooter." He pointed to a man lying on the floor facedown with two agents in suits and ties on top of him, their knees on his back and their weapons aimed at his head.

"The perp's gun is there," one of the men said, pointing to an automatic rifle on the ground beside him.

"Kick it over here," the Dallas officer said cautiously, and the man did. These two officers were well trained, but they had never been taught how to deal with something like this. They were so significantly outnumbered they had to take the CIA man at his word and assume everyone else was friendly. They breathed easier as five more police cars with sirens screaming pulled up in front of the hotel and a barrage of officers stormed inside.

"What the hell are all you guys doing here?" one officer asked an FBI agent who'd clipped his badge on his shirt. The cop had never seen so many armed government agents in one place, especially here in his hometown. What was going on? Was some celebrity here? If there was, the Dallas cops should have known about it beforehand. But no one did. And no one answered the cop's question.

The lobby was pure mayhem. Hotel guests still cowered behind furniture, unsure if it was safe to come out.

"Is anyone hurt?" one policeman yelled, glad that everyone seemed okay.

The shoot-out in a Dallas five-star hotel not only headlined the local news that evening, it was the lead for the national broadcasts too. No one had been killed, but the real story here was why it had happened. And that raised questions no one was willing to answer. Reporters interviewed a hotel guest – a businessman from Houston – who had been in the lobby.

"I saw some guy – dark, maybe a Muslim – walk in and toss something into a flowerpot. It started smoking like hell and people began yelling. I think it was a smoke grenade, and I'd bet it was to draw attention away from where he was headed. The guy pulled a rifle from under his coat, and I saw him fire two shots into the bar. I hit the deck at that point, but I heard other gunshots."

"Who did you believe the shooter was after?"

"I don't know. As I said, he fired shots into the bar and was walking toward it. The bar was packed – I'd just come out myself – so I don't know who he might have been trying to kill. The thing that surprised me was that once he started shooting, it looked like everyone in the lobby except me had guns too. I don't know if that's how our open-carry law in Texas is supposed to work, but it was like the gunfight at the OK Corral, do you know what I mean? Everybody had guns and some of them were shooting. They must have been shooting at the guy who started it, but while I was on the floor, I thought it was a terrorist attack and we were all going to die. Somebody just told me no one was hit. That's amazing, with all the lead flying around this place."

Developing news followed that eyewitness report. An FBI spokesperson said the agency believed that the perpetrator had acted alone. Neither his name nor his description were released, and he had been taken to an undisclosed site for questioning. The spokesperson said the men and women in the bar and lobby who had drawn their own weapons were government agents providing undercover protection for an unnamed person identified only as a high-ranking official. Agents refused to release any further information about that person, citing the need for security until the matter could be investigated.

Commentators speculated that the dignitary being protected was perhaps the President of Mexico or a Central American country. ABC pointed out that the sheer number of agents, both FBI and CIA, meant there was someone in the hotel who was very important indeed, and that person might not necessarily be an American citizen. That was all they had, and it wasn't much.

BILL THOMPSON

CHAPTER FIFTY-FOUR

Harry couldn't have been happier at how the first part of Operation Clawback had gone. He had assembled the island team – the Vice President and the Secretary of State – and this time Bob Parker joined them. All four were on the line with Don Case and the chief justice, who were again in Case's secure office. The only one of the group missing was Michelle Isham. No one had heard from her since she left the Senate after yesterday's vote. Harry wasn't going to push her to join them for more updates. She'd been through enough for now.

Nicole and Jennifer Harrison had also been invited to listen in on today's call.

Using prearranged codes, the director told the team that things went extremely well. Ox was safe in the Panda cage and Elvis was at Mama Bear's den. Elvis would give a concert, after which they expected him to be on the horn.

Everyone except the women whooped and yelled in mass jubilation. Having understood nothing, they were confused.

"Tell them," Harry said to his Chief of Staff. Bob took Nicole and Jennifer to the far end of the room, away from the boisterous and noisy celebration. Ox was Brian, he explained, and he was safe in the Panda cage. He was doing fine at a CIA safe house near the zoo in Fort Worth, Texas. Elvis was Zarif Safwan. He was at Mama Bear's den, an isolated hunting lodge in the Great Smoky Mountains, where the CIA was holding him under tight security. The government was about to release his identity to the media. His wealthy boss would be very, very unhappy that his security chief was in the CIA's hands. Once that happened, Don Case anticipated that Zarif would begin to "get on the horn" – to start talking. He might prefer to cooperate than to be a dead man when Amin Hassan found him.

As Nicole broke down in tears, Jennifer held her hands and hugged her tightly. For Nicole, the floodgates had finally opened. All the tension of the past few days, all the secrecy and fear, were finally coming to an end. She knew it wasn't finished, but the worst part – the part involving Brian – was over. He was safe at last.

———

Zarif Safwan sat in front of a crackling fire in the great room of the cabin nestled on the side of a mountain in Swain County, North Carolina. Four Suburbans were in the garage, and a helicopter sat on a nearby landing pad just in case anyone needed a quick exit.

Eleven CIA agents were guarding Safwan; the agency knew his boss would spare no expense to silence him. The agents had also been told that ultrahigh security measures had been implemented. All communications would come directly from Director Case. Code words would be used at the start of each message, indicating that no one was under duress. The agents didn't know who Safwan was, but given the security associated with his capture and detention, they would ensure the director's orders were followed.

Zarif spent the night in a comfortable but very secure room with no windows. Two agents sat in chairs five feet from his bed all night long, weapons at the ready. It took him a while to fall asleep with people watching him, but it finally happened. The next morning they took him back to the great room, offered him coffee and sat him down in front of a television so he could watch himself on the news.

The agency had given the networks nothing but Zarif's name, and Case was confident they would easily flesh out a story. The Dallas attack was so bizarre that people immediately thought of terrorists. Now there was a link to Syria – Zarif himself – and terrorism became even more of a possibility. Connecting the dots on this news release was as simple as googling his name and learning something extraordinary – his boss was a very well-known man. In the last few days the name of Hassan Group had been on the news frequently. It was about to take over a major company headquartered in Dallas, Texas, the city where the hotel shootings occurred.

Don Case called the prisoner. "You know Hassan will kill you. That's why I've had you taken to a place where no one can find you. Do you understand that? We brought you here for your own safety. If we put you in a jail cell anywhere in America, you're a dead man. Amin Hassan can make it happen, and you know that better than anyone. We'll help you if you'll help us."

He knew they were right, and he made his decision. He held all the cards, but they had no idea what he knew. He could deliver far more than they could have imagined.

Zarif hadn't uttered one word since they captured him. Now he opened his mouth and said, "Let's make a deal."

———

At nine that evening, Michelle Isham's daughter in Pennsylvania called the US Capitol Police. She hadn't heard from her mother since she voted for the Exxon bill yesterday. That was unlike her – the two of them were close and they chatted every evening. Last night the calls went to voicemail. The legislator hadn't shown up for work today, and her daughter's calls to the house still went unanswered.

Officers went to Senator Isham's Georgetown townhouse. The place was dark and no one responded to their bangs on the door. Her door had a keypad lock and her daughter had given police the code and authority to enter. They found the Senate Majority Leader dead in her bed with an empty medicine bottle in her hand.

Harry and his advisors took the news very hard. They had misread her. Her apparent strength, her outward signs of toughness, masked the depression for which she had secretly sought treatment over the years. They prayed together for her daughter and for the life of a woman who had stepped up to fight for America.

BILL THOMPSON

CHAPTER FIFTY-FIVE

The proceeds from Zayed al-Fulan's fifty-billion-dollar loan were sitting in Hassan Group's investment account at a major New York bank. Amin had arranged loans for thirty billion more. He'd had to mortgage everything the group owned, but it was all worth it. He had a war chest and he was ready to go.

When the market opened the morning after President Parkes signed the Exxon-Hassan bill, Amin's buy orders were the single thing everyone was talking about. On the floor of the Stock Exchange brokers yelled, screamed and pushed to buy billions of dollars of stock. Exxon opened at $82, but within minutes it was at $95, then $105. The buy orders stopped suddenly as the sellers in the market learned that Hassan had reached his limit. He wasn't paying more than $105, at least for now.

Analysts at Amin's office in Dubai kept a close eye on eleven brokerage firms worldwide that were placing Hassan's buy orders. There were small variances here and there, up and down, among the markets in London, Hong Kong, New York and Dubai, and the traders took advantage of them to allow Hassan to buy as much stock as possible at the lowest price.

Hassan Group now owned ten percent of Exxon and had spent almost fifty billion dollars. When the buy orders stopped, the price fell back a little, sitting now at just over a hundred dollars a share. Amin gave instructions and his men began buying again. He got the last five percent he wanted at an average price of $124 – around twenty-five billion dollars. He'd invested all of his partner's funds and all but five billion of his personal bank loans, and he had accumulated fifteen percent of Exxon's stock.

With his new ally Valgardo Capital, Amin controlled thirty percent of the company. The next largest shareholder owned less than two percent. Hassan now had effective control; he couldn't be outvoted unless a huge block of random shareholders banded together. In the world of corporate high finance, that simply never happened.

Amin had sequestered himself in his office all morning. Spending billions of dollars required absolute concentration, instant interaction with brokers worldwide, quick-response buy and sell offers and no distractions. He had made it clear there would be no phone calls, no visitors and no communication except with the trading desks at Hassan and the brokers executing his trades.

He had just bought the last shares when the door to his office opened.

"Get out!" he yelled to whoever was behind him without turning from his computer screen. He was furious that someone had disobeyed his explicit instructions.

"I beg your pardon?" Amin's business partner Zayed al-Fulan stood in the doorway. "You're a hard man to contact," he said sharply.

"Come in. I'm a little busy right now," Amin said in an attempt to appear minimally cordial. No one – not even Zayed himself – had the right to violate Amin's instructions. He was buying control of Exxon, and his partner should have respected that.

"We need to talk," al-Fulan said as he sat across the desk from Amin.

"Haven't you heard?" he shot back sarcastically. "I'm in the middle of something here. There isn't time –"

"I want my money back."

Amin laughed nervously. *What? What was he talking about?*

"That's not possible. Your money's invested, Zayed. You and I are the owners of fifteen percent of Exxon."

"Sell the shares. I'll sit here while you do it."

"Perhaps we should talk . . ."

"I couldn't agree more. Have you listened to the news this morning, or have you had your head buried in the sand, buying stock with *my* money?"

Amin's perplexed look gave him away. He had no idea what his partner was talking about.

The man continued. "Where is Zarif Safwan?"

"He's in Texas. He's doing some work for me . . ."

Zayed slammed his fist on Amin's desk so hard that his laptop crashed to the floor.

"Did you hear the news yesterday about the shooting at that hotel in Dallas? Do you remember they called it something about national security? The police wouldn't reveal why it happened or who did it."

Suddenly Amin was nervous. He had told his man to find Brian Sadler, but the news story from Dallas hadn't mentioned Zarif's name. In the exhilaration of preparing to spend billions of dollars, he hadn't given the story much thought, except that it didn't seem to be related to Amin's mission.

"A shooting in Dallas? It had nothing to do with me. Why are you bringing that up? And why are you so upset? What have I done except what we agreed? We now own control of the largest oil company in the world. Doesn't that excite you?" He forced a smile.

"You fool! You've locked yourself in your office and ignored the world around you. Are you ready for the news? Your man was the shooter at that Dallas hotel. He's being held by the CIA in a secret location somewhere in America. While you were sitting here spending my money – *my* fifty billion dollars – the national newscasts were broadcasting *your* picture around the world. Amin Hassan – the owner of Hassan Group – just got approval from President Parkes to buy Exxon. Zarif's picture is there too. Hassan Group's security chief – a trusted high-level individual in Hassan Group – tried to kill someone – someone yet unidentified but obviously someone important – in that hotel in Dallas yesterday."

Amin was genuinely scared now. This could be bad – really bad. He wanted to get this man out of here so he could think.

"Zayed, they can't possibly tie you . . ."

His backer spoke calmly and evenly. "You think not? My picture was on the news too. You sent your man to commit murder, to kill someone on American soil, and suddenly I'm involved. Everyone in the entire world knows

I'm your business partner. What idiocy! What were you thinking? The Exxon deal is over. Sell the stock and return my money. Now."

His mind was racing. How could he sell the stock literally hours after he'd bought it? The price would drastically plummet if he dumped the stock. He'd lose millions, billions maybe – money he didn't have and couldn't repay. He would lose everything he'd built during his entire life. If he did what his partner was demanding, Hassan Group would be finished. It would be bankrupt; its creditors would seize what they could and dump everything else, leaving him with nothing. Amin and his company were mortgaged to the hilt, and if that happened, the world would think he wasn't as smart or as rich as he had pretended to be. He'd look like a fool to every business magnate in the world, and he couldn't allow that to happen.

"You loaned me the money. You have no legal right to demand it back like this. And you know what would happen if I do what you ask. You saw how the price went up while I was buying. The same thing would happen in reverse when I dump six hundred million shares on the market. The price will collapse and you'll lose billions."

"Why would you think that?" Zayed responded. "I loaned you fifty billion dollars on a demand note. I have the right to call the loan at any time and that's exactly what I'm doing. It makes no difference what you did with the money I loaned you, but now that you're dragging me into the spotlight, I want out. Maybe you don't have to sell the stock, Amin. Maybe you can repay me from other assets." He smiled cruelly. "But you can't, can you? You borrowed every penny you could to buy more shares, didn't you?"

He stood. "Keep this in mind. I'm your partner and I know the banks from whom you borrowed your money. It would take me just minutes to call each one and explain that I'm demanding repayment of my fifty billion dollars. They'd be in a panic – they'd call your loans before I was off the phone.

"Twenty-four hours. Wire my funds back by noon tomorrow or I'm taking you and your little empire down."

"Don't threaten me, Zayed. If you carry out this threat, you'll never get your money back. My banks would dump the stock and come out whole, but you wouldn't."

"I have plenty more where that fifty billion came from," he replied with that same twisted smile. "But you don't. See you tomorrow."

Amin Hassan's shining moment – the greatest day in his business career – had ended as quickly as it began. He had to come up with a plan, and the one man he depended on most to get him out of trouble was in the hands of the CIA.

BILL THOMPSON

CHAPTER FIFTY-SIX

The minute Amin's wealthy partner left, his executive assistant buzzed him.

"Sir, Amina's called several times. She seems very upset and said it's urgent."

Of course she was calling. She'd obviously heard the news too.

She's the one that got me into all this mess.

"What do you want, Amina?"

"Father! Tell me what I'm hearing isn't true!"

"What, that I now control the largest oil conglomerate on earth? Yes, it's true, my dear."

"I'm talking about Zarif! Did you send him to Dallas to kill Brian?"

"Calm down! There's much about me that you don't know and that you'll never know. I've let you go too far, too fast. Your friend 'Brian,' as you affectionately refer to him, is not a friend at all. He planted listening devices in the receiving room. Brian got a warning from Zarif in Berkeley Square, but he wouldn't stay away. He disappeared for a time, but he came back. I sent Zarif to fix a problem *you* created, but he made a mistake. Because of your carelessness, my dear, I now have to repair this situation myself."

"How much does he know about you, Father? Can he hurt you?"

Amin shouted, "You stupid, silly girl! You have no idea who's listening to your calls. You didn't even know your new friend bugged your office, but Zarif did. Stop talking about this now! Go back to your lunches and your afternoon teas and I'll handle the real work. No, actually I want you to come here. Book the next available flight and come to me. Fly coach if you have to. It might actually do you good. We have a lot to talk about, my dear."

The last sentence was spoken so menacingly it made Amina shiver.

It also made the computer in the lodge up in the Great Smoky Mountains ding. Zarif's information-gathering systems were still in place. They brought their prisoner out of his room and asked him to check his computer. Five minutes later they listened to the call between enraged father and terrified daughter.

The lead agent called his boss at the CIA. Case in turn called Harry, and they agreed they had to extract Amina before she could go to Dubai. It was likely they'd never see her again otherwise.

A man walked into the bar of the Connaught Hotel, where Amina Hassan was engaged in her Friday afternoon ritual. Her second martini sat in front of her and she looked distraught, he observed as he took the stool next to hers. She glanced at him for a moment; there were plenty of empty seats, but he'd chosen that one. Men did this often, hoping for conversation or something extra, but it never worked. She turned away as the bartender took his order for a club soda.

"You're in grave danger," the person next to her whispered. "Don't look at me, Miss Hassan. Look at what's in my hand." Just below the bar he showed her his CIA ID and a badge.

"What do you want? You're scaring me. All I have to do is shout. The bartender's my friend."

"So am I. Please listen for a moment. The agency heard everything you and your father said during the call an hour ago. We have Zarif Safwan in a safe place, and he has damning information about your father's criminal operations. My boss believes you need protection immediately. Even though Safwan's not here, your father may have other people following you."

This was a risky mission; the CIA had no jurisdiction in situations involving citizens of another country, but there was no time.

She knew everything this man had said was true, just like the other things she knew in her heart. Her father was a ruthless man, cruelly indifferent to those who weren't important to him, and she had always feared him. She was certain he had ordered men killed, but she had chosen to ignore it. So far she hadn't followed Amin's order to book a flight; instead she came directly here from the office to have a drink and think about things. She honestly was petrified at the thought of going to Dubai. There was no telling what this man – her own father – might do to pay her back. He had to be getting desperate. His name had been all over the news, and now he was tied to the shooting in Dallas.

She whispered, "I'm afraid."

"We'll protect you. Would you allow me to call the CIA director? He wants to explain what we're offering."

The bartender really was her friend. He watched the stranger suddenly engaging in conversation with Amina and saw her look of fear, so he stopped by and said lightly, "Everything okay, Miss Hassan?"

"Everything's fine. This is a friend of a friend I hadn't thought about in years."

The agent handed his phone to her and she listened. Five minutes later she paid the tab, decided to trust these people and walked out of her father's life forever.

BILL THOMPSON

CHAPTER FIFTY-SEVEN

The agents interrogating Zarif knew all about his mission in Dallas. Amina's father, enraged about the bugs in her office and concerned that his daughter was getting too close to Brian and Nicole, ordered his trusted lieutenant to eliminate him. Zarif intended to create a diversion with the smoke bomb in the lobby. Then he'd go into the bar where Brian was sitting, kill him and disappear in the confusion.

When he walked in and tossed the grenade, he was more surprised than anyone to see a dozen pistols suddenly aimed in his direction. He got off two wild shots before what appeared to be tourists, business people and employees took him to the floor. Two of them fired back, but he wasn't hit.

Zarif had far more to offer the United States government than the discussion about Brian Sadler. He had everything on Amin Hassan and he negotiated for hours with Don Case. He traded his cooperation for Case's promise to ask for leniency. Zarif knew he'd be in prison for years, but it seemed logical to finally get something for the material he'd always kept as his final bargaining tool. And at least he wouldn't die for what he'd done.

All afternoon he answered questions and accessed an unbelievable cache of documents on a laptop they had provided. Case could see the computer screen and hear the conversation via remote access and a speakerphone. There were others watching and listening too – ones only Case knew about. A group of dead people – Harry and his team – was elated by what Zarif had. This would make Operation Clawback happen much faster than they'd thought. As they listened, each was beginning to realize he would be going home soon.

In the years he'd worked for Amin Hassan, Safwan had created his own life insurance policy. As head of security, he knew everything about Hassan Group's infrastructure. He knew all the passwords and all the secrets. From his office in London Zarif could access everything in the Dubai headquarters; he spent hours every day archiving things that might be useful in the future. Before the cloud, he stored things – pictures, emails, documents and the like – on USB flash drives and he recorded hundreds of phone calls. When cloud storage became available, everything was much easier, and now he had a vast collection of his employer's secrets.

Safwan linked Hassan to the Falcons of Islam. He demonstrated that Amin deposited fifty million dollars in the jihadist leader's account immediately following the disappearance of the planes. Cham Parkes's ten-million-dollar payment was there too. He followed the trail from the Falcons to the mosque in suburban DC. He showed them pictures of Ali and Mo, the two operatives who had recruited Joe Kaya, and gave them the conversations that tied Kaya to Master Sergeant Jeremy Lail in the plot. Amin Hassan had kept detailed records of everything. Blackmail was part of Amin's arsenal, and secrets were the catalyst for blackmail.

They didn't spend a lot of time on any one subject because the information was simply too vast. They got enough here and there to ensure they had what they needed to proceed with Operation Clawback. For every question they asked, their prisoner had a response that was perfect. For instance, there had been Case's question about what specific information might tie Amin Hassan to President Parkes.

Zarif laughed boisterously. "Where do I begin?" He clicked until he located a folder that held every communication between Parkes and Hassan, arranged by month and year. It was all there.

Next he talked about Lou Breaux. Amin had padded the Vice President's pockets too. He was a Louisiana senator, and there was a lot of oil in Louisiana. Hassan Group had bought up pipelines, offshore drilling companies and production rights thanks to insider information from a friendly source in Congress, a man who'd profited handsomely in return. Thanks to Amin Hassan, Lou Breaux also had offshore bank accounts, and Zarif knew where they were.

They had them both! This damning information was so hot that the director once again admonished the agents around Zarif about the confidentiality of what they were hearing. Secrecy was absolutely essential now. If this got out too soon, everything could be compromised.

It was time for Zarif to have some rest. He had handed the CIA everything it needed to implement the next phase. Case spoke privately with Harry and got approval for Operation Clawback to continue. It would take only one phone call to open the floodgates, and Case was really excited to be at this point. He picked up the phone.

It was four p.m. in Washington, one in Los Angeles. It was show time in Hollywood.

BILL THOMPSON

CHAPTER FIFTY-EIGHT

California had more Democratic delegates than any other state, and its primary was one of the last. That state's election was coming up the first week in June – ten days from now – only eleven weeks before the Democratic convention.

It was becoming more and more likely President Chambliss T. Parkes would be the nominee. He was only a few delegates short of the count he needed, and California's five hundred and forty-eight would put him way over the top. His opponent had suffered six defeats in a row, and he was now dismantling his campaign staff. Two hundred people had been fired, and the remaining ones were in California, desperately seeking to keep Parkes from winning the state and the nomination.

Hollywood had always been a great place for Democratic candidates. The majority of people in the entertainment industry were liberal, left-leaning, politically active individuals who had lots of money and were willing to share it with candidates they liked.

Parkes and his Vice President first learned about Zarif Safwan's detainment on the noon news. They were in the five-room bungalow Cham's campaign had rented at the exclusive Beverly Hills Hotel. Four Hollywood producers who donated a million dollars each to Cham's PAC were invited for lunch with the President. Cham and his guests were sipping mimosas by a private pool when Lou Breaux beckoned him inside, saying, "You're gonna want to see this."

He watched Amin's face on the screen and listened to the newscast. Zarif Safwan had been arrested and detained by the CIA in connection with yesterday's shooting in Dallas. The news was disturbing, to say the least.

The newscaster said, "Zarif Safwan is chief of security for Hassan Group, a company that has been in the news the last few days. Less than twenty-four hours ago the

Dubai-based oil conglomerate was given authority to purchase controlling interest in ExxonMobil, the world's largest oil company, by virtue of a bill signed into law by President Chambliss Parkes. Sources at the Stock Exchange tell us Hassan has purchased over seventy billion dollars of Exxon stock this morning. At noon Exxon's shares were up fifty percent from the opening bell just three hours ago."

Another picture now appeared next to Amin's. "Hassan's financial partner is Zayed al-Fulan. A billionaire like Hassan, al-Fulan is believed to be the wealthiest person in the United Arab Emirates. We attempted to contact both men for comments on this story but were unsuccessful."

The segment ended with a question about why Safwan had been in Dallas and who he was targeting. The fact that the CIA was involved raised more questions, an analyst said. Safwan was in the CIA's custody – that indicated there was a national security or terrorist angle to the events in Dallas. So far there was no statement from the agency.

Parkes glanced at three Secret Service agents sitting on a couch across the room and said, "Get out." They walked to the patio and kept an eye on Parkes through large windows.

"Goddammit," Parkes muttered through clenched teeth, demonstrating uncharacteristic restraint. He didn't want to alarm his guests. "What the hell's that crazy A-rab thinking, Lou? I set up everything so that Amin's takeover of Exxon would work perfectly. Everything he needed was in place, and everybody performed just like I told them to. Even that damned Michelle Isham came to her senses and kept me from having to work even harder behind the scenes. I did all that, just like I promised I would, and right in the middle of the best-orchestrated plan in history, he sends some gunman to do a contract killing in Dallas. What the hell, Lou? What the hell was he thinking?"

"This isn't going to help you," the Vice President replied without answering the question. "This is really bad, Cham. You just gave this guy carte blanche to buy Exxon, and this morning he did it. Now this attempted murder's tied to him."

"Maybe this Safwan guy was acting on his own. Maybe this has nothing to do with Amin."

Breaux shook his head. "You gotta be realistic. Number one, it *does* have something to do with Amin. You know that and everybody else knows that. Number two, even if it didn't, there's a shitload of negative publicity that's happening just as your buddy's buying the biggest oil company in the world. You gave him the keys and he drove the car off the cliff."

Cham didn't want to hear Lou's comments anymore. "Why don't you get off my ass? I picked you to be Vice President. Are you already planning how you'll take my place at the convention? You wanna be President, Lou? You can knock that shit off, buddy, because it ain't gonna happen. I go down, you go down too."

Alarmed at the President's anger, Breaux backpedaled. "Come on. You know better than that. I'm just saying you better start thinking about damage control. This is not just going away. The CIA has that guy somewhere –"

Cham interrupted him, suddenly knowing how he was going to deal with this. "Go out there and eat lunch with those guys," he said. "Tell them the truth if you want. They'll know soon enough anyway. Tell them I'm on a call with the CIA about what happened in Dallas."

There was a secure phone line in the bedroom. Within minutes he had Don Case on the phone. He didn't like Case and he knew the feeling was mutual. He was one of Harry Harrison's appointments, and Cham made a mental note to fire Case as soon as he got back to Washington.

"How can I help you, Mr. President?"

"Where's Zarif Safwan?"

Case had to stall for an hour. Everything would be over soon, but for right now he wished he'd simply not taken Parkes's call. It wouldn't have worked, he knew. One way or another the President would have caught up with him, so he'd better deal with this now.

"He's in a secret location, sir. Our agents are interrogating him. I assure you he's secure."

"I don't give a rat's ass how secure he is. Where is he? That's what I asked you."

"All I can say is that he's in a secure location."

Cham was just about to explode. His face was beet-red as he stood by the bed, holding the receiver. He literally screamed into the phone.

"Listen to me, you son of a bitch! I want to know where he is. Right now. After that go out and find some boxes. You can pack your stuff because you're out of a job when I get home, but for now you *will* tell me where he is."

Case hadn't intended to tell him anything, but he had to stall just a little longer. Giving him a bone would get the President off his back, at least until Parkes realized he'd been sent on a wild-goose chase. Hopefully that wouldn't happen.

"Safwan's in a safe house in Minnesota, a few miles from the Canadian border."

"A.J. will call you in five minutes. I want the exact location and directions on how to get there."

"Are you planning to go see him, Mr. President?"

Don't you worry what I'm planning, you impertinent jerk.

"Yes, Don," he said in a condescending tone. "Of course I am. I'm planning a little trip to Minnesota. Just give Minter the damned information and pack your stuff. You'll never work inside the Beltway again. I guaran-damn-tee it."

He called A.J. and gave him instructions. Cham was coming up with a plan. It would take some effort, but it would work. What he needed was for Safwan to admit he was acting solo. Hassan had nothing to do with this. That was what the shooter would say.

The last thing I want right now is to go outside and eat lunch with some big shots who want to kiss the President's ass, he thought to himself as he put on a big smile and returned to the patio.

"My apologies, gentlemen. The President's job never seems to slow down!"

When the Chief of Staff called, Don Case gave him a complete list of directions to get to a place that didn't exist. Now Minter waited by the phone for Parkes to tell him what to do next.

Around 1:30 the luncheon was winding down. Puffing on a cigar, Cham thanked the moguls for their support. Lou stood by his side, his mind on the news report. This could work out very well for him, he thought.

Half an hour earlier, while the men were having lunch, the CIA director had placed a call to his counterpart at the FBI. That man had been on standby, waiting for the signal.

"All green. All green. Proceed with the mission." Operation Clawback was about to end.

Cham and Lou accompanied their guests to the front door and everyone shook hands. As one of the Secret Service agents opened it, they saw four men in the doorway, wearing flak jackets and holding automatic rifles in one hand, federal badges in the other. The bodyguards started for their guns but paused when they realized everyone was on the same side.

"FBI! Stand back! You're under arrest!"

The President's initial thought was that one of his guests was in serious trouble. *This is going to be embarrassing for somebody. Damn stupid Hollywood guys.*

He waved the FBI men back and said, "Okay, boys. There's no need for so much fanfare. Why all the guns? Who's under arrest?"

The director of the FBI stepped in front of the agents. Cham was surprised. What was he doing here?

With a smile, the director replied, "You are, Mr. President. President Parkes and Vice President Breaux, you are under arrest for treason against the United States. I'm going to read you your rights now."

"You're going to regret this, you bastard," Parkes said, chomping his cigar almost in half. "You have no idea what a pile of shit you're in."

"On the contrary, sir," the FBI director replied exuberantly. "This is the best day of my life."

CHAPTER FIFTY-NINE

The decision to bring the team home had been made yesterday afternoon once the interrogation of Zarif Safwan was finished for the day. It was now becoming almost certain that President Parkes would learn about their plans. Case had engaged dozens of his agents for tasks that were directly related to Operation Clawback. If the President became aware of unusual activities or if he suddenly chose to remove Don as director, the entire plan would collapse. From here on out, everything had to happen at warp speed or it could all fall apart.

Conveniently, Parkes and Breaux had been together in Los Angeles. Don Case brought the FBI director, another holdover from Harry's administration, in on the secret.

"I'm in southern California too!" he had responded enthusiastically. The FBI chief was on vacation at his daughter's home in Malibu. "I'm handling this one myself!"

Don had expected his counterpart to dispatch agents from the LA Bureau to make the arrest, but he understood exactly why the director wanted to be present. Don wished he could be there too. After everything Harry Harrison and the others had gone through, Case would have enjoyed watching these despicable men hauled away in handcuffs.

———

Last night's double-whammy of negative news caused wild swings in the Asian financial markets. Around seven Eastern time the Dallas attacker Zarif Safwan had been positively linked to Amin Hassan who, thanks to President Parkes's support, owned control of Exxon.

An hour later Americans heard the shocking news that the President and Vice President were under arrest for treason. That story was still unfolding, but volatile news always meant a lower stock market. The Asian and European exchanges swung wildly, but there wasn't the severe negativity that happened when the planes disappeared. This was a crisis that could be dealt with. The markets closed down less than five percent, which allowed investors to be tentatively optimistic about the New York's opening at 9:30.

Once the news about Parkes and Breaux had broken last night, Harry Harrison called Vincent Valgardo and asked him to sit tight on his block of Exxon stock. Reminding Valgardo of the confidentiality document he'd signed, Harry disclosed that they would all be returning tomorrow. The world would learn he wasn't dead after all. That news would be released before the market's opening; Harry's advisors were optimistic it would counteract the negativity.

Harry explained what was going to happen. CIA Director Case had contacted the ruler of Dubai, who agreed to take Amin Hassan into custody on charges of stock manipulation. Extradition procedures would begin immediately to bring him to the States to stand trial on a dozen charges.

The Treasury Department would liquidate the Exxon stock Amin had purchased, requiring sellers to return the funds they'd received from Hassan and receive back the shares they'd sold. Those proceeds – Hassan's money – would immediately be seized by the US government to keep it out of Amin's hands. The government would guarantee that anyone who had sold stock to Hassan would not suffer a loss when they returned the shares. Whatever profit they had made by selling to Hassan Group, they could keep, courtesy of the US government.

The plan was bold, it solved the problem of a criminal enterprise owning a huge oil company, and it could be accomplished by a simple executive order if Harry were returned to the presidency. Valgardo agreed to keep his block intact, so long as he had the same guarantee against loss in case everything went to hell at the Stock Exchange tomorrow morning.

———

At 7:35 a.m. local time, a Boeing 737 touched down at Homestead Air Reserve Base in south Florida. The pilot, a colonel in the United States Air Force, had been sent on a secret mission to a remote Caribbean island to pick up a group of people. Although he'd been given no details, the pilot was accustomed to ferrying high-level government officials, but there was no hiding his amazement when he saw the missing President, Vice President and Secretary of State come on board. There were tears in his eyes as he shook hands with his passengers. He told everyone how important this moment was for America and how proud he was to be a part of history.

The Gulfstream would remain hidden on the island. There was plenty of time to bring it home once Operation Clawback was finished.

The only thing air traffic control and base officials were told about the incoming flight was that the jet was on a classified mission for the government. It was directed to a large empty hangar that had been outfitted with a desk and a secure phone. Everyone milled about killing time as Harry and Marty discussed final logistics with Don Case. Case called Defense Secretary Vernon and informed him that the team was alive and returning from Homestead to Washington momentarily. Vernon wasn't part of the team – all this was news to him, and he was thrilled to learn his colleagues were alive.

The Vice President walked across the hangar to the group and asked everyone to board in preparation for departure shortly.

Harry had one more person to contact. He couldn't place the call himself – not just yet. This would be his last call before the world learned the astounding truth about the disappearances.

With Harry on the line, the CIA director called Chris Wallace at Fox News. When Case told the operator it was urgent, the renowned newscaster was on the line in seconds.

"What's up, Don?"

"Are you sitting down? I have someone on the line who wants to talk to you."

CHAPTER SIXTY

Chris Wallace was a commentator for whom Harry had tremendous respect. He left nothing out – he gave Chris an exclusive interview, telling the entire story. He heard how the Air Force sergeant at Andrews allowed the planes to be sabotaged. He learned that the two Supreme Court justices had been murdered at the instructions of Amin Hassan. And he learned that Harry Harrison was on his way back to Washington to reclaim the presidency.

It was only 8:15 Eastern time. The Stock Exchange wouldn't open for over an hour, and Harry urged the newscaster to get this story on the air quickly. Wallace assured him that would not be a problem. An exclusive like this was a once-in-a-lifetime opportunity. It would take a few minutes to vet the situation; if this were a hoax Fox would be in a colossal mess. Wallace's producer called his contact at the CIA and was quickly transferred to the director, who confirmed everything was true. Harry Harrison was really alive and returning to DC.

All finished, Harry strode across the hangar with a huge grin on his face. He climbed the mobile staircase, stood at the front of the cabin where all his friends were seated, and said, "Let's go home!"

No one argued with that order.

As the 737 rose into the air, four fighter jets pulled alongside to escort them to Andrews. They were on hand courtesy of the Defense Secretary. Vernon was a strong, tough man with years of combat service under his belt, but he had wept profusely when he learned everyone was coming back. It was a glorious day.

This morning most Americans were still in shock from last night's news. The brand-new President and Vice President were in custody. Would a Speaker of the House become President once again? This was a wild, crazy and unsettling time, reporters reflected. Polls indicated that fear was once again sweeping the nation, only weeks after the tragic disappearance of President Harrison and the others.

Millions of people were eating breakfast or getting the kids ready for school or driving to work when yet one more breaking news announcement came.

What next? People would later recall the shivers of fear – the goose bumps – as they turned up the volume and steeled themselves to hear what had happened now in a country that only a month ago had been as calm and stable as any on earth.

PRESIDENT HARRISON AND VP TAYLOR ARE ALIVE AND RETURNING TO DC TODAY.

That was the banner that ran along the bottom of the screen as Chris Wallace reported the incredible story. He announced that he had spoken to President Harrison just moments ago. He and all the people on both aircraft would be arriving in Washington this morning.

At Harry's suggestion, Wallace had contacted the chief justice for a comment. The justice said he was confident Harrison and Taylor would be reinstated to their offices. Parkes and Breaux still held their positions, under the presumption of innocence until being proven guilty. There was neither precedence nor need for the Speaker of the House to become President, the chief justice opined. Parkes and Breaux would possibly resign voluntarily, upon which the justice would recommend Harrison and Taylor assume the positions since neither had been officially declared dead. If the jailed leaders did not resign, the chief justice would recommend temporarily reinstating Harrison and Taylor pending the outcome of their trials for treason.

Yes, the chief justice revealed, he had been involved in the mission from the beginning. So had Don Case, director of the CIA, and the late Senate Majority Leader Michelle Isham.

As Wallace reported all this news, it was impossible to miss the broad smile on his face and the positive tone in his voice. At last the media could give the public something upbeat – something to be happy about.

Finally it was time for the New York Stock Exchange to open. As expected, stocks opened lower; the Dow Jones Industrials fell around a hundred points in the first few minutes as sell orders that had been entered before the market's opening were automatically executed. Trading in ExxonMobil was halted for the day. That move was orchestrated between Don Case and the Secretary of the Treasury in the interest of maintaining an orderly market. By the time Exxon traded again, Harry Harrison would have announced the government's plan to sell Hassan Group's block.

The market today was reacting vastly differently than that day when the planes went missing. Today there were plenty of buyers. Institutional investors looking for bargains began snapping up stocks as the prices fell and the market shot upwards. It would end the day up over nine hundred points, buoyed by the news that twenty-five missing people were alive and well.

It was nearly eight in the evening in Dubai. Amin sat in his darkened office, watching television. He hadn't answered any of his wealthy partner's calls today, and Zayed's noon deadline to sell the stock had long since passed. He couldn't have sold it anyway; Exxon stock was halted on the New York exchange. And what did it matter? Suddenly that had become the least of his problems. This had been the worst day of his entire life. One crisis after another piled on Amin as the media announced each new astounding revelation.

The first news flash had been about Amina. She was shown at Heathrow airport in London this morning, leaving for New York in the protective custody of two CIA agents. Amin's daughter was going to cooperate with American authorities in their investigation of Hassan Group. Upon their arrival at JFK, reporters had mobbed her, but the agents whisked her away before they could push her for answers.

His own daughter, the ungrateful wretch. He had given and given and now she was going to help them attack her own flesh and blood? How could it have come to this?

Next had been today's email from the enforcement division of the Securities and Exchange Commission. It referenced the sweeping allegations of wrongdoing by Zarif

Safwan against Hassan Group and Amin personally. It demanded the divestiture of his holdings in ExxonMobil within five days and stated that a criminal investigation was commencing.

According to the news, Cham Parkes and Louis Breaux were in custody. Amin would have been elated if he hadn't been shown on TV as a coconspirator. The President was a detestable individual. Amin had hated every minute of kowtowing to the crude boor, but now it was over. All of this was over, once and for all.

As if that all wasn't enough, there had been the news about President Harrison and the others. All that work – all that money he'd spent – had been for nothing. Tariq the Hawk, the young smartass who thought he had pulled off the greatest terror plot in history, had ended up being nothing but a pawn in the US government's clever plan to ensnare Parkes.

He leaned back in his office chair and put his feet on the desk, reflecting on the powerful company he had singlehandedly created. *No matter how much you give people,* he thought wistfully, *they will stab you in the back if it benefits them. Trust no one. Not even your child.*

The night officer on duty in the lobby forty floors below buzzed him.

"What is it?" Amin asked, clicking to the video feed from the man's desk in the expansive public area. He saw a dozen uniformed men standing there.

"The police are here, sir. A lot of them. They're demanding I send them up. I . . . I want to be sure it's all right."

The guard's voice was shaky. He wasn't sure what to do. It wasn't his fault, Amin thought. The kid was merely doing his job, and he was doing it a hell of a lot better than Zarif Safwan had done.

"Of course. Send them up."

He had almost no time left. He reached into the lower left drawer of his desk, took out his father's old hunting pistol and held it lovingly in his hands. He'd spent some of his best times as a child in the company of his father. Maybe he'd see him in a few minutes and they could reminisce about those days.

He put the gun to his temple. Just as the officers rushed into his office, he pulled the trigger.

BILL THOMPSON

CHAPTER SIXTY-ONE

Everyone was glued to the TV screens on the 737 as Chris Wallace told the world that Harry and the team were on the way home. There were cheers, tears, champagne and a Bloody Mary or two on the plane. There were slaps on the back and an impromptu sing-along led by the President with accompaniment by one of the flight attendants who'd brought her guitar along. It was a festive mood and everyone was excited in his own way.

All the phones were returned, fully charged and ready to go. For the first time in weeks everyone had communication again. Most spent the rest of the flight reconnecting with friends and loved ones.

When the plane landed at Andrews Field, Jennifer looked out the window and began to cry. "Look, Harry. Look what they're doing."

As the plane pulled off the active runway, there were fire trucks lined up along the taxiway, spraying columns of water into the air as a tribute to the return of a beloved man once thought lost.

"Good thing Cham's in jail," Harry quipped. "He'd kick the ass of whoever thought that up!"

Before the door opened, Harry made a few heartfelt comments about how much he appreciated the contributions of this special group. Everyone hugged everyone else. At this moment they weren't cabin stewards or pilots or United States Presidents – they were people who had been through an incredible ordeal together and survived.

When the former President and his family descended the stairway, there was a lot of clapping. A crowd of reporters and cameramen were in a roped-off area. They were filming and broadcasting, but they were applauding too. It was a rare sight. Flanked by his Secret Service agents, Harry walked over and shook their hands.

"It's good to be back," was the only statement he made.

There was a tearful reunion between Secretary of State Clancy and his forty-year-old daughter, who until this morning had thought she would never see him again. He had called her from Homestead and arranged for her to be brought here from her home in Philadelphia. She stood at the bottom of the staircase right next to another person waiting for his loved one – Brian Sadler.

Brian and Nicole hugged the Harrisons one last time before they went to the lounge area. The same government jet that had brought Brian here this morning would soon take them home. They called family and their offices to let everyone know they were safely back. Then they boarded the plane, relaxed and talked about how nice it was going to be to get to work again.

Bob Parker was on his phone. When he finished, he caught Harry's eye and waved him away from the press.

"Parkes and Breaux just resigned," he said. "The chief justice has called the court into session behind closed doors."

"That'll be interesting," Harry responded. "They're four-to-three liberal. Wonder what they'll do?"

That answer came quickly. Less than ten minutes later Bob snagged Harry once again.

"They voted unanimously to reinstate you and Vice President Taylor, sir. I'd like to be the first to welcome you back, Mister President."

The two friends hugged for a long time. Harry told Jennifer about the decision and they turned to enter the lounge. Just then there was a frenzy of activity in the media area. Obviously they were just getting the news.

"Mister President! Mister President!" The yells happened all at once.

"I have to do this," he told his wife. "Give me a minute and we can go home."

The closest reporter raised his hand and asked, "Since you've just been reinstated, do you have a comment?"

"The same comment I made a few minutes ago still applies, folks. It's good to be back."

The Harrison family boarded Marine One for the short flight to the White House lawn. They landed, and as they walked toward the entryway, Harry and his family heard shouts behind them. They turned and saw hundreds of people lined up along the fence on the other side of the broad back yard. They were chanting, "Welcome home! Welcome home!" All four of them waved. Harry and Jennifer knelt, hugged the girls tightly, stood and walked back into their lives.

Over the next forty-eight hours the Democratic leadership fought unsuccessfully to overturn the Supreme Court's decision that reinstated Harry as President. Given this uncharted ground, dealing with circumstances that had never occurred before, they finally withdrew their opposition in the face of overwhelming support from the American people. Polls showed the populace - Democrats and Republicans alike - were united behind the President and Vice President.

This time it would be Harry and Jennifer who stayed in the Lincoln Bedroom for a few nights until Cham Parkes's two boys could come supervise the removal of their parents' belongings. Cham's wife, Karen, would never walk into the White House again. She was too embarrassed to even appear in public. She remained in seclusion on the family ranch outside Austin, as new allegations of corruption and kickbacks seemed to pop up against her husband every day. If it wasn't some sheikh in the Middle East, it was a corrupt governor in Mexico. If it wasn't a secret oil deal with his buddy Lou Breaux in Louisiana, it was a pay-for-play extortion of lobbyists.

BILL THOMPSON

EPILOGUE

The key players, nine months later

PRESIDENT CHAMBLISS T. PARKES refused to cooperate with the government's attorneys and did not take the stand during his trial. Investigators were able to locate more than twenty million dollars hidden in offshore accounts, all of which was confiscated. His bank accounts in the United States were also seized. He would receive no pension or other benefits normally afforded to past Presidents. His wife, who was deemed to have had no part in the plot, was granted an allowance of two thousand dollars a month for the rest of her life.

Zarif Safwan was on the stand for three days testifying against the former President. His shocking revelations kept the media on fire. Chambliss T. Parkes was convicted of treason, sentenced to death and is in solitary confinement on death row at the Federal Correctional Complex in Terre Haute, Indiana.

VICE PRESIDENT LOUIS BREAUX was willing to cooperate but the US Attorney didn't need what he had to offer. Zarif Safwan had already given them everything they required so there would be no plea bargain for Breaux. His assets were seized and he avoided trial by pleading guilty to one count of treason. He was sentenced to life without parole. He received death threats while in jail awaiting trial, and he is now in the protective custody unit at the United States Penitentiary in Hazleton, West Virginia.

WILLIAM HENRY HARRISON IV went to the Republican National Convention just weeks after his return. His parents sat in the audience with Brian and Nicole. After the opening ceremonies, Harry's three opponents stood together on the stage before an arena full of cheering supporters and announced they were withdrawing in favor of Harry. It was a magnanimous gesture, reflecting the admiration and respect most Americans felt for Harrison and his family after the ordeal they had endured. Harry won the general election in November with fifty-eight percent of the popular vote, one of the greatest margins in recent history.

MARTIN TAYLOR was formally reinstated as Vice President but immediately declared he would not join Harry on the ticket at the convention. The stress of Operation Condor and its successor, Operation Clawback, had caused him to decide there was more to life than this. He served the few months left in his term, attended Harry's inauguration in January, and then retired to Florida to enjoy a life free from politics.

BRIAN SADLER was Harry Harrison's first choice to be his running mate after Taylor declined, but Brian told his old friend he wouldn't do it. Bijan Rarities and his trips to archaeological sites were the things he enjoyed. Nicole and her continuing progress after the wreck were his top priorities. He'd had enough politics for a lifetime.

Bijan Rarities' auction *The Wrath of Vesuvius* reaped over sixteen million dollars and attracted thousands of bidders. It was no surprise that the broadcast on History Channel had more viewers than any of his previous events. Anyone who hadn't heard of him before certainly knew and respected him now. His fame and reputation increased exponentially once people learned the extent of his involvement and help with the mission.

NICOLE FARBER practices law in Dallas, improving mentally and physically every day after the debilitating car wreck that almost took her life. She vowed to take more trips with Brian, spend more time with her family and not take life for granted. She and Brian continue to talk about marriage, but it isn't top priority yet for either of them.

DONOVAN "DON" CASE, former director of the CIA, was Harry's second choice to join him on the ticket. His years of service to the CIA and his heroic efforts during the time Harry and the team were missing made him a perfect running mate for the immensely popular President.

He is currently serving as Vice President of the United States.

HASSAN GROUP After Amin's suicide, his daughter and only heir Amina took over Hassan Group, unwinding its operations. At the direction of the SEC, she sold the block of Exxon stock in small units over a few months, to avoid negatively affecting the price. She is cooperating with the governments of several countries that are investigating her father's criminal activities, all of which were made public thanks to the testimony of Zarif Safwan.

ZARIF SAFWAN could have been charged with far more heinous crimes, but the CIA director asked for leniency, as had been agreed. He pled guilty to conspiracy to commit murder in the deaths of the two Supreme Court justices and to the attempted murder of Brian Sadler. He also pled to racketeering – violating the RICO act. He is serving a thirty-year sentence at the Federal Correctional Facility in Lee County, Virginia. He continues to cooperate with the government regarding his activities and those of his former employer.

VINCENT VALGARDO increased his Exxon block, buying some of the shares previously owned by Hassan Group. His holdings have increased significantly in value as oil prices moved upward and the economy stayed buoyant.

AMINA HASSAN was rescued and kept in a safe house by the CIA until Operation Clawback was over. Although her father was dead and Zarif Safwan was in custody, Amin could have put something in place as payback for his only child's betrayal. Fortunately for her nothing happened.

Since then she has become close friends with Brian and Nicole, visiting Dallas three times. She helped the Vesuvius broadcast become the most watched of Brian's telecasts ever. Partly because of the notoriety surrounding her father and partly because she agreed to display her priceless relic *Cupid* from the House of the Genius in Herculaneum, the broadcast was a tremendous success.

Amina is now helping Brian develop clients for his London gallery, in much the same hostess function she performed for her father's operation.

ZAYED AL-FULAN, Amin Hassan's partner, received his fifty billion dollars back with interest, as Amina wound down Hassan Group. He remains one of the world's wealthiest men and survived his involvement with Amin Hassan with his reputation untarnished.

JOE KAYA cooperated with authorities but was unable to provide substantial help because he really knew nothing about who his handlers Ali and Mo were. Prosecutors turned down his offer for a plea bargain, and he was convicted of treason. He is serving a life sentence without parole in the protective custody unit at the United States Penitentiary in Leavenworth, Kansas.

TARIQ THE HAWK His mentor Mohammad al-Joulani learned that Tariq personally received Hassan's fifty million dollars, money that was intended for the Falcons of Islam. He made plans to kill his protégé Tariq, but the young man struck first. Mohammad was ambushed and killed at the safe house in Edlib, and Tariq is now the leader of the Nusra Front, al-Qaeda in Syria. He is on Interpol's list of the ten most wanted men worldwide.

Bill Thompson's next book is coming in Fall 2016

Want advance information before it's released?

Just go to
billthompsonbooks.com
and click "Sign Up for the Latest News"

Thank you!

Thanks for reading Order of Succession. If you liked it **I'd really appreciate a review on Amazon, Goodreads or both.**

Even a line or two makes a tremendous difference so thanks in advance for your help!

Please join me on:
Facebook
http://on.fb.me/187NRRP

Twitter
@BThompsonBooks

Books by Bill Thompson

Printed in Great Britain
by Amazon